"YOU BELIEVE
YOU'RE . . . DEAD?"—

—Chief Engineer Geordi La Forge asked.

The music of the young woman's laughter brightened the garden. "Starlord, you are gracious. You condescend to tease me. Have I not said that the flesh still holds me? Of course I am not dead!" Then her lovely face sobered. "But I hope to be. Is it for that you have come, great starlord? To free me from the shell of flesh that weighs me down?"

Before he could answer, she threw herself forward into Geordi's arms and locked her mouth to his in an impassioned kiss . . .

STAR TREK
THE NEXT GENERATION®

TO STORM
HEAVEN

ESTHER FRIESNER

POCKET BOOKS
New York   London   Toronto   Sydney   Tokyo   Singapore

An *Original* Publication of POCKET BOOKS

POCKET BOOKS, a division of Simon & Schuster Inc.
1230 Avenue of the Americas, New York, NY 10020

This book is published by Pocket Books, a division of Simon & Schuster Inc., under exclusive license from Paramount Pictures.

ISBN: 0-671-56838-8

First Pocket Books printing December 1997

10 9 8 7 6 5 4 3 2 1

POCKET and colophon are registered trademarks of Simon & Schuster Inc.

Printed in the U.S.A.

*This book is dedicated to my mother, Beatrice C. Friesner,
and to the memory of my father, David R. Friesner,
for their constant love, support, and belief in me*

TO STORM
HEAVEN

Prologue

"DEATH!" OLD SE'AR MOANED, writhing in pain on her pallet. "Ay me, death is coming!"

"Hush, you're ill. Lie quietly," the maiden soothed, kneeling on the hard floor of beaten earth. "You must save your strength if you want to get well, Mother Se'ar, you know that."

"Well . . ." The old woman repeated the word as if it were one of the local oberyin's magical healing chants. She shook her head. "Do not lead me astray with false hopes, child. I am old. I know what I know, and I have always known when death would come." A hollow chuckle escaped her fever-cracked lips.

Yes, she thought wearily. *Death has been to me the best of friends. The best of husbands as well. Has not death himself fed me, clothed me, provided for me all these years? I know when it will come, when the soul will leave the shell and find the glories of distant Evramur. Always before I have been right in my predictions, but always before it was another's death I saw approaching.* Aloud she said, "Now it is my turn at last."

"Don't speak of that," the maiden insisted. "Your time has not yet come."

"And how would you know?" A sudden burst of indignation flared up from the old woman's fading spirit. She made a great effort, heaving herself up on one elbow, and stabbed an accusing finger at the girl beside her. "Don't give yourself airs, just because I've taken you in. For your mother's sake I've let you share my roof, my bread, the fear-offerings of our friends and neighbors, but you don't share my gift! How dare you presume—" A sudden fit of coughing racked her bony body and she sank back down onto the sweat-stained sheet. The reeking straw beneath the coarse cloth crunched and crackled.

The maiden got up swiftly, gracefully, and fetched a clay bowl full of fresh milk, the cream beaten back into it to fortify the sick woman. She set it to Se'ar's lips and helped her drink. Only when the old woman had had enough and waved her off did she say, "I didn't mean it that way, Mother Se'ar. I know I have no gift like yours." She lowered her head as if in submission to the will of the gods, but beneath the fringe of blue-green hair, her eyes blazed with resentment.

The old woman seemed not to have heard the girl's words. Outside the hut the sun was setting, staining the sky pink and purple. Her life ebbed with the day's dwindling light, but her thoughts were elsewhere.

I was never wrong, never. When I said that such a one would die, he was as good as dead. In time, the people knew this. Was I wrong to turn my gift to trade? Ay, what choice did I have? I was widowed young, no sons to labor for me, my daughters all wed to shepherds

even stupider than the usual run of such shell-skulls.
Well, I suppose it was the best they could do, poor girls,
with no dowry worth the name.

"A shepherd's wife," she mumbled. "Nothing lower
could befall any woman." Her eyes rolled aimlessly
from side to side as her mind wandered.

The maiden at her side wrung out a cloth that had
been soaking in a bowl of water nearby and laid it
across the old woman's brow. It soon turned warm
and she gave it another cooling dip. "Be at peace,
Mother Se'ar," she soothed. "Let nothing trouble you.
You did what you had to do to live, as we all do. Don't
worry about it now."

Without warning the old woman siezed the maiden's hands in an iron grip, pulling herself upright so
that their eyes met. "You don't understand!" she
wailed. "I took what was holy and sold it as if it were
milk or fleece or grain! Because I could foretell death,
my neighbors thought that I could also forestall it.
They came to me with food and drink and cloth,
begging me to spare the lives of their loved ones."

She paused, panting for breath as painful memories
assailed her. *Fools. Sorry fools. Those who were bound*
to die, died anyway, despite my silence. When that
happened, I told them it was because the gods willed it,
and they had caused me to utter the doomed one's
name in dreams. How could anyone prove otherwise?
Who would stand against the way of the blessed
Balance? They did not understand, and I let them live
on in ignorance because it suited me, and because it let
me lead a life of comfort, plenty, respect.

"Nothing can justify what I have done," she
wheezed, shaking her head. "Nothing!"

"You are not responsible for what others choose to
believe." The maiden slid her arm under Se'ar's back
and tenderly lowered her to the pallet once more,

feeling the nubs of her spine poking against the age-slackened skin.

The old woman gazed up into the maiden's tranquil face and sighed. "You are a good girl, Ma'adrys. I wish I could tell you how often I have prayed to the Lady of the Balances to work her holy transformation on you and make you my own blood. But she would not hear the prayers of a cheat and a trickster."

"It doesn't matter," the maiden comforted her. "Even though I am not your blood kin, in all these years you have never begrudged me a single mouthful of your bread."

The old woman sighed. "I only hope that you haven't suffered for sharing it. It was contaminated with the taint of how I earned it. Oh Ma'adrys, what if that's it? What if that's what's kept you from your heart's desire? What if that's the flaw that Bilik saw in you when he forbid you to——?"

"Hush," the girl repeated, dabbing at the old woman's waxen face with the damp cloth. "Don't upset yourself. That's over and done with."

"But you're such a clever girl, such a *good* girl, you shouldn't be excluded just because——"

"Mother Se'ar, what good will it do either of us knowing why my petition was refused?" the girl asked quite reasonably. "It won't change the way things are."

"True, true." The old woman's voice trailed away like water trickling through stones. Her eyelids lowered. It seemed that she slept. The maiden settled back to oversee her rest.

The old woman's words came suddenly, taking the girl by surprise. "Maybe it wasn't my fault after all," Se'ar murmured, her eyes still closed. She spoke as if she were alone in the hut with none but herself to hear. "The girl's kind, yes, but headstrong, too bold about speaking up to the men, too demanding. Well, who can hold her to blame for that? Father lost in the winter storms before the Feast of Flowers, mother died birthing her, poor youngling left to run wild . . . Not that she ever had a proper mother to start, that one. Easy to see where the daughter's strange ways come from. Yes, everyone knew. Where that mother of hers came from, I'll never know. Mad, most likely, and driven out of her own village by folk with more sense than we ever had. All her high-sounding talk, all just ravings, ravings. Offensive to the Balance, her life thrown back into the scales to pay for her words, poor soul. Poor mad soul."

Beside the deathbed, the maiden Ma'adrys sat back on her heels, her back unnaturally stiff, her face drained of all expression. She tried to exclude the old woman's babbling from her mind, but she could not. It was nothing she hadn't heard before, all the village talk of her dead mother. As a child she'd gotten into more than a few fist fights with the other children when they'd taunted her by repeating the things they'd heard their parents say. She'd lost more battles than she'd won, and the elders had always punished her afterwards for the few fights she did win. When she was a little older, she'd tried to train herself to play deaf to the gossip and the snide remarks, the whispers she always heard behind her back, but it was beyond her best efforts. In time, she'd learned that there was only one safe thing to do when someone— even a dying woman no longer responsible for her own ramblings—spoke of her mother.

"I'll be right back," she announced, rocking back on her heels and standing without needing to push herself up from the ground. "The air in here's too sour to do you any good. We should burn some dawnsweet flowers to freshen it. It's early in the season for them, but I think I saw a patch in bloom in Avren's meadow yesterday. I won't be gone long." She was out the door before Se'ar could utter a word to stop her.

The old woman never noticed her departure. Her eyes remained closed, her wrinkled lips moving over words that were no longer audible to any but herself. In time she drowsed.

In dreams she was young again, a maiden herself, a girl whose brilliant golden eyes ensnared half a dozen suitors. She was sitting on the steps of the village shrine to the Six Mothers, whispering delicious secrets with her girlfriends—*Dead now, all long since dead!* a wraith of reality moaned through the dream—when a shepherd came by, down from the mountainside, and the girls paused in their chatter to tease the lad. Like all shepherds, he was slow witted, with hardly more brains than the beast that led his flock. Everyone made fun of the shepherds, no one thought anything wrong about doing so, and the shepherds themselves lacked the intelligence to understand that they were being ridiculed.

But something was wrong: This shepherd understood. He heard the dream-young Se'ar's taunts and scowled darkly at her. She was taken aback for an instant, then shrugged her misgivings aside. *He can't possibly understand!* she thought. *He's only a shepherd. Ma says if you give one of them a piece of bread, he'll be as likely to stick it in his ear as in his mouth. No hurt's possible where there's no wit to mind what's said.* Having reassured herself, she launched another verbal barb at the lad, and capped it with a rude gesture with both hands.

But she was wrong. He did understand. He let out a roar of anger and leaped for her, siezing her by the shoulders and shaking her while her girlfriends fled screaming.

She wanted to scream too, but she was helpless, voiceless. Her captor shook her harder, harder still, until she fell down and her teeth chattered together and her head banged against the steps of the Six Mothers' shrine. She could still hear her girlfriends screaming, only now their screams had turned into her name, shouted over and over while the enraged shepherd tried to batter the life out of her bones.

"Se'ar! Mother Se'ar!"

She snapped back into the waking world, a hand on her shoulder shaking her, but gently. She looked up into the broad, bland face of Kinryk, the innkeeper's son, and what she saw there made her forget to breathe. Easygoing Kinryk, lazy Kinryk, slack-faced Kinryk who everyone said was only a half step off from shepherdhood himself, this same Kinryk had become transformed. His whole face was alight, radiant with bliss, and his squat, flabby body quivered with the effort of trying to contain some astonishing piece of news.

"She's gone!" he gasped. "Oh, Mother Se'ar, I was there. I saw it myself. She's gone! She's been taken!"

"Who?" A veil of shadow passed over the old woman's eyes, the sign that always visited her when she knew that a death was coming to the village. She knew: "Ma'adrys." It was a whisper, like a fall of pebbles into one of the mountain crevasses.

She went to gather flowers to sweeten my sickroom, Se'ar thought. *Avren's meadow. The main track up that side of the mountain's fine, but the shortcut's still half gullied out by the winter storms. She would take the shortcut, my wild one, in a rush to come back to tend me, and now—*

"Have they . . . fetched her body?" The old woman tried to sit up, her thoughts roiling. *Taken so young, poor unlucky orphan. No man's child, a mad mother's*

7

daughter. Ay! As if a hard life were the fee to let us purchase the hour of our death! Lady, in mercy give me back only a handful of my old strength. Let me see to the proper arraying of her corpse. She gathered breath with a great effort and panted, "That—that box by the hearth. My wedding dress. She shall have it for—for her burial. Take it. Take it and—and bring it to—"

Kinryk laughed as if Se'ar had told him the best jest in all the world. "Dress, Mother Se'ar? Ma'adrys needs no dress where's she's gone. I saw them take her, the shining ones, and the light almost blinded me, but when I got my eyes back I saw her clothes left there in the grass, all in a muddle. No need for any but the robes of star and sunlight where she dwells now."

Se'ar's almost toothless mouth gaped. What was all this gabble? Some of the village wags must have put the boy up to it. Their idea of sport, setting the innkeeper's slow-brained son to play a prank on a dying woman. Passionately she wished for strength enough to flay this fool alive with curses. *But I am too weak . . . too weak,* she thought. *And my poor Ma'adrys is gone.*

"Evramur!" the boy sang out, and from outside the old woman's hut she heard a chorus of excited voices echoing the holy name. "Our own Ma'adrys, worthy to be taken living into the eternal garden, the shining city, the undying refuge Evramur!"

"Evramur," Se'ar repeated, unable to believe with her mind what her heart had at last accepted. From the time she'd been old enough to hear the good teachings, she'd heard the name of Evramur, haven of all blessed spirits after death. Yet sometimes a spirit appeared whose great goodness couldn't wait for death to free it from the flesh. That spirit's power was so intense that it cried out until the servants of holy

Evramur came seeking it and took it, flesh and all, to its rightful home. Se'ar had heard of folk so blessed, but such privileged ones always seemed to live leagues away; they were the stuff of legend.

No longer. Se'ar still saw the veil of death before her eyes, but now she knew it was not for Ma'adrys. She gazed at the innkeeper's thick-witted son with pity. "Kinryk," she said softly, "carry me into the air."

Beaming with joy, he scooped up the old woman's frail body and carried her out of the hut. Night had fallen, one moon already visible high above the horizon, the other two lagging behind. By rights all the villagers should have been in their own homes, eating their evening meal, getting ready for another day of hard life and harsh labor. Instead, the narrow, crooked path that led up to Se'ar's hut was choked with people, all chattering and wide eyed. When they saw the old woman, they surged forward, hands outstretched.

As if my touch could make them holy because she *touched me,* Se'ar reflected. She tilted her head back and looked up into the night sky.

Yes, there it was, beyond the glimmering disc of the lone risen moon: the red-gold sphere that the good teachings named the Gate of Evramur. She imagined that if she stared at it long enough, hard enough, she could almost see the laughing face of her lost Ma'adrys waiting for her just beyond the threshhold.

I have bartered holy gifts for gain, Se'ar thought. *I will never see you again, my dear one, for I have made my spirit unworthy of Evramur.* The realization broke her heart and she began to weep.

No, Mother Se'ar. Was it an illusion or did she truly hear Ma'adrys's voice in her ear? *Recall the good teachings: It is never too late to make your spirit worthy. Not even now. One last time, use your gift as it was meant to be used.*

"Yes—" The old woman's word was lost in the clamor of the crowd closing around her. While they strove to reach her, she placed her lips close to Kinryk's grimy ear and whispered, "Listen to me, boy. I have seen the veil of your death before my eyes." She felt him freeze and quickly added, "Don't fear it. It's yours no more. For her sake I will take it from you, take it upon myself. For the sake of the one who walks the shining gardens of Evramur in flesh and spirit. For Ma'adrys—"

The breath caught in her throat and was gone in a gurgle and a sigh. Se'ar was dead. Kinryk burst into sobs, crying out the news of the old woman's final prophecy and the blessed Ma'adrys's first miracle. At the back of the crowd, the oberyin Bilik surreptitiously wiped his cheeks and called down a curse on any villager who might dare to pillage the blessed Ma'adrys's own miserable dwelling in search of relics.

Overhead, the red-gold Gate of Evramur looked down impassively upon the wailing villagers, as distant from their deaths as from their lives, and on the hillsides the shepherds danced and dreamed.

Chapter One

"WHAT IS THE REASON for this delay?" Legate Valdor of Orakisa slapped the conference table, leaving a ghostly impression of his splayed palm on the formerly spotless surface. The cluster of multicolored crystal baubles at the base of his official topknot—each one the mark of a successfully completed diplomatic mission—chimed and jangled against each other. "This is unbearable! A deliberate insult! When we return, I will file a complaint with the Reclamation. I will not be treated in such a way by a mere—"

"Father, please." The younger Orakisan at Legate Valdor's elbow spoke in a voice so burdened with embarrassment as to be almost inaudible. His own pale silver topknot was adorned with a single, lonely crystal pendant small to the point of invisibility. "I am sure that there is a perfectly logical explanation for her absence."

"With respect, I agree with your son, Legate," Captain Picard put in. "Ambassador Lelys herself requested that we call this briefing. She would gain nothing by delaying it on purpose."

"Nothing but another chance to remind me that—" The legate's voice dropped to angry, incomprehensible mutterings. From his place directly across the table from Valdor, the android Mr. Data observed the older Orakisan's sulks and grumblings with marked interest.

At that moment, the door to the conference room opened as Dr. Crusher entered, followed by a tall, alien woman of striking height and exotic beauty. "Sorry to be late, sir," Dr. Crusher said, taking the chair between the captain's and Counsellor Troi's. "Ambassador Lelys made it a point to call for me in person, but just as we were about to leave, I was unavoidably detained." A mysterious smile flickered over her lips.

"Unavoidably?" Captain Picard echoed, regarding her closely. He preferred his mysteries solved.

Before Dr. Crusher could reply, the alien woman spoke up. "Captain Picard, I accept full responsibility for our lateness. If you must undertake disciplinary action against anyone for the offense—"

"Madam Ambassador, I assure you that nothing was farther from my mind," Picard replied. "I only wished to know—"

"Good," the Orakisan woman cut in. "Then we can proceed. Captain, if you please." She wore a gown that held all the brilliant shades of an Earth sunset, the sleeves mere wisps of iridescent drapery secured at wrist and shoulder with sunbursts of faceted gemstones, and when she extended one slender hand bearing an information chip it was with the sinuous grace of a trained dancer.

"Certainly, Ambassador." Picard felt a momentary twinge of irritation at being interrupted, but he quickly put it aside. He inserted the chip into the control unit at his fingertips, and immediately a holographic projection of a gold, blue, green, and white planet set against a field of stars materialized in the center of the conference table.

"Ah. Skerris IV," said Mr. Data automatically.

"S'ka'rys," the ambassador corrected him. She glided to the head of the table where a chair stood empty at Captain Picard's right hand. Instead of sitting in it she passed it by in favor of the vacant seat next to the younger Orakisan male. As soon as she settled in beside him, he took an intense interest in his datapad. The crystal pendant in his hair trembled violently.

Ambassador Lelys noticed none of this. "I beg your pardon," she said to Mr. Data. "I did not intend to make you feel inadequate. I should not have expected you to know how the name is pronounced in the old style."

"Quite the contrary, Ambassador." Mr. Data replied. "In preparation for your arrival aboard the *Enterprise,* I thoroughly familiarized myself with Old Skerrian as a matter of course, as well as all variations of that language as currently spoken throughout the Skerrian daughterworlds. As I understand it, it has become the fashion for the Reclamation colonists on S'ka'rys to adopt old-style ways as much as possible, although I must confess I fail to see a practical purpose." He cocked his head briefly to one side, then added, "S'ka'rys. I believe that means the mother in the old language."

Ambassador Lelys inclined her head in agreement, a charming smile illuminating her face. Silky hair the color of a storm-ridden sea swept forward, clusters of crystal droplets making their own music. Like her colleagues, she too wore a topknot, but hers was the merest tuft of hair caught up in a tiny golden ring. She was not the sort of person who needed to rely on official symbols to establish her authority. "You are a credit to the Federation, Mr. Data. I am privileged to count you among our most valuable resources. With someone like you helping us, I feel certain that our mission will succeed."

"Thank you," the android replied. "However, given the nature of the problem that your colonists are facing, I would say that Dr. Beverly Crusher will be a much more valuable resource than I."

"Why do I suddenly feel like a med probe?" Dr. Crusher murmured to Counsellor Troi behind latticed fingers. The Betazoid declined to comment.

"Yes, of course," Ambassador Lelys was saying, turning the power of her smile on Dr. Crusher. "As soon as I volunteered for this mission, I made it a point to request transport by the *Enterprise,* chiefly because I knew you were assigned to this ship. Your reputation as a xenobiologist is extraordinary, and we may well need the extraordinary before we are done. I can not begin to tell you how unnerved I was when we were informed that you might not share this voyage with us."

"I was attending the Ark conference on Malabar Station," Dr. Crusher explained. "I received direct orders from Admiral Mona to return immediately. Unfortunately, the orders didn't include more than the barest briefing. I know that there's a health crisis of major proportions on Skerris IV"—she didn't even attempt to pronounce that world's name in the old style—"but if that's so, I don't see what we're doing in this sector, nowhere near the Skerrian system, and heading farther from it by the minute."

Ambassador Lelys sighed, her eyes full of sorrow as she gazed at the holographic projection slowly turning on the conference table. "How beautiful," she said, the ornaments in her hair chiming softly. "And how great a pity that we did not appreciate its beauty soon enough." She fell into a heavy silence which no one—not even the impatient Legate Valdor—tried to break.

From his place, Captain Picard, too, regarded the slowly turning projection of Skerris IV. The story of that lovely world's ugly fate was a familiar one—far too familiar—in the scope of universal history. Once a thriving world, Skerris IV had made great technological progress, conquering interstellar travel and seeding countless other worlds with her colonies.

"What fools we were," said Ambassador Lelys with a sigh.

"Fools?" Legate Valdor snapped out the word, his pale skin darkening with rage. "Is this how you speak of the Ancestors? Mark me, Ambassador Lelys. Disrespect to me is one thing, but disrespect to the Ancestors must and will be reported to the—"

"Very well, Legate," Lelys said with the patience of a mother dealing with a fractious four-year-old. "Report me with my blessing. You have done little this entire trip but collect incidents, evidence, and assorted sins I have supposedly committed. By the time you present the full catalog of my offenses, I will have retired from the diplomatic service, so by all means, enjoy yourself."

The legate's fleshy lips pressed together, the dull orange irises of his eyes expanding until the thin rim of white surrounding them was no longer visible. He started to rise from his chair, fists on the table.

"Father—" The younger male tentatively reached out to sieze the legate's arm. "Father, Ambassador Lelys only said the same thing that you and I have heard many times from the lips of respected Council members. She speaks within the law. The glories of the Ancestors are holy, but the follies of the Ancestors must be acknowledged."

"A fool's law," Legate Valdor muttered, subsiding. He jerked his arm away from the younger male. "Small wonder *you* know it so well, Hara'el."

The younger male bowed his head and meekly said, "Yes, Father."

"But is it not true, Legate Valdor, that any law that allows us to extract present wisdom from past errors is not only valid but essential?" Mr. Data asked. He received a venomous look from the Orakisan for his troubles.

"What are we to learn?" Valdor demanded. "To this day, no one is certain of precisely what became of Skerris IV." He pronounced the world's name Federation style, and gave Ambassador Lelys a look that defied her to correct him.

"You are quite right, Valdor." Again she rose above the potential confrontation with her subordinate. "We do not know the precise chain of events that led up to the complete annihilation of our motherworld. For many, it is enough to know that such a disaster happened, that it did not need to happen, and that we must strive to ensure that it never happens again. The death of S'ka'rys was more than the death of a world, it was the death of knowledge."

"Not—not *all* knowledge, Ambassador," Hara'el ventured. For this, he was rewarded with one of Lelys's warmest smiles.

"Your pardon," she said kindly. "I did ask you to handle this briefing, didn't I? Yet here I am, in love with the sound of my own voice." She did not notice how the color rose up Hara'el's neck when she said *love*. "Please proceed."

Hara'el cleared his throat and fidgeted in his chair, then stood up and tried to compensate for his nervousness by adopting a professorial pose. With an unnecessary gesture at the holograph, he said, "Orakisa was one of the more recently founded Skerrian colonies, relatively speaking, and was an extremely prosperous world from the first. We were very fortunate on both those counts, since prosperity allowed our founders the leisure to preserve history. Otherwise we might have come to believe that we had no roots beyond Orakisa after S'ka—Skerris IV— destroyed itself." He, too, used the Federation style pronunciation after an uneasy sideways glance at his father "All knowledge of the motherworld—and thus of our sister colonies—would have been lost."

"What I don't understand," Dr. Crusher began, "excuse me for interrupting, but Ambassador Lelys told me some of this on our way to the conference room and I didn't quite follow her. What I don't understand is why Orakisa didn't know of the other Skerrian colonies until recently."

"In their wisdom, the Ancestors would have it so," Valdor intoned. His expression made it clear that, as far as he was concerned, that was enough of an explanation for anyone.

Ambassador Lelys disagreed. "We can only theorize from recovered and reconstructed information, but most likely it was one of our Ancestors' deliberate policies concerning colonies. As far as possible, new daughterworlds were kept in ignorance of older ones, and more established daughterworlds were not informed of new foundations, which was an easier task."

"Yes, but why?" Counsellor Troi asked. "What did the motherworld hope to gain?"

"Independence." Hara'el spoke up, and most of the

17

people at the conference table did a double take, as if they'd forgotten his presence even though he was standing right in front of them. "If you believe that your settlement is isolated from all others, if you don't even know that there are any others, you will develop self-reliance because to your mind, you have no other choice."

"And diversity," Legate Valdor put in. "Nothing evolves, nothing progresses without diversification, not even a culture. Our Ancestors, in their wisdom, realized this. If every daughterworld were a clone of her sisters, then any cataclysm capable of wiping out one would be able to destroy the rest. But if the daughterworlds were forced to evolve separately, then in time of crisis, one colony might have developed the resources to save her sisters."

"Except for the fact that no daughterworld was aware that her sisters even existed," Ambassador Lelys amended. "I am afraid that our Ancestors' motives were far less noble: If the daughterworlds couldn't possibly rely on each other, they would have to rely on S'ka'rys. Until a colony was secure enough to be totally self-supporting, there would be no chance of the motherworld losing control of it."

Legate Valdor shot out of his seat, the pendants in his topknot clattering loudly. "I will not allow myself to be subjected to this—this *pollution!* You may defame the Ancestors all you like, Ambassador, but you can not force me to bear witness to such sacrilege." With that, he stormed out of the conference room, the door hissing shut behind him.

Hara'el stared after his father's violent departure. The younger Orakisan male looked ready to sink into the floor. Ambassador Lelys patted his arm. "Proceed," she said.

"But—but if he's gone how can I?"

"The purpose of this meeting is purely informational. All Starfleet personnel crucial to the success of our mission must have a complete view of the situation on S'ka'rys. While your father has served Orakisa capably for many years as a diplomat, he has never been able to present the facts as they are, without benefit of emotional coloration. An unfortunate shortcoming, and probably the reason why he's still a legate. Since we don't need to reach any sort of decision or accord at the moment, we don't need him." She spoke with a cool, logical detachment worthy of a Vulcan. "Go on with your presentation, Hara'el."

Hara'el took a deep breath before obeying his superior. "As I was saying, Orakisa was one of the last colonies founded before the fall of Skerris IV. In time, we came to think of the motherworld as a legend, but a legend that might have some basis in reality."

"Atlantis," Captain Picard murmured.

"What?" Ambassador Lelys's luminous amber eyes were suddenly on him.

"A legend of Earth," he explained. "Supposedly all early cultures were colonies of a superior civilization that was lost when the continent of Atlantis sank into the sea."

"And did any of your people believe that this Atlantis was more than just a legend?"

Picard nodded. "Many. Some even mounted diving expeditions to locate the sunken land. Unfortunately, most of their discoveries were of dubious scientific worth. Some legends are merely legends."

"Ours was not," the ambassador said demurely. She indicated to Hara'el that he should go on.

By now the younger male was so ill at ease that he adopted the terse, thoroughly unemotional delivery of someone reading aloud from an encyclopedia: "The first Orakisan expedition to Skerris IV revealed planet-wide extinction of our founding civilization, but also that the motherworld was on the path to ecological recovery. The expedition's report caused a great stir on Orakisa. Once it was determined that the legendary motherworld did exist and that it was once more capable of supporting life, there was a great movement to reclaim and resettle Skerris IV."

"I remember reading about the medical aspects of the Reclamation movement," Dr. Crusher said. "I can't say I approved of some of the more radical adaptation procedures your people used."

"We had no choice," Hara'el responded. "Even though the motherworld was no longer barren, the radiation levels were still somewhat heavier than our people could bear."

"They could have chosen not to go," Dr. Crusher pointed out.

"Out of the question, Dr. Crusher," Lelys said. "Well, perhaps not so, if viewed from a strictly practical standpoint, but in the days of the rediscovery and the Reclamation no one on Orakisa was in a strictly practical mood. The Reclamation was not a sober, carefully considered undertaking. It was a crusade. Those who decided to resettle S'ka'rys were willing to have their bodies genetically altered so that they and their descendants could survive existing conditions on the motherworld, even though the procedure meant that they would be unable to live anywhere else. As you yourself said, Dr. Crusher, it was a radical adaptation, a strain that no body could undergo twice and survive, but the colonists had no intention of going back. They were determined to take an irreversible stand. They said that S'ka'rys gave Orakisa birth and now it was time for Orakisa to give S'ka'rys rebirth. True, nothing forced our people to return to the motherworld. Nothing but a dream. But we will give up much for the sake of dreams."

Dr. Crusher was silent.

"The Reclamation enjoyed great initial success," Hara'el resumed. "The Orakisan crops and stock animals that the settlers brought with them did better than expected. They not only flourished, they acheived nontraumatic coexistence with the native plant and animal life that had survived the devastation."

"Hardly surprising," said Mr. Data. "I assume that when Orakisa was first settled, the colonists brought plants and animals from Skerris IV. The Reclamation settlers no doubt wished to avoid any problems that might arise from importing truly alien life-forms to their new home. They must have taken the precaution of bringing back only the descendants of originally transplanted stock."

"As you say." Hara'el nodded. He was beginning to lose a measure of his nervousness, and when he spoke on, he no longer sounded younger than his years. "The Reclamation was going well. Optimistic reports from the first comers encouraged more settlers to join the movement, which in turn made it necessary to scout out more land that had recovered enough to support communities. It was during one of these explorations that they made their most momentous discovery: They unearthed Miramik, chief city of the motherworld."

"And among the ruins of Miramik we found our history," Lelys said. She made a small, self-effacing gesture. "I beg you to forgive me, Hara'el; I spoke out of turn. But the discovery of Miramik is a source of unpardonable pride for me, since it was my own brother who led that expedition."

Hara'el's recently reclaimed self-control vanished

as soon as Lelys addressed him directly. Flustered, he stammered out, "Why, why, yes—yes, of course it is. It—it ought to be! Your brother—the honor—perfectly pardonable, any pride you take in—all that followed." He was making a fool of himself and judging from the look on his face, he knew it. With a great effort, he stopped babbling and said, "It would be only proper for you to speak of it." He sat down with the air of a man who would not open his mouth again if his life depended on it. Counsellor Troi gave him a sympathetic look, but his eyes were resolutely lowered and it was wasted on him.

"What we—what my brother's expedition found in the ruins of Miramik was astonishing," Lelys was saying. "More than astonishing, a miracle! As they were investigating the sublevels of an apparently unimportant structure on the outskirts of the city, they stumbled across a door almost entirely buried in rubble. They would have ignored it—they had no time for more than a cursory exploration—but for the fact that my brother caught sight of the sign attached to the wall beside it. He was an academic when he still lived on Orakisa. He'd studied the written form of the old tongue as it survived in our records, and the moment he interpreted the sign, he knew that they had to get into that room. He was right. The blocked door guarded a treasure greater than anyone could have imagined, a government data bank, shielded and sheltered, almost perfectly preserved, with most of its information intact and retrievable. It was only an auxiliary backup unit—the main storage facilities had been destroyed utterly—but it contained the official records of all colonies ever seeded from the motherworld. That was how we learned that we were not the only child of S'ka'rys. The universe thronged with her daughters. We had given life back to the planet that had given life to ours, and we had been rewarded. Orakisa rejoiced and immediately began plans to contact our long-lost sisters."

"It was my privilege to attend one such ceremony of reunion, when Orakisa reestablished ties with Kikal," Counsellor Troi said.

"We still recall your service with gratitude," Lelys said. "Kikal is one of the oldest colonies, and her ways have become very different from ours. Thanks to you and to the Federation we were able to convince a world of strangers that they are truly our kin."

"And to bring that world into the Federation," Picard commented, "among others. The discovery of the S'ka'rys data bank may lack the glamor of King Tut's tomb, but on a galactic scale it has proven itself to be infinitely more valuable."

"King Tut's tomb?" Lelys inquired.

"The multi-chambered burial site of King Tutankhamen, a major archeological find of the early twentieth century," Mr. Data provided. "The discovery of a virtually undisturbed royal interment belonging to Earth's ancient Egyptian civilization was an event which greatly enhanced contemporary knowledge of—"

"Thank you, Mr. Data. Ambassador Lelys can pursue the references in the ship's library for herself if the subject interests her," Captain Picard interrupted. He turned to Dr. Crusher. "Unfortunately, the troubles on Skerris IV began soon after the Miramik find."

"Tut's curse," Dr. Crusher murmured under her breath. It was still loud enough to be heard. This time both Mr. Data and Ambassador Lelys regarded her quizzically. She smiled briefly and said, "Just a story. When the archeologists opened Tutankhamen's burial chamber, some people claimed that their invasion of

23

the site invoked a curse. Supposedly, when the Egyptian priests sealed the king's tomb, they used magic spells that would destroy anyone who disturbed their royal master's eternal rest."

"And this curse, is it truly just a story?" Lelys asked.

"Naturally," the doctor replied without hesitation.

Counsellor Troi gave her a knowing look. "Is it?" she echoed.

Dr. Crusher colored slightly. "There were a number of incidents following the discovery of the tomb—tragedies touching members of the expedition—but as for hard evidence, well," she shrugged, "people will believe what they want to believe and interpret facts to suit their own preconceived ideas. A romantic would choose to believe in the magic of an ancient Egyptian curse rather than in mere coincidence." Before Troi could question her further about her own views on the subject, she quickly asked, "What happened on Skerris IV? A medical crisis, I know that much, but what are the specifics? Did the opening of the sealed data bank room release some sort of dormant microbes? We've handled similar cases on other worlds many times before this. A Federation medical team should have been able to take care of it easily."

Ambassador Lelys shook her head. "We contacted the Federation as soon as the first problems manifested themselves among the colonists. That was their initial analysis, soon proved wrong. My brother's expedition hadn't released any curse out of S'ka'rys's past. In fact, if we hope to save our motherworld from a second obliteration of her children, the answer will come from the Miramik find."

She signalled Captain Picard, who touched a control, altering the projection in the center of the table.

Now Dr. Crusher saw the face of an Orakisan woman. "My brother's wife, Vi'ar," Lelys said.

Dr. Crusher studied the ravaged face before her. Vi'ar's hair was dull and brittle, her eyes lusterless. Orakisan eyes were mostly composed of gloriously colored iris with only the smallest rim of white, but this woman's irises had dwindled and paled until it was almost impossible to see them. Her skin was muddy gray, like tissue paper stretched over her bones.

"How old is she?" the doctor asked.

"A little younger than I," Lelys replied. "I know it doesn't seem possible, looking at her, but it's true."

"Malnutrition," Dr. Crusher concluded. "Starvation induced, I'd say."

"So." Lelys agreed. "And yet she eats well, plentifully. There is no shortage of food on S'ka'rys."

"To starve in the midst of plenty . . ." Dr. Crusher mused. "A metabolic disorder, then."

Again Lelys nodded. "Your Federation scientists concur. For some reason, the alterations necessary to allow our settlers to return to S'ka'rys had a disastrous side effect on their digestive systems. They are no longer able to extract the nutrients their bodies need from the crops they raise. Unfortunately, this effect did not become evident until it was too late, with too many Orakisans no longer able to live anywhere but on S'ka'rys." She lowered her voice. "To say nothing of their children."

"How—" Dr. Crusher couldn't take her eyes off the tormented, haggard face of Lelys's young sister-in-law. "How many have died?"

"Almost a hundred. Does it matter? Unless our mission succeeds they are all doomed. None of them can leave S'ka'rys and live; none of them can remain on S'ka'rys and survive."

"And the stock animals? The ones they brought back to Skerris IV from Orakisa? Have they been dying off as well?"

"The beasts don't seem to be affected," Lelys told her. "The Federation team explained it to us in detail, but my specialty is diplomacy, not biology. Besides, I don't believe in questioning luck. The herds have no trouble metabolizing the native vegetation, which allows our people to get some nourishment from eating the animals' meat. It's only a temporary solution, though. Meat alone can't provide them with all their nutritional needs, and the animals can't reproduce fast enough to keep everyone fed."

"Couldn't Orakisa send more stock?" Troi suggested.

"The beasts must first be adapted to bear the higher radiation levels of S'ka'rys, just as the settlers have been. The process is time consuming and impractical. We must find an answer elsewhere or stand by and watch our motherworld die all over again."

"But we *have* found the answer." Hara'el asserted so unexpectedly that all eyes snapped onto him. Under this sudden scrutiny, he pushed back into his chair and meekly added, "Father told me so. He said that the Federation medical teams on S'ka—Skerris IV—know what's wrong and have informed our government how to correct it."

"You have the answer?" Dr. Crusher looked puzzled. "Then what—?"

"An answer is not a solution," Mr. Data commented. "According to the reports that I have assimilated, Federation scientists had little trouble determining the cause of the Skerrian settlers' problem. Their bodies fail to produce a particular enzyme that would permit them to effectively metabolize plant nutrients. The stock animals suffer no such inability."

"I take it that we've already tried synthesizing this enzyme from the animals?" Dr. Crusher asked.

"The enzyme in question has a unique, highly unstable configuration. While it can be synthesized, the process is complex, inefficient, and does not yield sufficient quantities to meet the existing demand."

"What about replication?"

"That, too, was tried as a matter of course. The synthesized enzyme broke down under artificial replication." Although Mr. Data's face seldom revealed much, for an instant he appeared to wear an expression that implied, "I could have told them that."

"But we do have an answer *and* a solution," Hara'el insisted. He motioned for Captain Picard to change the holographic image a third time. Dr. Crusher felt a whisper of relief, followed by a pang of guilt, when Vi'ar's face was replaced by a green sprig of vegetation with wide, sawtoothed leaves and abundant clusters of pink-edged purple flowers.

"N'vashal." Lelys stared at the image and breathed the alien name as if it were a holy thing. "The life of S'ka'rys, if we find it. And if not . . ."

The humble flower turned slowly under their eyes, carrying the weight of untold lives on its fragile petals.

Chapter Two

"NOWHERE?" COMMANDER RIKER REPEATED, incredulous. "Not on *one* of the Skerrian colonies?"

"Not so far as the Orakisans have been able to find out," Counsellor Troi replied, and sipped her drink.

"I don't know why you're so surprised," Dr. Crusher put in, running her finger down the side of her empty glass, tracing patterns in the condensation. The three of them were sharing a table at Ten Forward, enjoying each other's company along with the view. "It's not unheard of for an entire species of plant or animal to vanish. The original Skerrians destroyed themselves and most of their planet; they just happened to destroy the n'vashal plant at the same time."

"So now it seems they'll be taking their Orakisan descendants with them too," Riker remarked.

"Oh, *you're* an optimist," Dr. Crusher said.

Riker hastened to defend himself. "I'm only making an assumption based on what you told me. I'd love to be wrong."

Troi sighed. "So would the Orakisans. The delegation maintains a mask of hope, but I sense that each of them is fighting despair in his or her own way. Legate Valdor uses his anger and resentment against Ambassador Lelys to distract himself from thinking about this mission, and how it seems likely to have the same unlucky end as all the others he has served on already. His son Hara'el, the junior legate, focuses on Ambassador Lelys too, although in a more friendly manner."

"Friendly doesn't begin to describe it." Dr. Crusher smiled. "The boy's in love."

"The boy?" Riker echoed with a little grin. "I met him when the ambassadorial party first came aboard. He's an adult male Orakisan."

"Not when he's anywhere near Ambassador Lelys," Dr. Crusher said. "Or when he's near his father, for that matter. I'd say that Hara'el has some growing up to do."

"Is that your considered opinion as a physician?"

"As a physician, a parent, and a woman."

"Well, that about covers it." Riker returned his attention to Troi. "What about the ambassador herself? How is she coping with the situation?"

"Of the three, she appears to be the one most in control of her feelings, but only on the surface. Her brother is one of the colonists, he and his family. She also has a younger sister who underwent the alteration process before the Orakisans realized what was happening on Skerris IV. The girl is barely out of childhood, and when she was still small, Lelys's family lost their parents. Lelys herself raised her sister. If she dies, the ambassador will lose both a sister and a daughter."

"Ambassador Lelys never mentioned a sister," Dr. Crusher said. "Not during the briefing. Not even when she came to bring me to the conference room. She always struck me as the friendliest of the three, very outgoing, eager to make contact outside of official business. I thought we were friends." She sounded vaguely disappointed.

"I am sure that you are friends," Troi reassured her. "If Lelys didn't tell you about her sister, it's just to keep from thinking of her. The only reason I know about the girl is because I consulted the background records of the Orakisan delegation. Ambassador Lelys has enjoyed a spectacular career, rising through the ranks to her present position in barely half the time Legate Valdor has been in the diplomatic service."

"So it looks as if Valdor's resentment against Lelys is more than just a coping device," Riker observed. "I hope our lovely ambassador knows enough to watch her back."

"She won't have to bother," Dr. Crusher said. "If this mission fails, she told me that as its leader she'll be held personally responsible, demoted, and—given the severity of the crisis—possibly asked to resign."

"You're kidding. Isn't that a little severe?"

"That's the Orakisan way. Reward success and make an example of failure. It's no worse than some practices we've encountered, and much better than a few from our own past. In ancient Babylon, if a doctor failed to cure a patient, they chopped off his hand, and if the patient died—" She allowed Riker and Troi to reach the obvious conclusion.

Riker let out a long, low whistle. "Now that's severe."

"If hardly the way to encourage many people to go into the medical profession," Troi added. "Hmm.

Tut's curse, ancient Babylon, the mysteries of Earth's past . . . You *are* a romantic, Beverly."

"Just an amateur student of Earth history. I like to think of it as my small contribution to conservation. Ideas can become extinct too. So much has been lost, so many things that we could still learn from." She was not aware of the rising passion in her voice, but her friends were. Riker and Troi exchanged a look of amusement.

"Another expert diagnosis, Counsellor," he said. "The patient is definitely an incurable romantic."

Dr. Crusher made a face at him. "Fine. Guilty as charged. I'd rather be a romantic than a cynic any day."

"Who said I was a cynic?" Riker spread his hands. "You can be a romantic and practical at the same time. Nothing in Starfleet regulations against it. Besides, romantics never lose hope. I can't believe that in all the universe—or at least in all those colonies Skerris IV founded—there isn't one place where they still grow n'vashal."

"I agree with Commander Riker," Troi said. "According to Hara'el, the unearthed data bank contained the complete records of all colonial expeditions, including the ships' manifests. The settlers took many of their native plants and animals with them for propagation. There were several listings of n'vashal seeds included in the agricultural inventory."

"Most of those colonizing expeditions happened long ago." Dr. Crusher pushed her glass away. "You know, when a species becomes extinct, it doesn't always happen through deliberate destruction. Some things die out through simple neglect and disuse. N'vashal was never a staple of the Skerrian diet; it was only used as a seasoning, in minute quantities, and then only in certain ethnic dishes. It's like—Well, have either of you ever heard of a spice called galingale?" One look at their faces told her that they hadn't. "It was popular during the Middle Ages, found in the kitchens of almost every European nobleman. But nobles were not in the majority. Galingale was a luxury, and when tastes changed, it was no longer worth the trouble and expense of importing it."

"So you're saying that it became extinct?" Riker asked.

"No, just extremely rare. On the other hand, there was a kind of parsnip called skirret that did die out entirely because people stopped cultivating it, and a type of small onion, and a certain breed of English peas—"

"And you call yourself an *amateur* historian?" Riker teased.

Dr. Crusher smiled. "Don't be fooled. I didn't even know there were such things as galingale and skirrets before I attended the Ark conference. Malabar Station has one of the Federation's most comprehensive archives of plant and animal DNA, and the cloning facilities—" Her face fell. "It's a shame that they don't have a sample of n'vashal either. It's the synthetic enzyme that's unstable, not the naturally occurring one found in the plant itself. If we could get our hands on one living n'vashal plant, we'd have no trouble producing enough clones to treat the immediate problem on Skerris IV. Once they recovered their health, the Reclamation settlers could grow a more genetically diverse crop and take care of themselves."

"*If* we could find that one plant," Troi said sadly. "The Federation has been helping the Orakisans contact every colony that carried n'vashal with them from Skerris IV. The plant couldn't grow on some worlds, on others it grew, but was destroyed by native wildlife."

"And on some it grew unmolested until the colonists decided to cultivate something else instead," Dr. Crusher finished. "Now there's only one colony left for them to search: Ashkaar."

"At the risk of being called a pessimist again, I don't think much of their chances," Riker said. "I've seen the navigation specs. Ashkaar is the fourth planet from a sun that's about as far from Skerris IV as you can get and still stay in the same quadrant. Do the Orakisans know whether the colony itself survived, let alone the n'vashal?"

"That is what we're going to help them find out," Troi answered.

"Much as I hate saying it, I'm inclined to agree with Commander Riker on this," Dr. Crusher said. "For a last chance, Ashkaar really isn't a very good one. I've been talking to Data about the information taken from the Miramik find. It was more than just a list of ships' manifests and colony coordinates, it also contained progress reports received from the individual settlements. As you said, Ashkaar is the most distant of the Skerrian daughterworlds, and for good reason: The colonists who undertook the voyage had some very definite goals in mind. They were cultural dissenters, people who disliked and disapproved of many elements of life on Skerris IV. It's an old story, really, wanting to escape, start over, make a new, simpler life for yourself, for your children."

"Like the Pilgrims," Riker supplied. Then, seeing Dr. Crusher's searching look he added, "I'm a bit of an amateur history buff myself."

"Or like the Min-hau. The desire to escape a corrupting cultural influence is not unique to Earth history," Troi said. "Nor is the desire to put as much distance between the new settlement and the old, to avoid the temptation to return and the possibility of contagion."

"That was how the Ashkaarian colonists must have seen it," said Dr. Crusher. "They wanted to keep communications between their new world and Skerris IV to the bare minimum. However, the Miramik find records reveal that it was the policy of the colonial office to demand quarterly reports from all new settlements. The motherworld liked to keep track of her daughters. Failure to receive these reports would set off all sorts of alarms, and an investigative mission would be dispatched to the silent colony as soon as possible."

"Let me guess," Riker said. "No reports from Ashkaar."

"There were some at first, all received at the proper intervals, but then . . . nothing." Dr. Crusher leaned her elbows on the table and rested her chin on her clasped hands. "And then, before anyone could be sent to discover the reason for the sudden silence, the war broke out and Skerris IV was destroyed."

Riker pressed his lips together. "So we're taking the Orakisan delegation in search of a colony that might not even exist to look for a plant that might be extinct." He stood up from the table. "I enjoy being an optimist, but at times like this it's too much work. My break's almost over. I have to get back to the bridge. If you'll excuse me, Doctor, Counsellor." He made a gallant, if archaic bow and left.

Dr. Crusher sighed. "It doesn't look very hopeful, does it?"

A half smile touched Troi's mouth. "Someone told me a riddle the other day; it seems appropriate now. What is the difference between an optimist and a pessimist?"

"Does this have anything to do with whether the glass is half full or half empty?" Troi shook her head. "All right, then, I give up."

"The optimist says that this is the best of all possible worlds. The pessimist agrees. Even if we believe there is no hope for the mission to Ashkaar, Beverly, we must still act as if there is."

"You know I will." Dr. Crusher settled back in her chair. "Who told you that riddle?"

"Alexander. He didn't know whether or not he ought to try it on his father." Troi's smile widened. "He isn't quite certain if Klingon warriors approve of riddles."

Dr. Crusher got a peculiar look on her face. "I can tell you one thing that Klingon warriors definitely do *not* approve of," she muttered.

"Oh?"

Before Counsellor Troi could make further inquiries, Ten Forward resounded with the clear, unmistakable tones of the *Enterprise*'s chief of security. "Doctor!" Lt. Worf boomed, bearing down on the doctor like a Tauridian thunderdust storm. "I have been looking for you everywhere. You and I must talk." He folded his arms across his powerful chest and glared down at her.

"Talk?" Dr. Crusher met his scowl with a look of limpid innocence. "What about?"

"It is not honorable to feign ignorance." His eyes narrowed. "I attempted to speak with you about it earlier, but you were on your way to the conference room with the Orakisan ambassador. Now we are both free and we must settle the matter. You will have to take it back."

"Take what back?" Counsellor Troi asked, wondering what Dr. Crusher could have done capable of angering Lt. Worf this much.

"The gift." Dr. Crusher looked at the ceiling. "The one I gave Alexander when I came back from Malabar Station."

"A gift?" Troi looked from Dr. Crusher's face to Lt. Worf's. Despite the Betazoid's inborn talents, both were unreadable. "What kind of gift?"

"A highly unsuitable gift, and one that must be returned at once," Lt. Worf decreed. "I cannot permit my son to keep it."

By now Troi was completely at a loss. "Beverly?" she appealed to the doctor.

Dr. Crusher rose from her seat. "Lt. Worf, if you insist that I take back the gift I gave to your son, I'll do it. However, I think we ought to have Counsellor Troi present when you tell Alexander about your decision. He may become upset."

"He will not!" Lt. Worf was scandalized at the very thought. "He will understand my reasons and obey. He does not want such a gift."

"Then why did he seem so pleased when I gave it to him?"

"He was—he was only being polite," Worf huffed. "He did not wish to offend you. Now that courtesy has been served, you may take the beast away."

"What beast?" Troi asked.

"An improper one," Worf maintained.

"Come with us and see for yourself." Dr. Crusher's eyes shone with barely concealed mischief.

In Lt. Worf's quarters, Counsellor Troi brought her face close to the transparent wall of the cage. "Is that a tribble? I thought they were extinct." she marvelled aloud.

"It's not a tribble," Dr. Crusher told her. "If it were awake and uncurled you could see its eyes, ears, and paws. It's a hamster. Dr. P'tann of Vulcan presented a fascinating paper about them at the Ark conference. They lived on Earth undiscovered in the wild until the mid twentieth century, when they first became widely used laboratory subjects, then popular pets. Of course there's no longer any call for them in the laboratory, but if anything, their numbers have increased. Dr. P'tann used them as a prime example of how biological success often defies the rules of logic."

Troi tilted her head, trying to get a better look at the dozing creature. "But it's adorable!" she exclaimed.

Lt. Worf snorted. "I am in complete agreement with the Vulcan. There is no reason for Alexander to harbor this creature. It is small, it is easily damaged, it sleeps most of the time, and when it is awake it deals with its food in an unseemly manner."

"Hamsters stuff their food in their cheek pouches," Dr. Crusher explained for Troi's benefit. "I admit it can look frightening." She looked at Worf meaningfully.

"It did not frighten me," he said with more heat than necessary. "At the time, I was concerned that the creature would ingest too much and explode. In any case, that is irrelevant. The point is, my son will not learn anything to advance his training as a warrior by tending such a weak and helpless animal. It will be a needless distraction from his studies. Please remove it."

"If you insist," Dr. Crusher said. She picked up the cage. "And what will you tell Alexander when he comes home from school?"

Lt. Worf wore the resolute air of every parent who has ever determined that he knows what is best for his offspring. "I will tell him the truth, that you took it away."

Dr. Crusher set the cage down again. "That's it? That's all?"

Lt. Worf looked surprised. "That is all there is to say about the matter."

"No, Lt. Worf, that is not all there is to say. Not unless you also intend to tell him that I took away his pet because you told me to do it. As a matter of fact, I won't remove this hamster until Alexander comes home and knows what's going on." She took a stance that broadcast that the only way either she or the hamster was going to budge was if Worf himself laid hands on them.

The Klingon was not happy with this turn of events. "I fail to see what will be gained by having my son present. I do not require his consent in this matter."

"Then *you* remove the hamster."

"Very well, I will." Worf picked up the cage and started for the door.

"Where will you take it?" Counsellor Troi called after him.

"To sick bay," Worf answered. "You heard for yourself, it was once a laboratory subject. It belongs in a laboratory."

Dr. Crusher stepped neatly into Worf's path, blocking his way out the door. "Not in my lab," she said. "Not without Alexander's permission."

"I told you, I do not require Alexander's permission to—"

"But I do and sickbay is my territory."

"Then I will take it elsewhere."

"And where might that be?" Dr. Crusher's face hardened. Although she said nothing, her expression made it clear that she was thinking of Klingon cuisine and daring Lt. Worf to deny that he had been thinking the same thing.

Counsellor Troi automatically fell into the role of intermediary in an increasingly tense situation. "Perhaps it would be best to wait until Alexander returns from school, Lt. Worf," she suggested. "If your son will accept your decision as reasonably as you predict, there will be no harm in waiting."

"There is no need for waiting," Worf insisted. "He is my son, and if I say that this animal is not a fit example for a warrior, then I know what I am—" His diatribe was interrupted by the chirp of his communicator. In its cage, the hamster burst from its nest of wood shavings at the unexpected noise. Worf gave the startled beast a scornful look, set the cage down on a side table, and touched his badge. "Worf here."

"Lt. Worf, report to bridge immediately." Captain Picard's voice came through loud and clear.

"Aye, sir. Worf out." The Klingon looked from the cage to Dr. Crusher. "We will settle this later," he growled, and strode from the room. He was not sure, but he could have sworn he heard the faint sound of Dr. Crusher's suppressed laughter before the door shut behind him.

"Lt. Worf reporting as ordered, sir." The Klingon's practiced eye took in the scene awaiting him on the bridge. All three members of the Orakisan delegation were present. There was a pervasive air of excitement about them. Even the normally dour Legate Valdor seemed tempted to smile.

"You're just in time, Lt. Worf," Captain Picard said from the command chair. "I wanted you to be here for this."

"For what, sir?"

The captain indicated the scene currently displayed on the bridge viewscreen. Seven worlds and their attendant moons orbited a G-class star. "We have just entered the Ashkaar system. Ashkaar itself, the Skerrian colony we came here to contact, is the fourth world from this system's sun. When cursory long-range sensor scans of the planet's surface revealed scattered concentrations of humanoid life-forms, I had Ensign Kolb open hailing frequencies."

Worf looked at the Orakisan delegation. Ambassador Lelys was beaming, her face radiant with hope as she gazed at the viewscreen. "I assume you received a response, sir?"

"Yes. An extremely brief transmission from an observatory on the main continent. They requested that we repeat our transmission as soon as they could notify the government of our presence. We are presently waiting to receive the official response from that government."

"Signal coming through now, sir," Ensign Kolb said.

"Put it on screen, Ensign," the captain ordered.

At once the viewscreen was dominated by the smiling image of a well-fleshed, middle-aged male who might have passed for Legate Valdor's distant cousin. The luminous irises of his eyes were the bright gold of sunflower petals, and his thinning hair was pulled into a willow-green plait slung over one shoulder like a pet serpent.

"Greetings, my friends!" he cried, making an all-embracing gesture of welcome with his plump hands. "I am Udar Kishrit of the Masra'et. I welcome you with joy. When we were first informed of your presence, we could not believe that the gods had seen fit to grant us such a blessing. It seemed like a dream, and yet—But there you are. Can you see me all right?"

"Yes," Picard replied. "I trust you are receiving our transmission satisfactorily also?"

Udar Kishrit chuckled. "Yes, yes, praise the Net of Blessings. You understand, our own system of communications is limited to this world. I did not expect it to be powerful enough to send or receive off-world signals so well."

Ambassador Lelys stepped forward, her face still alight. "Udar Kishrit, I greet you in the name of Orakisa, your long-lost sisterworld, like Ashkaar, a daughter of S'ka'rys."

"Ashkaar?" Udar Kishrit repeated. His amiable look collapsed into a frown. "There is no Ashkaar. This is Ne'elat. Ashkaar is dead."

Chapter Three

COUNSELLOR TROI WATCHED ATTENTIVELY as the fourth
delegation of Ne'elatian children approached the center of the vast civic gardens where the ceremony of
welcome was taking place. In their long, white robes,
their carefully braided hair ornamented with silver
starbursts, the young ones were a beautiful and
charming sight. They came forward singing, their
arms laden with flowers, and added these to the
imposing pile of blossoms already mounded at Ambassador Lelys's feet.

"Don't worry, my dear, they are the last," Troi
overheard Udar Kishrit whisper in the ambassador's
ear. "Your visit is a gift to us, and this ceremony is our
gift to you. Our teachers say that one gift must be met
with another or harmony is lost."

If Lelys responded to this information at all, Troi
could not hear her. The Betazoid shifted her attention
elsewhere, first to her right, where Captain Picard and

Commander Riker completed the ambassador's entourage, then to her left, where the five other members of the Masra'et—the governing council of Ne'elat—attended their leader, Udar Kishrit.

It was as Udar Kishrit had promised. The fourth group of children was the last body of Ne'elatians to participate in the formal rites of welcome. As soon as they were gone, he spoke a few words to officially conclude the ceremony, then offered Ambassador Lelys his arm and personally escorted her into the nearby palace of government. The others followed.

The palace of government seemed to have been made of air and light rather than stone. Shining pink pillars of elfin slenderness soared to support ceilings that had been painted to resemble spring skies. Tiled floors offered up scenes of unknown gods casting golden nets out into the depths of space to snare a dazzling catch of comets and suns and planets, with here and there the silvery sliver of a starship like a minnow tangled in the strands.

They passed many Ne'elatians in the palace halls, some hefting scrolls and books and papers, some carrying piles of thin, inflexible tablets that clattered together, and others still speaking into hand-held communication devices. In short, they saw all stripes and breeds of bureaucrats, hard at work or at least trying to give that impression. Udar Kishrit and the other members of the Masra'et paused now and then to detain one of the scurriers. Always their interview began with the proud and joyous presentation of Ambassador Lelys as "she who has given us back the stars."

At last they reached a private room where a long, low table made of transparent crystal gleamed like a sheet of ice. Backless chairs with high armrests and overstuffed cushions stood waiting. Udar Kishrit seated the Orakisan ambassador at what had to be the place of honor, a gracefully curved indentation on one of the table's longer sides. Then he and the other council members took seats facing her. There seemed to be no formalities now, though as head of the Masra'et, Udar Kishrit's place was directly opposite the ambassador's. The representatives of Starfleet were allowed to choose their own places.

Either they have called off all ceremony or they have decided that we are no longer important, Troi mused. *And yet when Udar Kishrit first invited us to the planet's surface—insisted on it, in fact—he was almost too deferential. I've seen this kind of behavior before. This man has a face for every occasion.* She glanced sidelong at Captain Picard. To judge by his bearing he had reached the same conclusion as she concerning Udar Kishrit, and was wary.

Udar Kishrit himself was seemingly oblivious to the scrutiny of his character. He leaned across the table, all goodwill, his whole body transformed into one giant, ongoing embrace to enfold the ambassador. "I thank you, gracious lady, for your patience with our rites," he told her. "I realize that our welcome must have been tedious for you, but we had no other choice. All guests are sacred, their coming to be hailed and honored, and such a guest as yourself! But now that we have served the teachings, we can speak freely. How we have dreamed of this day! It has been too long in coming. Take no offense, but you come to us like a creature out of the old legends, a wonderful impossibility. Until your arrival, we did not know that such a world as Orakisa existed, seed of our common mother."

"And we did not know of Ne'elat's existence either," Lelys replied. "Not at all." A dark look crossed her face like a passing cloud.

"You are troubled," Udar Kishrit said in a most ingratiating tone. "How can I ease this?"

"Udar Kishrit, I will not dissemble. We did not come here seeking our sisterworld for its own sake. If circumstances had been otherwise, we would have put off reestablishing contact with you for years yet." In as few words as possible, Ambassador Lelys went on to describe the situation on Skerris IV.

As Lelys spoke, Counsellor Troi could sense the Orakisan's mounting emotional stress. *Her diplomatic training is good, but she has held the mask of professional neutrality in place for too long. The lives of all her family depend on her and she knows it, just as she knows that the n'vashal seeds taken along by the colonists of Ashkaar are their only hope. But Ashkaar is dead. The question is, did the seeds die with it?*

Udar Kishrit heard out the ambassador's story, his face the perfect image of concern. "N'vashal?" he repeated when she was done. "Ah, my lady, is that all? How small a thing! You shame us by asking for so little—you, our beloved kin, who will restore to us the means to reunite with the stars. I hope you will not think me impertinent, but if sometime before we part you would permit me the supreme honor of viewing the blessed vessel which brought you to us—"

Ambassador Lelys lowered her eyes. "That is not for me to say. It is not an Orakisan ship, but a Starfleet vessel."

"Not yours?" A tiny crack appeared in Udar Kishrit's jovial mask, but was quickly patched away.

"No Orakisan starship could have brought us here as swiftly as the *Enterprise,* and speed was—is of the essence."

"Orakisa has long been a valued member of the United Federation of Planets," Captain Picard said. "Starfleet has been requested to do whatever possible to aid their colonists on Skerris IV. We were glad to be of service."

"Starfleet. The United Federation of Planets." Udar Kishrit repeated the names with a childlike awe, then erupted into fresh smiles. "Ah, so much, so *very* much for us to learn! Great things. Our sisterworld must be powerful indeed if she commands such servants."

"Oh no, Udar Kishrit, you mistake me," Ambassador Lelys said quickly. "The Federation stands ready to aid and defend all its members, regardless of the individual planet's importance."

"Is this so?" The head of the Masra'et considered this new information, then made a discreet motion for the council members at either side of him to lean in. They whispered among themselves for a short interval, then settled back on their cushions. Udar Kishrit's expansive smile had spread to his colleagues like a case of Denebian swamp fever.

"We rejoice in the good fortune of our sisterworld to have earned the favor of so mighty a shield as your Federation. We pray that you will enrich us by describing how it was you won this prize."

"Udar Kishrit, I'm afraid you don't understand," Picard said. "Orakisa did nothing extraordinary to earn membership in the Federation. When a world wishes to join the United Federation of Planets there are, of course, the proper channels for application, but these are open to all. If any world should desire to—"

"Any world?" The Ne'elatian waved his hand over the tabletop and a panel irised open to allow a hidden platform to rise, bearing refreshments. He poured a thin, blue liquid from a decanter like a giant emerald and passed walnut-sized silver cups to all present.

However, he made sure to serve the first cup to Captain Picard. "Even this?"

"Yes." The captain responded in a guarded manner.

"But we are so—so primitive, by your standards."

"We have seen a good deal of your city since our arrival," Picard replied. "I would hardly call it primitive. I confess, I was not expecting to encounter this level of technology. The surviving records on Skerris IV indicate that the founders of Ashkaar left to establish a simpler way of life."

"That was long ago, Captain," Udar Kishrit said, abruptly solemn. "I cannot vouch for the intentions of my ancestors. As to our technology, it would be an insult to compare it to yours. Your ships sail the stars! Ours are confined to this system alone."

"How is that possible?" Commander Riker asked. "The Skerrians had starships with warp drive. Your ancestors couldn't have come this far from the homeworld on impulse power; they'd still be in transit."

Udar Kishrit sipped his drink. "You came here seeking a world called Ashkaar; Ashkaar is lost. So, too, the secret of the ship that brought us there, and from there, here."

"How did it happen?"

He nodded to the man on his right. "Meeran Okosa is our council historian. In harmony, it is his place to speak of it."

Meeran Okosa crossed his hands before his chest, thumbs touching, so that if a light were shone behind them their shape would look like the shadow of a dove. Bowing his head over them, he said, "In the name of the six moral treasures, I will tell it." He raised his eyes and in a lilting voice recited, "Our fathers and mothers swam from star to star, seeking new hope in a new world. Those who had gone before them from the homeworld saw Ashkaar, fourth daughter of the blessed sun, and gave it good report. So our ancestors came after, on the word of the scouts, and settled there, giving thanks for the kindliness of the climate and the fertile land."

He paused in the telling, all eyes on him. Not one of his auditors disturbed the perfect silence of the room by so much as the clink of a glass being set down on the sleek tabletop. Meeran Okosa seemed pleased by such attention and went on:

"But surfaces deceive and the warmest smile tells nothing of the heart beneath. Time revealed what the scouts could not have known: The ground of Ashkaar shook with the writhings of unquiet spirits, it split apart the pleasant fields, cast up poisonous vapors, and in the end drove our fathers and mothers back into the black sky-sea. In their lone ship they sought another land and found it in the blessed sun's fifth daughter, which they named Ne'elat, which means the new sustainer. Ne'elat was no golden land. It wanted the warmth of Ashkaar, but it also lacked Ashkaar's evil eruptions. To live here would take work, but our ancestors did not fear that. What they feared was that the world we had left would not know what had become of them. And so our fathers and mothers took council and said, 'Let us send our starship home again to tell our kin that we have chosen a different world, and also to bring us back what aid they can, for we lost much when we left Ashkaar, and Ne'elat demands more to sustain us until we have learned her ways.'"

He took a breath and concluded, "So the ship was sent, and the ship was lost, and with it the homeworld and all help except what came from the gods." He laid his hands palms down on the table.

"You see how it was, Captain Picard." Udar Kishrit

resumed control of the meeting. "When their ship did not return and when no word came from the home-world, our ancestors realized that they were truly on their own. Building a new ship was out of the question. They had left S'ka'rys seeking a simpler life, as you say. No one with the knowledge for building starships would join such an expedition. Likewise they lacked the materials and the means to obtain them. Apart from all this, they had to devote all their efforts to the more immediate problems of survival on a hostile world."

"I'd say they more than succeeded," Captain Picard remarked, sipping his drink. It was tart on the tongue, though it had an almost honey-like bouquet.

"A limited success. There are some who say that we have betrayed the dream of our ancestors." Udar Kishrit gave Meeran Okosa a look short and sharp as a dagger blade. "But what choice did we have? A simpler life requires a kinder land. Could we stand by and watch our children die from cold and hunger and sickness when we had the knowledge to prevent it?"

The council historian snorted scornfully. "You mouth one of the nine deaths of S'ka'rys, Udar Kishrit. The teachings recall that our fathers and mothers left the homeworld precisely because they were surrounded by too many people speaking the same evil."

"Our ancestors were surrounded by some of the most brilliant minds in the universe," Udar Kishrit replied hotly. "The teachings themselves speak of the discoveries and inventions, the pure knowledge that S'ka'rys brought into the light!"

"Into the darkness, you mean. The teachings do not mention S'ka'rys for praise, but to give us warning. They held themselves too high, the ones our ancestors fled. Because their hands created ships to sail the stars, they forgot who had created the stars they sailed. And in the end, did they not create their own destruction?" He looked to Ambassador Lelys for confirmation.

She bowed her head. "That is so."

Udar Kishrit made an impatient sound with his lips. "We are not S'ka'rys, Meeran Okosa. No new thing comes from our hands without the blessings of the gods. We have the ceremonies to anchor each discovery of the mind to the realm of the spirit. We will not repeat the errors of the past. Neither will we sacrifice the future."

But what will you sacrifice to gain *the future you want, Udar Kishrit?* Counsellor Troi wondered. Looking at the head of the Masra'et, she felt a distinct chill trickle down her spine. There was something more to him than a strong will or the wish to bring his world out of isolation. When he spoke, she heard the roaring of a fire, a blaze without limits that would devour anything that stood between him and his desires.

Anything . . . or anyone.

She forced herself to shake off the warning chill in time to hear Udar Kishrit say, "I pledge you my word as head of the Masra'et that we will do everything in our power to help you in your search. I regret that I am not familiar with the name of the plant you seek, but then, I do not pretend to know much about flowers. There is also the chance that we have another name for what you call n'vashal. I am certain that our combined efforts will be rewarded." He rose, and his fellow council members followed his lead. The meeting was obviously coming to an end.

Ambassador Lelys and the rest stood as well. "May it be so, and soon," she said. "Our gratitude to you would be immeasurable. Our sages too teach that gifts must be given when gifts are received. If your world can give us back the lives of our dear ones in peril on S'ka'rys, then our world will give yours the path to the stars."

As they all filed out of the chamber, Riker managed to draw Counsellor Troi aside. "What's wrong?" he asked. "I know that look. What did you pick up on in there?"

"I am not sure," she answered. "Nothing that will affect the Orakisan mission."

"But *something,* yes?"

"Only that Udar Kishrit can be a very... determined man."

"Well, that might be all to the good as far as the mission's concerned. As soon as he heard about Starfleet and the Federation he was all ears, eager to get Ne'elat in. I'll bet he thinks that if his people can produce some n'vashal, it's a done deal. He'll make sure they give one hundred ten percent to the search now."

"Perhaps." The Betazoid picked up her pace, leaving Riker behind, until she drew level with Udar Kishrit. The head of the Masra'et was walking between Captain Picard and Ambassador Lelys, chatting affably with both, offering the full hospitality of the capital to any and all who might desire it.

"I will not hear of a refusal," he told Captain Picard. "A starship is a marvel, but it is a place of containment. It would be my pleasure, my honor, to offer your crew the freedom of our city. The teachings say: The rich man paints his ceiling to resemble heaven, the poor man steps out of his hut and has heaven for the asking."

"A generous offer, Udar Kishrit," Captain Picard replied. "Thank you. We will consider it."

"And a beautiful sentiment," Troi said, insinuating herself between the captain and the chief councilman.

"Although I must say, I have not seen anything remotely like a hut since our arrival."

"Dear lady, you are blessed with the second moral treasure, which is kindness." He gave her an indulgent look. "We thank the gods for our prosperity. That is one of the older teachings, from the days when our ancestors first came here from Ashkaar."

"All of them?"

Udar Kishrit stopped short. "What?"

"Before you answered our hail, we scanned your sun's fourth world for signs of humanoid life. We found them."

"That's true," Captain Picard said. "At the time we didn't pursue the matter, but now that Counsellor Troi mentions it—"

"Oh, *that.*" Udar Kishrit burst into peals of laughter. "They're nothing, nothing at all."

"Are you saying that there is no life on Ashkaar? That our sensors picked up a false signal?" Picard asked. His eyes concealed any hint that he already knew the true answer to that question. The *Enterprise*'s sensors were in perfect working order. If they detected humanoid life-forms, those life-forms were there. If Udar Kishrit denied it—

"No, of course not. There are Ne'elatians living on Ashkaar. Not many, and some not worthy to be named. Criminals, mostly, of the more dangerous sort. I trespass against the sixth moral treasure of forgiveness when I say this, but I sleep better at night knowing that there is more than just a wall between them and me."

"There seemed to be quite a high number of readings," Picard pressed, although he gave every impression of reluctance. "I suppose if we count the guards that must be stationed there as well . . ."

"Ah, I see that you, too, are a master of the second

moral treasure, Captain Picard." Udar Kishrit's eyes twinkled. "We do not have that many criminals on Ashkaar. The majority of your readings must be our military training encampments. The terrain is rough and the conditions harsh, but that is an advantage when you wish to produce a good soldier."

Captain Picard nodded his agreement. By this time, they had passed through the palace of government and out into the plaza where the party from the *Enterprise* had first materialized on the surface of Ne'elat. Picard contacted the ship and told the engineer on duty to prepare to beam them back up, but before he gave the command to energize he told Udar Kishrit, "With your permission, I think I would like to take you up on your kind offer of hospitality. How soon can you accommodate any visitors from my ship?"

"At once and with joy!" Udar Kishrit exclaimed.

Shortly after, as they were stepping off the transporter platform, Riker turned to Picard and said, "That was unexpected."

"What was?"

"That decision to turn this into a shore leave."

Captain Picard turned his head; his eyes met Counsellor Troi's. "I have my reasons," was all he said.

Chapter Four

GEORDI LA FORGE HAD NEVER thought of himself as a spy. Still, here he was, getting ready to beam down to the surface of Ne'elat and—there was no other word for it—spy on the natives. Well, all right, to observe them. Closely. Captain Picard had been quite specific about that *closely* part.

At least I can't say I'm too surprised by this, the Enterprise's chief engineer thought as he checked the readings on the warp drives. (If he had to spend any significant length of time ashore, first he was going to make sure he left everything in his division ship-shape.) *I'm no cadet. It's not the first time I've been handed an assignment that's outside the boundaries of my original job description.* He shrugged. Starfleet officers were always prepared to do whatever was required of them as long as it served the greater good and did not violate regulations.

True, no one involved had ever come right out and

used the word spying, but how else to describe this assignment? He wasn't due for shore leave, he had no training in diplomacy and even less in botany. And if there's some other field of expertise with any bearing on the mission to Ashkaar, no one bothered to tell him about it.

Ne'elat, he mentally corrected himself. *As a colony, Ashkaar's gone.*

That was what the Ne'elatians claimed, anyhow, and the Ne'elatians were the last hope of the Orakisan colonists on Skerris IV. *I'm no more a diplomat than I'm a spy,* Geordi thought, *but even I know it's not the smartest thing to come right out and accuse people of lying when they've got something you need that badly.*

He checked out a flickering bank of telltales. *Not that there's any proof that the Ne'elatians are lying, just suspicions.*

He remembered the reaction when Captain Picard and the others from the first Ne'elatian visit had reported their findings to a small group of handpicked crewmembers and the two remaining members of the Orakisan diplomatic mission in the captain's ready room. He could still feel Legate Valdor's angry words burning his ears:

"So what if there were life-form readings on Ashkaar? They are irrelevant! Soldiers and prisoners will not help us fulfill our mission; Udar Kishrit and the Masra'et will. You waste my time and yours by speaking of this when you would do better to join your resources to theirs in aid of the search for n'vashal."

Geordi didn't need to rely on his visor to tell that Picard was not pleased with the Orakisan's outburst; he could hear the captain adopt a distinctly more controlled and formal tone to his reply, as dead a giveaway as the brightest warning beacon to those who knew their commander well.

"We have already attempted to place our own people side by side with the Ne'elatians whom the Masra'et members have assigned to the project. Our offers of help were refused—pleasantly, but firmly."

"For someone who seems to be so eager to show off his world, Udar Kishrit's still got plenty of Keep Out signs posted," Riker commented, his eyes following the graceful water ballet of the fish in the ornamental aquarium. Geordi wondered whether the lieutenant's casual attitude was deliberate, intended to soften the already hostile atmosphere. "Not in so many words, but the message is still crystal clear."

"Perhaps he has something to hide, but perhaps not. We may be mistaken in how we interpret his actions," Ambassador Lelys spoke up. "It is plain to see that Udar Kishrit wants nothing more than to have Ne'elat taken into the United Federation of Planets as soon as possible. I believe he is under the impression that if the Ne'elatians, alone and unaided, succeed in locating the n'vashal plant, this accomplishment will somehow guarantee their immediate induction."

"Let him think so, then!" Valdor snapped. "It will be to our advantage. Would you interfere with something that could save the lives of our brethren on Skerris IV?"

"That is not the point." Geordi was taken aback by the sudden bite in the Orakisan ambassador's tone. Lelys had the uncanny ability to change from a blossom to a blade in an eyeblink. "I have already conferred with Captain Picard and Counsellor Troi and we are in agreement. If we cannot trust Udar Kishrit's honesty about the life-form readings on

Ashkaar, do we dare to trust his promises of help with our search?"

"Conferred with them, you say?" Valdor's brows came together. "You have had secret meetings—meetings of which I was purposely kept ignorant?"

In the face of Valdor's indignation, Hara'el attempted to play the peacemaker. "Father, please, it was no great thing. Ambassador Lelys did not seek to exclude you—us—from any vital information. By tradition, as senior representative, she was the only one of our party whose presence was required at the first encounter with the Ne'elatians. It was all done according to strictest protocol. I am sure that this discussion she had with Captain Picard and Counsellor Troi took place then, while they were on Ne'elat and we remained here."

"That is so," Troi confirmed. "Any secrecy touching our conference was purely accidental, not planned."

"Certainly not planned by me." Lelys met Valdor's hard look with one of her own. It was neither a defensive statement nor an apology. Privately Geordi decided that if this confrontation worsened, his money would be on the lady.

Valdor was unmollified. "And yet this is the first I hear of it! You and I, Ambassador, and my son Hara'el are a single entity in the eyes of our brethren on Orakisa. Three voices, one mind; three bodies, one heart. You know the dictates as well as I do. To keep anything from us betrays our unity."

"Nothing has been kept from you." Ambassador Lelys's eyes took on an icy glitter.

"Not kept, no, not exactly. But information that is delayed is almost as—"

"Then you are in agreement with us, Legate Valdor." Captain Picard was swift to step into the widening breach between the Orakisan envoys. "You, too, understand the importance of bringing the whole truth of Ne'elat to light."

Unwilling to surrender so easily, Valdor insisted, "I still do not see that the Ne'elatians are hiding anything. Not from what you have relayed to us."

"Perhaps they only seem to be hiding something," Hara'el said. "In the same way you believed that Ambassador Lelys was deliberately—" A curt gesture from his father stopped Hara'el's words cold. The silence was deep enough for Geordi to pick up the faint sigh of the fishtank filter.

Ambassador Lelys was less easily cowed. "If we are wrong about Udar Kishrit, we will make amends. But if the cracked vessel will not hold water, why should we assume it will hold wine? If he has lied to us about one thing, why not another? How can we trust that he will fulfill his promise to find us n'vashal?"

Valdor laughed contemptuously. "Why would he want to lie about helping us?"

"Why would he want to lie about Ashkaar?" Troi countered.

The elder Orakisan's face darkened. "What makes you think he *is* lying about that?"

"May I, sir?" Mr. Data turned to Captain Picard and received permission to speak. "As repeated here, Udar Kishrit's explanations for the life-form readings on Ashkaar are not logical. Ne'elat is not overpopulated, therefore if the authorities wished to keep dangerous criminals in custody far from law-abiding citizens, they could construct prisons in any of a number of remote sites on the planet itself. To transport them to another world is neither convenient, economical, nor necessary. Moreover, from your descriptions of Ne'elat, it does not seem to suffer from poverty, ignorance, or intolerance, therefore I would not expect it to be a particularly lawless society. It is my theory that were we to inspect the judicial records, we would find that what prisons the Ne'elatians do maintain on their world are not filled to capacity."

"Next I suppose you'll tell us that the Ne'elatians have no military training outposts on Ashkaar either," Valdor sneered.

His sarcasm had no effect on the android. "It would surprise me if they did. The Ne'elatians enjoy a united planetary government of apparent political stability. They may have a domestic security system in place, but with no threat of war, they do not need to train an army."

"And what of the possibility of an off-world invasion?" The Orakisan legate acted as smug as if he had just made the winning move in a game of chess.

Geordi suppressed a smile. *Wrong game to play with Data if you want to win, Legate Valdor.*

Mr. Data promptly proved the engineer right: "They also inhabit a remote world of little strategic or material value, except to themselves. Even supposing that some alien power wished to invade and conquer their system, such a power would have to possess warp drive to reach Ne'elat in the first place. Any troops trained on Ashkaar would be outmaneuvered and probably outgunned in short order."

"In other words, it would make about as much sense for the Ne'elatians to train troops off-world as it would for us to maintain a Roman legion," Riker commented so softly that Geordi wondered whether he'd been the only one to hear it.

Having his every argument so casually demolished sank Valdor even deeper into his usual state of cold-eyed, smoldering resentment. He said nothing more for the rest of the debriefing.

On the other hand, young Hara'el seemed to gain courage from his father's silence. "We are indebted to Starfleet for your help in this mission. We will be guided by your suggestions concerning the reliability of the Ne'elatians. They are our brethren, but blood is no guarantee of truth. It will do no harm to investigate any misgivings you might have, especially if you suspect they might affect the ultimate success of our quest. I recommend that we give Orakisa's official approval to whatever plan our allies suggest." He made an elegant gesture of deference to Captain Picard.

"Well said, Hara'el." Ambassador Lelys was the tender-petalled flower once more. Her approving smile sent the younger male into a new attack of agitation, which she ignored. "I concur. Legate Valdor, will you join with us?"

"I will not add my voice until I have heard what their plan might be," Valdor snarled.

"We have been given an open invitation to visit Ne'elat," Captain Picard said. "I suggest that we use it to our advantage. All of our misgivings can be put to rest by information, and we can gather that information for ourselves, through close and careful observation of the true state of things on Ne'elat. We will send several parties of crewmembers to the surface, some of them instructed to look and listen attentively for any evidence to confirm our suspicions of Udar Kishrit and the council or—and I hope this will be the case—to dismiss them entirely." It was shortly after that that Geordi found himself tapped to be one such observer.

"In other words, a spy," he muttered as he wrapped up his tour of inspection. He shook his head over the whole situation. Truths, half truths, hidden truths, lies that were deliberate or accidental or truth wearing a mask . . . It was all too complicated for his liking. Why couldn't people be more straightforward, like machines?

That thought brought a fleeting image of his good friend Data to mind. Geordi smiled. Did the two of them get along so well because or in spite of the fact that each, in his own way, had one foot on either side of the human-machine borderline? There was a saying in Starfleet that a good engineer understood machines almost as well as he did people, but that a *great* engineer understood people almost as well as he did machines.

I've got to get out more, Geordi told himself. *Maybe it's past time I started paying more attention to people. Maybe this shore leave is just what I need after all, no matter why I'm getting it. I know I won't be a very good spy, but there's no reason I can't explore Ne'elat, meet someone new, just have a plain, ordinary, good time.* With that resolution in mind, Geordi headed for the transporter room.

"*Now* will you admit we're lost?" Ensign Yee demanded. She pointed to the floor-to-ceiling wall panel, a panoramic landscape, every line and shape of it a carefully inlaid piece of semiprecious stone. It dominated the high-domed chamber where six corridors intersected. It was not a landmark you could forget, especially if this was the fourth time you had found it. "*Now* will you ask someone for directions?"

"A Starfleet officer is resourceful," Ensign Blumberg countered. "We can find our own way."

Ensign Yee looked doubtful and dismissed Ensign Blumberg's words by turning to Geordi and asking, "Please, sir, can't we stop one of our hosts and ask which way to the gardens? The concert's supposed to start soon and—"

Geordi restrained the urge to laugh, not at the two quarreling ensigns, but at himself. Ensign Yee was right, they were definitely lost and they should have asked for directions long ago. The government palace of Ne'elat was like a three-dimensional example of any sufficiently advanced bureaucracy, a labyrinth to those uninitiated into the secret plan underlying it all.

Very well then, he'd ask directions. But from whom? Geordi glanced around the huge, circular chamber. Unlike most of the areas in the Ne'elatian palace of government, this one seemed virtually deserted. During the four unsuccessful attempts Geordi and his party had made trying to find the gardens, they had passed through corridors and anterooms where it was almost impossible to get by for all the Ne'elatians rushing here and there on their own errands.

"Wait here," Geordi directed. "I'll see if I can find someone who can help us." He started up one of the six entryways.

Behind him, he heard Ensign Blumberg declare, "I can find my own way," followed by the sound of retreating footsteps. This was in turn followed by Ensign Yee's loud, heartfelt sigh of resignation, and then her voice calling, "No, not *that* way! We just came *out* that way! You're going to get yourself lost even worse than . . ." More retreating footsteps reached Geordi's ears, the rapid beat of Ensign Yee taking off after Ensign Blumberg.

Wonderful. Now I've lost them, too, Geordi thought. *We'll probably have to have the ship's sensors locate us all, one by one, when it's time to go back. Some shore leave. And some spy I am. I can't even find any Ne'elatians to ask directions from, let alone to observe.* He shook his head, marvelling over his bad luck.

That was when he became aware that he was not

alone. The sensors in his visor that served him in lieu of eyesight touched off an uneasy feeling that he was being watched. He looked all around, but there was no one there. The corridor he had chosen to explore was empty, though there were several doors lining it, as well as many pillared alcoves made to display an assortment of Ne'elatian art treasures.

He considered knocking on one of the closed doors, in case anyone was in who could help him on his way, but Blumberg's words echoed in his ears and he stopped short. It was one thing to ask directions of a Ne'elatian encountered in the hallway, quite another to go hunting up a native guide. Geordi couldn't have explained the difference if anyone had asked him, but he knew at the gut level that doing the latter was tantamount to surrendering something very precious to him. A Starfleet officer was resourceful—took a healthy pride in being resourceful—but a Starfleet officer who was blind knew that resourcefulness was another word for independence, and independence was the most precious thing he owned.

As he stood there in the hallway, a cool breeze brought him the scent of alien flowers. Cautiously he followed his nose. *Maybe I can find the gardens without asking directions after all,* he mused as the scent grew more distinct. *I should have thought of this before I lost Yee and Blumberg. It's getting stronger. We must've been closer to the gardens than we thought.* The flowery perfume led him on until it reached him at a sharp angle, from a doorway to his left. Now it was so intense that he was sure that he was on the threshold of the palace gardens. He turned and went through, expecting to feel the sun on his face and to hear the sounds of the musicians tuning their instruments for the promised concert, an event specially staged to honor the visiting Starfleet crew.

Instead he felt the same cool, perfumed breeze and saw neither gardens nor musicians nor fellow crew-members, but the startled face of a young Ne'elatian woman. She wore a plain green robe, and her hair was hidden by a veil of the same color, its gauzy material held in place by silver netting. She was very lovely.

Geordi smiled. "Excuse me, but could you please tell me how to get to the palace gar—?"

She dropped to the floor before him, face pressed to the cold stone, arms extended and crossed above her head. "Let there be mercy for this one, unworthy as I am to hear your words, starlord," she said. She sounded as if she were on the verge of tears or panic or both.

Geordi's smile was gone. He squatted down on his haunches and looked at the woman closely. "I'm sorry, I didn't mean to scare you. I'm just lost. I want to find the palace gardens. Could you please—?"

She moaned and wrapped her arms over her head, as if cowering in anticipation of a blow. "Starlord, forgive me for having displeased you in this or in any desire you might have." The words were muffled, but Geordi still managed to hear all she had to say. "My spirit is still imprisoned by the flesh; its flaws have led me astray. My glorious teachers warned us that we would do best to keep to our rooms while you deigned to walk with them in the undying light of Evramur. I disobeyed. I heard there was to be music, and there is no sweeter sound than the celestial songs of Evramur. My greedy spirit thought it would do no harm to go secretly to hear it. I should have known that there is no thing that can be kept secret from the glorious ones. My sins are many. I admit them freely and give myself up to any penance necessary, even though it might be exile from the joys of Evramur." Her slender shoulders shook ever so slightly as she began to cry.

Geordi stayed where he was, staring at her, completely at a loss. At last he reached out his hand and touched her gently. "Don't cry," he said. "Please."

She lifted her face, copiously streaked with tears, and asked, "Is this—is this your will, starlord?"

"Yes. And also that you stop calling me starlord." He stood up, giving her a hand to help her rise with him. "My name is Geordi La Forge. What's yours?"

The irises of her brilliant turquoise eyes dilated with a mix of consternation and fear. Then she ducked her head and said, "I must go." She jerked her hand from Geordi's grasp and ran away.

He never knew what possessed him to race after her, he only knew that he couldn't let her escape him. Her robes were long and voluminous, hardly the best thing to wear for efficient running. He caught up with her easily. As soon as his hand fell on her shoulder, she hit the ground again, alternately imploring mercy of the starlord and declaring her unworthiness to receive it.

Geordi leaned back against a pillar and slid down it until he was seated cross-legged beside her. Very patiently he said, "I think there's been a mistake. I told you, I'm not a starlord, whatever that is. I'm Geordi La Forge, chief engineer of the *U.S.S. Enterprise.* You don't have to tell me your name if you don't want to. I'm sorry, maybe I was out of place asking that. I don't know the customs here on Ne'elat. I'm here on shore leave, just visiting your planet, and there's supposed to be a concert taking place in the palace gardens. I'd like to hear it. Would it be all right for you to take me there?" He felt odd, talking to the back of the young woman's head, but she was so tightly curled up into a protective ball that it didn't look as if he would ever get to see her face again.

Pity, he thought. *It's a very beautiful face.* He settled his shoulders more comfortably against the pillar, ready to wait as long as it took for a reply.

His patience was rewarded. After a time, the young woman tilted her head sideways and looked up at him out of the corner of one eye. He tried his luck at luring her back into the open with another smile. This time she raised her head and slowly uncurled her body until she was seated on her heels, facing him with a look no longer fearful, but merely uncertain.

"Ne'elat?" she asked. "Why do you call this place Ne'elat?"

Her question took him aback. He'd never had to explain the name of a planet to one of its own inhabitants, especially not when he knew that it was the same name the inhabitants had given that planet in the first place.

Maybe she thinks I'm talking about the palace itself, he reasoned. *They might have an official name for it, like the House Adorning Peace on Canis II or the Talking Lodge on Lamech V. She probably thinks I've confused the name of the government palace with the name of her planet.*

"I'm not calling this *building* Ne'elat; I'm talking about this whole *world,*" he said. He accompanied his words with an expansive gesture and hoped he had set things straight between them.

"World?" She shrank into herself as she echoed the word, panic edging back into her voice. "How great is your realm, starlord, if you can call boundless Evramur no more than a world?"

Now it was his turn to be bewildered. "What are you talking about? Evramur? I've heard you use that name a couple of times already. What's Evramur?"

She bowed her head reverently and folded her hands on her bosom in much the same dove-shaped sign that Meeran Okosa had used when he recited the saga of lost Ashkaar. "Holy Evramur, blessed Evramur, realm of untold sanctification, Evramur who shows herself robed in beauty on the evening horizon, Evramur from whose mouth the breath of life bathes us, her unworthy children. Here in her bosom our spirits never hunger, here our lips never thirst, here we find rest from all labor and know the peace that all pilgrims seek."

"You make it sound like ... paradise," Geordi said, and when she shyly asked the meaning of that alien word, he explained it for her as best he could.

When he was done, she smiled. "But that is Evramur, your paradise: refuge and rest of the deserving spirits who have left the flesh, haven to those less worthy, whose flesh still anchors the spirit, such as I."

"You—?" Geordi wasn't exactly sure of whether or not he wanted to ask the next question. He was a little afraid of the answer he might get. This young woman was as charming as she was beautiful. Unfortunately, charm and beauty were no guarantee of sanity. No, there was no help for it, he gained nothing by willful ignorance. He had to ask. He had to know. "You think you're there? In Evramur? You believe you're ... dead?"

Her laughter brightened his world. "Starlord, you are gracious. You condescend to tease me. Have I not said that the flesh still holds me? Of course I am not dead!" She spread her fingers and held them like a latticework between them, then said, "But I hope to be. Is it for that you have come, great starlord? To take me from the shell of flesh that weighs me down? To free me at last from tears and sleep and breath?" Her hands fell to her knees, revealing a face transformed with holy ecstasy. "Oh yes, it is so! It must be so! Starlord, take what you have come to take freely, with all my will! Tears, sleep, breath!"

She threw herself forward into Geordi's arms and locked her mouth to his in an impassioned kiss.

Just before he gave himself up to the sweetness of it, Geordi had the flicker of a thought: *I wonder how I'm supposed to cover* this *when I make my report to the captain?* And then: *Who cares?*

Chapter Five

Counsellor Troi was enjoying a moment of solitude in one of the pocket gardens adjacent to the Ne'elatian palace of government when she looked up and saw Geordi hurrying toward her. She rose from the intricately carved stone bench and greeted him warmly. "There you are! We missed you at the concert."

To her surprise, the ordinarily affable engineer didn't do her the courtesy of so much as acknowledging her friendly greeting. "Where can we talk?" he demanded. "Privately."

Troi could feel anger, confusion, and urgency radiating from Geordi in almost palpable waves. There was another emotion there as well, an underlying current that she could not yet identify. She sat down again in the shade of a lacy-leafed tree and patted the bench beside her, saying, "I believe that this place is private enough."

Geordi's glance swung quickly from left to right, surveying the little garden for possible security breaches. Only then did he accept her invitation. "You were right," he said grimly. "You and Captain Picard and the rest."

She didn't need to ask about what. It was obvious. "You've found proof?" She kept her voice low. He nodded. "What is it?"

"I don't think we should talk about it here," Geordi said. "It would be better if I showed you, but I can't show you here either. Especially not here."

"We could return to the ship."

"We'll have to. But first—" He clenched his fists, briefly enough to release a little of the tension holding him, long enough for Counsellor Troi to notice. "Can you do something for me?"

"What do you need?"

"Go back to the ship now. Tell Captain Picard I'll be coming aboard soon to make my report."

"To him alone?"

"No. It's only a secret *here*. I've found the answer we were after. He should have everyone involved present for this."

Troi regarded him closely. "From the way you are speaking, I would say that this answer does not . . . flatter our hosts' integrity."

Again Geordi ignored her words. "One more thing: Before you inform the captain, speak to Ambassador Lelys. Tell her to show Ensign Kolb one of her gowns—nothing fancy, some sort of simple day wear that we can easily replicate. On my signal, he can use my communicator as a homing device to beam the package down and—"

"Ambassador Lelys is not the sort to whom one gives such commands," Troi said. "I very much doubt she'd want to give Ensign Kolb a tour of her wardrobe. More to the point, what am I to tell her is the reason for an officer of the *Enterprise* treating a person of her rank in such a high-handed manner?"

"I'm sorry." Geordi's fists tightened again. "I made it sound like an order, didn't I? But she has to do it."

"All right" Troi said slowly. "What size is your 'answer'?" She saw by his reaction that she had hit it precisely. She touched his arm. "Who is she?"

"That's what I'm still trying to figure out," Geordi replied, a rueful half smile on his lips.

"Geordi, whoever or whatever this 'answer' is, we must tread carefully. If you wish to bring her aboard the ship undetected, we need to find another way than by disguising her. Disguises always carry the risk of discovery. If that were to happen, how would you explain it to the Ne'elatians? We can't afford a diplomatic incident."

"Well, she won't be able to speak to anyone from Starfleet while she's here," Geordi maintained.

"Except you," Troi stated.

Geordi agreed without saying a word. "If I speak with her, I can pass on what she tells me, but the Orakisans will want to hear this straight from the original source before they'll believe it."

"Ambassador Lelys would take your word as a Starfleet officer."

A breeze stirred the branches overhead, casting a network of shadows over Geordi's face. "She's not the one I'm worried about."

It took no psionic gift to realize who Geordi meant. "Legate Valdor."

"You were there, you heard him. If that man doesn't have an ax to grind—"

"Legate Valdor is significantly older than Ambassador Lelys," Troi said. "Despite this, she has surpassed him as a diplomat and is his superior. He resents being obliged to obey someone young enough to be his daughter. Aside from that, I believe he senses that his son, Hara'el, is attracted to the ambassador and views this as disloyalty."

"Okay, then he's got a whole lot of axes," Geordi opined. "All the more reason to have him hear the real story about this world firsthand."

"I agree." Troi thought it over, then said, "I have it!"

"What?"

"This will only work if she is familiar with the palace."

"She is."

"Good. Then have her meet you at the northeast corner of the grounds, at a place called Bi'amma's Tower. One of our Ne'elatian hosts has been serving as my guide; he showed it to me earlier today. We only viewed it from a distance. No one actually goes to visit it. My guide told me that the structure is old and unstable, but allowed to remain unmolested as a historical monument. That whole sector of the grounds belongs to the first foundation of the palace."

"You're assuming that I'll be able to find my way there too," Geordi said.

"Easily. The old walls surrounding it are no more than scattered heaps of stone, and the tower itself is clearly visible. You can reach it without needing to go through the palace itself, and," she smiled impishly, "you will not need to ask directions."

"Don't be afraid," Captain Picard said, standing behind one of the chairs in the conference room and motioning for the girl to take a seat there. "You're perfectly safe here."

Geordi looked down at the shivering body pressed tightly against his own. "It's all right, Ma'adrys," he whispered. "We're all your friends. Nothing's going to happen to you." Then, scarcely understanding why the words escaped him, he added, "I won't let it."

The girl slowly unburied her face from Geordi's shoulder and looked around the room. Her gaze passed over those faces already familiar to her from the palace—the captain, Troi, Riker, Lelys—lingered somewhat longer over those new to her—Dr. Crusher, Data, Valdor, Hara'el—and came to a dead, eye-popping halt at Lt. Worf.

"What *is* that?" she demanded of Geordi, stepping out of his embrace to point at the Klingon. Oddly, she sounded more indignant than afraid. Worf's expression at being the object of such a rude question was unreadable.

Geordi made haste to answer her question and to complete the introductions. By the time he finished, she had recovered full self-possession and had taken the seat Captain Picard offered her. Her eyes were wide with a lively interest in all the new and alien things surrounding her, and she met the curious looks of the others with a steady, unflinching gaze.

"So, Ma'adrys," Captain Picard said. "Have you been told where you are?"

"When I met Geordi at the tower, he told me where I would be taken," the girl replied calmly. "I did not believe him. The scroll of the trickster Yaro teaches that the Lady of the Balances bore a son whose destiny was to pour lies into one pan of his mother's blessed scales and undo the peace of the world. He did this by filling the world with his own children, whom he sired on mortal women. Less than gods, the children of Yaro envy us because we have been given the good teachings that will one day bring back the joys of Evramur to Iskir. So they use their beauty and their lies to lead us away from the good teachings."

She shrugged. "In the tower, when Geordi told me where he was going to take me, I assumed that I had fallen in with one of Yaro's children, but then the light came over us and it was too late to flee."

"And now?"

She looked around the conference room a second time, considering everything in it from the people to the furnishings to the contours of the Lamechian crystal flask and tumbler already set at her place through someone's thoughtfulness. "Now I am still not sure. When we first had word of your coming to holy Evramur, our teachers told us that you were the starlords, the children of the Six Mothers and the Three Fathers—although when I was small, I never heard of the Three Fathers." She made a small, dismissive gesture. "All teachings are perfect only in holy Evramur."

"What is this Evramur you keep mentioning?" the captain asked.

"It's her word for paradise," Geordi cut in. "It's also her word for Ne'elat. The same way Iskir's her name for Ashkaar," he finished grimly.

"She is *from* Ashkaar?" Hara'el half rose from his place at this news. "How did she escape?"

"She didn't," Geordi said. "She was taken."

Valdor studied the girl closely. "She does not look like a criminal, not a dangerous one."

"Now I suppose you will say she must be a soldier," Lelys remarked.

The legate snorted. "What I was going to say is that not all dangerous criminals look the part. Also, that perhaps Ashkaar serves our Ne'elatian brethren in a third role as a haven for disordered minds. See, she does not even know the proper name for her world!"

"That's hardly a gauge of mental health," Dr. Crusher said. "The natives of a place don't use the same name for their home that visitors do—or invaders."

"Do you mean to say that there were native lifeforms on Ashkaar when the Skerrian colonists first arrived?" Commander Riker asked.

"If there were, this girl isn't one of them," Dr. Crusher replied. "Look at her: She's the image of the Ne'elatians."

"Let her speak," Geordi said. He had taken up a defensive position behind her chair and now he placed one hand on her shoulder. "Tell them what you told me, Ma'adrys."

She looked up at him for a moment before beginning her story. There was no longer any awe or uncertainty in her eyes, but only the purest trust. Her smile rivalled Ambassador Lelys's for its power to charm any who saw it. She reached up to touch his hand as if it were some talisman, then spoke.

"My name is Ma'adrys of Kare'al village. My people like to brag that there is no settlement built higher up the flanks of the holy mountain than ours, for we guard the shrine of the Six Mothers at its peak. My father was a man of the village, dead before I was born. My mother came from beyond our mountains and died giving me life. I was raised by the village— mostly by old Mother Se'ar the deathspeaker."

A slight cough interrupted her story. Geordi hastened to pour her a little water from the crystal flask. She sniffed it suspiciously, sipped, then continued: "When I was growing up, I was always curious. I wanted to know why the village men who went into the lowland towns came back sick with the dry cough that killed their children but left them alive. I wanted to learn why the winter fevers never seemed to gather as many spirits for holy Evramur as the spring ones. Whenever anyone would come to ask Mother Se'ar to tell them whether their sick kindred would die, I went along and watched. I saw how there were always certain signs on the bodies of those poor folk she said would depart, and that when the same signs were on the bodies of the rich, they too departed even though Mother Se'ar claimed they would live. When I spoke to her of this, she beat me and told me I was wanting in reverence."

"Or ready for med school," Dr. Crusher said under her breath.

"She was right," Ma'adrys said. "I was flawed in spirit and it shamed me. More than anything, I wanted to become an oberyin, to enter the closed teachings, but when I was old enough for the judging and the choosing, our own oberyin, Bilik, said that my pride had made me an unfit vessel, ready to shatter and spill the precious teachings." She bowed her head, every eye in the conference room fixed upon her. "And I proved him right then and there by accusing him of making a false judgment against me for his own ends."

Riker leaned nearer to Dr. Crusher. "Nice guy, this Bilik."

"What is an oberyin?" Captain Picard asked.

"They are our healers, our teachers, our guides to the good teachings," Ma'adrys answered. "Each village has at least one, and the larger settlements boast more. They offer the burning leaves, they bless the fields, the forges, and the kilns, they know the secret thoughts of water, wind, and fire, and they help us to walk with the gods."

"They almost sound like shamans," Dr. Crusher remarked.

"It takes long years of study to become an oberyin," Ma'adrys went on. This time she was the one to pour herself a fresh drink and downed it without hesitation. "First, of course, you must come to the notice of your village oberyin and be found worthy. Sometimes the choosing comes to you before you know your own wishes. Bilik is only a little older than I, because he was only six years old when he was chosen. *He* never had to ask for the honor, or be rejected." She sounded bitter, but quickly realized this and changed her tone to one of businesslike indifference. "I do not know how many of them there are in all the settled lands of Iskir, but I do know that the seat of the Na'am-Oberyin lies less than a day's journey from Kare'al." She could not help sounding proud of this.

"Is the Na'amOberyin their leader?" Commander Riker wanted to know.

Ma'adrys looked at him as if he had sprouted antlers. "How can one alone lead?" she replied. "That goes against the good teachings. Not even the Lady of the Balances rules without taking counsel of her kindred, and who are we to act against the example of the gods themselves? The Na'amOberyin is a council of those nine oberyin who hold the highest favor with the gods."

Captain Picard nodded. "I see. Go on with your own story, please."

Ma'adrys spread her hands. "There is little more to tell. After I was found unworthy of the high studies, my life went on as it had before. That is—" She seemed to be on the point of revealing something, but then she blushed and said, "Yes, exactly as before. I lived in the house that had belonged to my father, and to my mother after he took her in and came to make her his wife. It was not very big or very solid, but it was mine. Mostly, though, I stayed with Mother Se'ar, helping her, sometimes helping our village herbwife, La'akel. I was unworthy of the closed teachings, but nothing forbade me to learn what I could elsewhere.

La'akel said that I had good hands for birthings, and she praised the blend of herbal tea I made to ease a laboring mother's pain. It was my own invention. I also found that if you boil the root of the n'shash plant and mix it with new milk, it helps wounds heal fast and clean."

"N'shash?" Ambassador Lelys was all attention. She produced a small datapad, tapped out a rapid sequence on the keys, and shoved it in front of Ma'adrys. "Does it look like this?"

Ma'adrys drew back from the datapad until Geordi leaned over her shoulder to whisper a few words of reassurance. The silence in the conference room became a living presence while the girl studied the picture of a sample of n'vashal in full bloom. All that could be heard was the soft hum of the great starship's systems, the breath of the *Enterprise*. At last she shook her head. "Nothing like it. N'shash is a weed that grows beside our mountain streams. It has no blossoms. In fact, I have never seen any plant like this one." She gazed at Lelys closely. "Why do you ask?"

"Never mind." The Orakisan ambassador retrieved her datapad, doing her best to hide her disappointment.

Geordi felt Ma'adrys' shoulder stiffen under his hand. "Do you test me too, starlords?" Her voice was tense with resentment. "Do you, too, brush aside my questions to teach me humility? Have I failed again by seeking to learn too much? I know I am far from perfect; I am too curious. My teachers often warn me of this. They say it would be a shame if I could not master the prying spirit when that is my one remaining flaw."

"I wouldn't call healthy curiosity a flaw," Dr. Crusher said.

"Who are these teachers of yours, Ma'adrys?" Geordi asked quietly. This was a part of her story he had not yet heard.

"The blessed ones who teach all those like me in Evramur."

"What do you mean, all those like you?" Captain Picard leaned forward, intent on her answer.

"You ask this?" She was only a little surprised. "So it is a test. Very well, since that is your pleasure, starlord. The others like me who were brought there, flesh and spirit. See, we all wear the green robes, to set us apart from the sacred guardians. It is a great boon, to be taken into Evramur while still alive, but it is also a great burden. Although we walk the holy streets and see many wonders, we may not behold the faces of our loved ones who came there before us until we have cast off the final imperfections clinging to our bodies."

"What nonsense!" Valdor exclaimed.

"Legate Valdor, if you will not restrain your tongue out of simple courtesy for another's beliefs, then keep silent on my orders," Ambassador Lelys said through gritted teeth. Her colleague gave her a poisonous look, but shut his mouth. She turned a pleasant face to Ma'adrys and said, "You are mistaken, child. We do not test you and we are not the starlords of your people's tales. Look about you again. Can you not see that we spring from many worlds?"

Ma'adrys once more took in the different faces ringing the table. "Yeeeesss," she said cautiously. "And Geordi told me what—who that is and where he comes from." She nodded in Lt. Worf's direction. "Many worlds." She pressed the dove-sign to her chest and bowed to Lelys. "Forgive me. All my life I was raised to believe that there was only one world,

Iskir, and the holy realm of Evramur, and the star road of the gods. It is not easy to change the teachings of a lifetime."

"Think no more of it," Lelys soothed.

"Please, Ma'adrys, tell them the rest of your story," Geordi said.

Was it his imagination or was her smile even warmer now? Geordi felt his heart leap. She was so beautiful, with a keen, quick mind. As for what she believed . . . *It doesn't matter,* he thought. *Whatever she believes—whatever lies she's been told—none of that matters. Not so long as she knows that I would never lie to her.*

She was speaking again, repeating the same tale she'd told him earlier, in the palace, in the abandoned tower: "When Mother Se'ar lay dying, I went to gather dawnsweets to freshen her house. I climbed the mountain where Avren pastures his flocks, seeking the flowers, but when I had gathered enough for my needs there was suddenly a great light all around me, and a shining messenger stepped out of the light to tell me that I had been called to holy Evramur. Then he cast a handful of glittering dust over me and I fell into a deep sleep. When I awoke, a great lady was bending over me. She told me that for my virtues I had been lifted up, flesh and spirit, into Evramur."

"And you believed this?" Valdor rapped out harshly, in spite of Lelys's orders for him to keep silent.

Ma'adrys regarded him serenely. "Of course not. How could I? I knew I was not worthy of that highest blessing. I said so to the lady, but she only laughed and told me that if I had believed myself worthy to enter Evramur, I would still be picking flowers in Avren's meadow."

"Ma'adrys, you know that *this* is not Evramur, don't you?" Captain Picard asked, indicating the conference room and the wall surrounding it.

"Oh yes," the girl responded without hesitation. "Geordi told me that he was going to bring me aboard a starship. I was not afraid. In Evramur I often saw pictures of such things. Our teachers told us that they were the way that the gods brought their children safely to Iskir when Yaro tried to destroy them." She paused in thought a moment, then added: "But Geordi told me that you are not gods, and you tell me that you are not starlords. You are like me. How, then, do you come to master such a ship?"

"I think perhaps that Geordi—Mr. LaForge— might be the best person to explain that to you," the captain said with a friendly smile. "Mr. LaForge, why don't you show our new guest around the *Enterprise?* Just a brief tour. It wouldn't do to detain her here too long. She'll be missed."

"Yes, sir!" Geordi could hardly contain his enthusiastic response to the captain's orders. He gave Ma'adrys his hand, though the gesture was unnecessary, and led her out of the room. She went with him gladly, only pausing at the door to turn and make a deep obeisance to the others. Then, with a final, inquisitive stare at Lt. Worf, she left.

Commander Riker laid his hands on the table. "Well, that answers *my* questions about the Ne'elatians' honesty," he said. "They lied to us about Ashkaar, for starters. As for Ma'adrys, why they went to the trouble of kidnapping her from her own world and letting her believe she'd been transported to her idea of heaven—"

"So she says," Valdor broke in. "You yourself admit you can see no reason for our Ne'elatian kindred to do such a thing. Why should they? The girl is ignorant, worthless, the expense of bringing her to Ne'elat is considerable. Why do it?"

"Then how would you explain her story, Legate Valdor?" Dr. Crusher asked.

"She must be insane," the Orakisan answered, his tone implying that he would accept no other explanation.

"She didn't strike me as irrational," the doctor said.

"Then she is a very clever liar."

"To what purpose, Legate Valdor?" Captain Picard said. "What does she gain by such a story?"

"What would the Ne'elatians gain by lying to us about Ashkaar?" the Orakisan countered smugly.

"Mr. Data, what's your opinion of the situation?" Captain Picard asked.

"I could not give a satifactory analysis at this point," the android replied. "There are still too few facts available to make a reliable evaluation."

"Then we will obtain the facts." Captain Picard rose from his seat. "Dr. Crusher, go after Mr. La Forge and the girl. Offer to show her sickbay and give her a covert examination. If she is from Ashkaar, I want to know what sort of life-form we're dealing with."

"A very fascinating one, judging by Geordi's behavior," Riker murmured to Dr. Crusher. She gave him one of *those* looks, then crisply acknowledged Captain Picard's order and left.

"Commander Riker, I want you to assemble a small Away Team and beam down to the surface of Ashkaar," Picard continued. "Find the village Ma'adrys comes from and make inquiries—if there is such a village."

"Yes, sir." Riker, too, rose to his feet. "I'd like to take Mr. Data and Counsellor Troi in order to—"

He was interrupted by a signal from the captain's communicator. Ensign Blumberg's voice rang out in the conference room: "A message from Udar Kishrit, sir."

"Put it through."

Now the room filled with the Ne'elatian leader's plummy tones. "Captain Picard, I apologize for this intrusion. I was under the impression that you and our Orakisan brethren were still among us." He sounded slightly annoyed by this. "I have news for you."

"News?" Ambassador Lelys took notice. "You have found n'vashal!"

"Ah, Ambassador!" Udar Kishrit's voice changed; even without visual contact it was almost possible to see his sorrowful face. "How I wish—how I *pray* I might say that!"

"No." Lelys made a gesture of rejection, refusing to accept the words that dashed all her hopes. "There must be some mistake. Your world is not fully settled. There are parts of it that you can not possibly know." Her voice rose with her mounting desperation. "I ask—I *beg* of you, allow Captain Picard to deploy Federation technology to explore every last—"

"My dear, dear Ambassador Lelys, to what good?" Udar Kishrit asked, all polite regret. "True, our world is not thickly settled, our knowledge of the native plant life is far from complete, but that fact has no bearing on this. N'vashal came here with our ancestors. It would not grow anywhere that they did not plant it, and they could not plant it anywhere that they did not settle."

"With respect, Udar Kishrit, you may be mistaken," Captain Picard said. "On Earth, the seeds of many plants are frequently carried to most remote locations by wind, water, animals—"

"Carried, yes, Captain Picard. I do not doubt you. But do they always take root, sprout, thrive? If we have not found any n'vashal in all our gardens and ploughlands, or even in the wild places near our settlements, can we honestly hope to find it growing freely elsewhere? This is not a gentle world, Captain; we occupy only the most favorable portions of it. If the seeds of our ancestors' n'vashal plantings ever did blow far from here, much as it pains my heart to say so, I do not think they could have survived. That is—" A reflective note came into his voice. The conference room stilled while Udar Kishrit pondered a wayward thought. Then: "Ah!"

"What is it?" Lelys clung to the edge of the table as if to a life raft in a stormy sea. "Tell us!"

"A chance," Udar Kishrit said. "How good a chance it may be . . ."

"Better than no chance at all. Go on," Captain Picard directed.

"The gardens," Udar Kishrit said. "The gardens of Bovridash. Captain Picard, your ship has scanned our world, you have seen the mountain chain to the north of our capital?"

"Far to the north, yes."

"When our ancestors left the motherworld, they came here seeking a simpler life, as you know. Alas, the demands of our climate led most of us to sacrifice simplicity in favor of the more comfortable means of survival. However, once we were well established on this world, there were some among us who decided that they wanted to serve our ancestors' original dream. They went into the mountains and there founded the community called Bovridash. It is actually composed of several small enclaves, each dedicated to simplicity and the service of the gods. The men and women who choose to live there have dedicated their lives to the preservation of much that we have set aside as no longer useful. They are our living history, and proud of it. Their gardens boast many plants found nowhere else on Ne'elat. I am a fool for not having thought of this before, and yet it would not have done much good if I *had* thought of it."

"Why not?"

"Because as I said, the keepers of Bovridash are proud of their achievements. They turn from those of us who lack the strength of spirit to renew our ancestors' dream. They receive no requests or petitions at second hand. They demand that anyone desiring their aid come before them in person so that their virtue may be judged according to the ancient practices."

"Then I will go to them at once," Ambassador Lelys declared.

This time Udar Kishrit's silence was awkward to the point of pain.

"Well?" Lelys demanded. "What is wrong?"

"The keepers—the keepers of Bovridash will only accept petitions from the highest. Forgive me, Ambassador, but if you go before them, they will shut their faces against you."

"Why? I am the senior official of our embassy here!"

"But your presence here depends on the Starfleet vessel that brought you, and you are not that vessel's senior official."

For the first time, Legate Valdor took umbrage for Lelys rather than against her. "Hmph! And how are they to know that, tucked away in their mountain retreat? If Ambassador Lelys tells them she is the master of this ship, how could they learn otherwise?"

Udar Kishrit's voice dropped. "The keepers of

Bovridash who preserve our past are always informed of great events, for the chronicles. As soon as we established contact with you, we sent word to them. It would be both rude and foolish to attempt to deceive them now."

"There's no need for any deceit," Captain Picard said. "If my presence is needed to secure the keepers' cooperation, then I'll go gladly."

"May you be blessed, Captain Picard!" Udar Kishrit fairly sang with relief. "It is not an easy road to Bovridash, but we will supply you with everything you might need for the journey."

"That won't be necessary, Udar Kishrit. Our transporters are quite capable of—"

"Oh, but you must not use those! It would offend the keepers. Your transporters may leave you at the Namlal Gate that begins the pilgrim's way, but from there I am afraid that you must travel according to the customs of all petitioners."

"Then so I shall."

"And so shall I," Ambassador Lelys said.

"Er," A distant sigh fluttered through the room before Udar Kishrit said, "Perhaps it might be better if one of your colleagues accompanied Captain Picard, honored Ambassador. You see, when one takes the pilgrim's way, it is not accepted custom for males and females to travel togeth—"

"Very well, very well, let it be according to your customs." Lelys looked at her legate. "Valdor, will it please you to accept—"

"Ambassador Lelys, please, do not send my father!" Hara'el's unexpected exclamation took everyone by surprise. The younger Orakisan male blushed at the sudden attention he had drawn to himself, but went on doggedly, "If the road to Bovridash is as rigorous as Udar Kishrit claims, I am the better suited to stand its hardships." He cast a nervous glance at the stone-faced legate and added: "That is, if you do not mind, Father."

"Mind?" Valdor repeated. "Why should I mind? If these keepers would insult us by refusing to receive our senior official, then we *ought* to send them you."

"Uh, thank you, Father." Hara'el sounded as if he were not entirely sure whether he had just been praised or slapped.

"Excellent, excellent!" Udar Kishrit exclaimed. "I will dispatch messengers to Bovridash at once, Captain Picard, so that you may receive the finest of welcomes. And of course you know that our invitation to your crew still stands."

"Thank you, Udar Kishrit. They have been enjoying your hospitality. We are grateful. Picard out." He cut off communication with the Ne'elatian leader, then addressed Ambassador Lelys: "I hope that you're not too upset by these developments?"

"Rest assured, Captain Picard, if it meant the difference between the success and failure of our mission, I would allow these Ne'elatians to do far worse to me than a simple snub. Besides," she looked at the three members of the Away Team, "I am sure that while you and Hara'el are looking after our interests on Ne'elat, I can find something equally important to occupy my time."

Chapter Six

"DO YOU THINK that is Ma'adrys's native village?" Ambassador Lelys asked as the Away Team trudged up the steep mountain road.

"The possibility is excellent, based on the information she gave us," Mr. Data replied. "This mountain range lies in the heart of the settled areas on Ashkaar, this peak in particular is the tallest, and the village we are now approaching is the settlement closest to the summit. There would also appear to be a modest complex of buildings located even higher up the mountain, which most likely form the shrine of which Ma'adrys spoke."

"At least *she* is no liar," Ambassador Lelys said bitterly. "Prisons! Military bases! Those Ne'elatians must have taken us all for fools. When they apply for membership in the Federation, I will make it a point to be there to warn our fellow members against them."

"With all due respect, Ambassador, there may be a perfectly legitimate reason for why the Ne'elatians tried to mislead us about life on Ashkaar," Riker pointed out.

"I do not see what it could be."

"Nor do I, yet. Whatever it is, it is something we all hope to learn, in time," Counsellor Troi told her. "But be aware that even after we discover it, we still might not be able to understand it."

"How could we fail to understand?"

"Often the motivations of an alien culture are not fully—"

"Alien culture? That is no alien culture! Ne'elat is our sisterworld!"

"A long-lost sister, in terms of time as well as space," Troi said. "Both are factors that can change much about a people."

"Some things are too much a part of us to change. There is nothing Orakisans despise so much as deceit," Lelys said hotly.

"And yet was that so for Skerrians as well, or did your ancestors only come to hate lies so violently because they had escaped a world that tolerated them, to its ruin?"

Lelys pulled her traveller's cape closer around her neck. "I do not pretend to know all there is to know about our motherworld's history, and now much of it is lost to us forever. I must be more concerned with the present, and that means finding help for our Reclamation colonists. Lies will not help them."

"Then let's hope we can find the truth there," Riker said, nodding toward the village. He stuck out his hand, inspecting the tint that had colored his skin to match Ma'adrys's. "Do you think I'll pass for a native?"

"The resemblance is remarkable, on a superficial level," Mr. Data said.

"Superficial? Oh now *that's* what we need to hear."

"You are displeased by my evaluation?" The android looked bemused. "I was referring to the fact that the lenses we are wearing may simulate the enlarged irises of the natives' eyes, but the size of the artificial iris is fixed. It can not adjust to reflect emotional changes, which is a reaction we have observed to occur in all Skerrian descendents. I do not think that this will be a problem unless the natives pay close attention to such details. However if my evaluation of the situation distresses you, Commander, perhaps I should attempt to dissemble, for the benefit of morale."

"No, Data, don't do that. I think we've got all the lies we can handle right now." Riker got a firmer grasp on his walking stick and looked up the road. A young man in a much-soiled tunic was coming down the same path, preceded by a small herd of animals that resembled Earth sheep. "On your toes, everyone, here comes our first audience."

"Honored guests, the rooms are pleasing to you?" The innkeeper of the only public accommodations in Kare'al village rubbed his hands together and beamed at his newly arrived customers.

Commander Riker looked up at the slivers of sky visible through the thatched roof, then down at the single, sagging bed, the water bucket beside the rickety table holding the washbasin, and the empty bucket in the corner that was all the room's provision for a guest's basic needs. Troi and Lelys were already installed in a similarly appointed chamber at the other end of the narrow, unlit hall that ran the length of the inn's upper story. He looked at the innkeeper and smiled.

"We couldn't ask for more."

"Good, good, and I trust that you will also find our evening meal just as pleasing."

"We can hardly wait."

The innkeeper bustled away, thumping down the stairway that was little more than a thick ladder nailed to the wall at a slant. As soon as he was gone, Riker and Data joined the women in their room.

"Chalk up another success," Riker reported. "Our friend the innkeeper had no trouble accepting us for pilgrims to the shrine."

"Let us hope that the other villagers will do likewise," Ambassador Lelys said. "Back on the road, I was very much afraid that all our plans were destroyed before they were even begun. That shepherd! The way he stared at us! And how he stood there gaping when we asked the way to the shrine of the Six Mothers, as if he had never heard of such a thing!"

"There was something peculiar about him," Troi admitted. "It was as if his mind could not hold on to our questions long enough to answer them."

"Strange," said Mr. Data. "My initial reaction was that he suffered from some advanced form of short-term memory loss. I have never seen so radical an example of the affliction. And yet he was just as obviously holding down a position of responsibility within his community. He must take good care of his flock, despite all indications to the contrary, or he would not have them in his charge at all."

"Maybe he's not the only one who minds that flock," Riker suggested. "He could have help, humanoid or animal, whatever's the local version of a sheepdog. We just didn't happen to run into his partner, that's all." He shrugged. "In any case, we'd do better to forget about him and find some villagers who can confirm or deny Ma'adrys's story."

"At least we know that this is her village," Troi said. "That is a good start. Let us go downstairs and have our evening meal in the taproom. I think we will find plenty of the local people there seeking diversion."

"If they want diversion, we'll give it to them," Riker said with a grin. "New faces in a village always do."

It was as if he'd been granted the gift of prophecy. The village inn was also the village tavern, the local magnet for as many work-weary souls as could pay the price of a drink. There were already several groups of people occupying the long plank tables in the low-ceiled, smoky room when Riker and the others came downstairs.

He observed the locals carefully before allowing his party to seat themselves at a vacant table near the great stone hearth. If men and women on this world would sooner die than eat or drink in each other's company, he wouldn't let his teammates reveal themselves as interlopers over such an easily determined detail. He was intensely aware of how little they knew about the social customs of Ashkaar. All he had to go on were the facts he knew concerning Orakisan etiquette, but he knew better than to rely on using that as a guide.

He let out a deep sigh of relief when he finally sank down onto the hard, split-log bench and noted that while the locals were slyly studying the newcomers, no one was gasping, pointing, or muttering in that threatening key that was usually the prolog to many an Away Team's quick escape via transporter beam. Two of the younger men present were even smiling, although their friendly overtures were aimed specifically at Troi and Lelys.

The Away Team was halfway through their dinner—a simple but filling meal of bread, soup, a few slices of well-roasted meat, and some unidentifiable root vegetables boiled almost to mush—when the two would-be swains gathered up their courage and came over to the table. They stood there awkwardly, swaying from side to side like sailors trying to keep their footing on a storm-tossed deck, until one of them found his voice.

"Good evenin', friend," he said, trying to pretend he was interested in talking to Commander Riker. "New to Kare'al, are you?"

Lelys and Troi kept silent. If this young man chose to speak to Riker first—no matter what his actual desires were—it could mean that local women were expected to wait for a male to invite them to join the conversation.

Or it could simply mean that this boy is too terrified of women to risk talking to one, Riker mused.

"Yes, we only just arrived here this afternoon," the commander replied affably. He shifted over on the bench so that the young men could join the table, if they wished. He didn't have to urge them. They slid their long legs under the boards in a wink and promptly made themselves the life of the party.

"Hoi, Sekol!" the taller of the two called out to the innkeeper. "Bring us all a pitcher of the old ale, here, the good stuff. Not every day we have visitors, not in this season. I'll pay." He leaned over to Mr. Data and said, "Too early for the shearing, too late for the hides, and not a single trader's pack beast with you anyway. What *does* bring you up our mountain? If you don't mind my asking."

"Not at all," Data replied. "Feet."

"Feet?" The young man's puzzlement broke into a loud, raw laugh. He gave the android a hearty slap on the back that didn't budge him an inch. "Feet! That's a good one! Then if it's a trek you've made of it, you needn't say anything more. No shepherds in my family, eh, Misik?" He raised one hand, thumb and ring-finger touching. It had to be the Ashkaarian equivalent of a knowing wink, for his companion made the same sign back at him.

"None at all, V'kal, none at all. So you're pilgrims, then?" He began by aiming the question at Lelys but lost heart and wound up asking it of Riker.

"Pilgrims to the shrine, yes," the commander replied, doing his best not to smile at the shy lads' bumbling and fully stalled attempt at flirtation.

"Which one?"

V'kal's inquiry took Riker by surprise. "Which—?"

"We are going to the shrine of the Six Mothers," Lelys said demurely. "We know of no other."

"Oh." V'kal swallowed hard, several times, before he found his tongue again. "Oh, well, you wouldn't. Not if you're not from the mountains. And even then, if you've come any great way."

"No, that's not right to say, V'kal." Clearly Misik didn't like to see his friend attracting all the attention, even though he was doing it so ineptly. "Word went to the Na'amOberyin the day it happened, sent by our Bilik his own self, and word came back sanctifying it not two weeks later. Wherever our vistors come from, might be their own oberyin brought them word of our great blessing. Is that what happened, friend?" Like his companion, Misik tried to address Troi, failed in short order, and wound up talking to Data.

"Undoubtedly," Data replied.

"You know, it really would be best—more sacred, some might say—if V'kal and I were the ones to guide you there." Misik lowered his voice, speaking in tones that were meant to be reverent and dignified but that came out sounding merely pretentious. "See, everyone in Kare'al knows that her father was V'kal's third cousin's brother-in-law, on his stepmother's side."

"Really?" Riker smiled. "In that case, it would honor us if you would consent to be our guides. That is, if it wouldn't be an imposition?"

"Oh none! None at all!" Misik and V'kal were falling all over each other, like puppies, in their eagerness to impress the ladies with their gallantry. Both spoke at once, a flood of chatter that made it impossible for the Away Team to distinguish who was saying what. "The honor'd be ours, friend. Wouldn't it, Misik?—Oh yes, without doubt, V'kal. Bringing the first pilgrims to *her* shrine, but the ground up that end the village street's rough going, it wouldn't do to let such fine ladies venture there alone, twist an ankle. Terrible, that'd be, eh V'kal?—Oh, not to bear thinking of, Misik!—And then we could escort you on to the Six Mothers, no trouble, an honor, tomorrow morning be all right?"

The young men finally ran out of steam and sat there grinning. As solemnly as he could manage, Commander Riker thanked them and accepted their gracious offer.

The next morning, before daylight had banished all the last night's shadows from the streets of Kare'al, Riker was roused from sleep by the innkeeper's summons. Sekol came into the room bearing a jug of hot water in one hand, a tray laden with small bowls of fresh milk and a platter of steaming rolls in the other.

"They're here for you, sir," he said, setting down his burdens on the one small table. "The fellows from last night, Misik and V'kal. Nice boys, they are, good family, not well-to-do but well meaning."

Riker sat up in bed. Beside him, Mr. Data continued to feign sleep. "Well, isn't that always the better of the two?" he remarked pleasantly. "My friends and I were just saying last night, before we retired, that one of the best benefits of making a pilgrimage— besides the spiritual, of course—is getting to meet new people."

"Your friends, honored sir?" The innkeeper coughed discreetly into his fist. "Then the ladies are no kin to you by blood or marriage?"

I never thought I'd actually say this to anyone, Riker thought. "We're just good friends." A moment later, he felt like giving himself a good, swift kick for not having taken the opening Sekol had offered and claiming the women as distant cousins. He said a silent prayer that the Ashkaarians wouldn't consider their travel arrangements to be scandalous or—worse yet—suspicious.

"Ahhh." Judging by Sekol's placid reaction, there was nothing unusual or improper about mixed-sex groups of pilgrims with no ties beyond simple companionship. Either the Ashkaarians in general assumed that the sacred nature of such excursions would keep the pilgrims' minds on holy things, or else the innkeeper in particular had decided that it wouldn't be smart to antagonize his paying guests by questioning their morals.

Riker swung his feet to the floor. "Speaking of the ladies, have they been woken up too? If not, someone ought to do it. It wouldn't be polite to keep our guides waiting downstairs."

"That's been seen to, good sir," Sekol reassured him. "I had my little girl Shisha bring 'em their breakfast and all they'll need for the morning rites." He sniffed the air and smiled with satisfaction. *"There* they go."

Riker sniffed too. The pungent aroma of spicy, bitter smoke reached him. *Morning rites,* he thought uneasily. *It smells like they're burning incense in the other room. Are Data and I supposed to be doing something like that too?* He glanced at the table. *Nothing there but wash water and breakfast, nothing for us to use in any kind of ritual. I hope. Unless we're supposed to do something with the milk and bread.* He saw that the innkeeper wasn't making any attempt to leave—was in fact deliberately loitering, his eyes fixed on Riker. *Is he waiting for me to do something? What? Uh-oh. All right, let's stay calm. If he calls me on this, I can always explain that we do things differently in the lowlands. If he buys that—*

Purposefully, Riker got up and walked over to the breakfast tray. He raised one bowl of milk in what he hoped looked like a reverent manner, and let a few drops fall to the ground.

"Oh, let me see to that, sir!" The innkeeper dropped to his knees, whipping a rag out of his apron belt, and mopped up the spill quickly. "No harm done, no harm at all."

So much for that, Riker thought. He decided to take the direct approach. "Is there something on your mind, innkeeper?"

"Well . . ." Sekol looked ill at ease. He stood there twisting his apron in his large, square hands, then coughed again and said, "I don't like to say, being as how they are of good family and all, and it's only that they're young and in high spirits. You must remember what it's like, being young?"

Remember what it's like? Oh, thanks a lot, Sekol, Riker thought. *Maybe I ought to get rid of this beard after all.* Aloud he asked, "Are you talking about V'kal and Misik?"

"They're good lads, truly," Sekol insisted. "Only—
Well, even if the ladies aren't your kin, perhaps you
ought to let them know that no matter what those two
say, there's no holy decree that says only two folk may
enter Ma'adrys's shrine at a time, and that with the
door closed after 'em. And there's nothing yet been
laid down by the Na'amOberyin about the proper
rites for honoring her in her own shrine, so if they try
telling those good ladies the same fleece-mouthed
story they handed my younger sister about how a kiss
in Ma'adrys's shrine means a rich husband within the
year, just see to it that those rascals get a clout in the
ear for their pains!" The innkeeper gave one final
chuff of righteous indignation and barrelled out of the
room. Riker waited until he heard the man's footsteps
clumping down the stairs before he enjoyed a good
laugh.

"He told you, eh?" V'kal scratched his head sheep-
ishly and toed the dirt outside the rundown hovel at
the uppermost edge of the village.

"Can you blame him?" Riker said.

"That bit with his sister, yeh." The two natives
nodded, looking more embarrassed by the minute.
Misik cleared his throat and asked, "S'pose it
wouldn't do to tell you that she was the one came up
with the whole story when he caught us up here?"

Riker patted him on the back. "Why don't we say
no more about it, instead? I understand. I was young
myself, once." He caught the look Counsellor Troi
was giving him and shrugged.

"This does not look like any of the shrines we have
seen in our travels," Troi said, stepping forward to
examine the humble structure.

It was a hut like many others in the village, the

dwelling places of the poor. Sekol's ramshackle inn was a palace next to those, and they in turn were mansions when compared to this. It stood so far removed from its nearest neighbor that it seemed as if the very houses of Kare'al village had agreed to shun it for its poverty. And yet, though the daub walls were so worn that their timber underpinnings were showing through in many places, the beaten earth threshold was strewn with flowers, cakes, clay images, and even a few pieces of jewelry.

"Oh, it don't look like much now, that's true," V'kal admitted. "But it will, in time. There's plans made already to do proper honor to the saintly Ma'adrys as soon as we've got the means to do it. It's not every village has one of its own taken up, flesh and spirit, to Evramur," he ended proudly.

"Did you know her?" Lelys asked.

"Know her?" Misik echoed. "Why, we grew up together! All that time, and who would've thought it? A saint for our playmate!"

"A saint you pushed in the brook," V'kal reminded him.

Misik glowered at him. "And a saint *you* used to call more thick witted than a shepherd!"

"Friends, that doesn't matter now." Riker stepped in to patch things up before it all degenerated into pointless bickering. "I'm sure that she forgot about it long ago."

"So she would." Misik nodded vigorously. "She could scarcely ascend to Evramur with a load of resentment in her heart, and over trifles. Patience and forgiveness, that's the best road to bliss, according to the good teachings."

"Kindness, too," V'kal put in. "No one kinder than Ma'adrys, while she lived among us. Always helping

Mother Se'ar, always there to help nurse anyone ailing, always with her eyes high. She should have been made an oberyin. Pardon me for saying so, but Bilik did wrong to prevent her, and there's not a soul in Kare'al but knows why he really did it."

"Bilik?" Troi pretended ignorance to draw him out.

"Our oberyin. He's got a house just a little ways down the road from here."

"He was in love with her, that's what," Misik declared. "He knew that if he let her become an oberyin, she'd have to go off for the training. Then, when she was done, the Na'amOberyin would send her to care for some other village, who knows where?"

"Yeh, they'd never let two trained oberyin live in a village this small," V'kal said. "So he said she wasn't good enough for the training, hoping that she'd stay put and marry him instead. I guess he knows better now! The gods will find their own."

"May we enter the shrine?" Troi asked.

"Please. Only not all at once." V'kal caught Riker's warning look and grinned. "Only because it's so small and cramped inside, that's why. You go on and look. Misik and me, we'll wait out here."

The interior of Ma'adrys's abandoned home was even less prepossessing than the outside. There were no windows and no chimneyed fireplace. A ring of stones in the middle of the floor contained a shallow layer of ashes. The smoke from any fire kindled in that primitive hearth could only escape through the soot-caked hole in the roof. The bed was nothing more than a heap of straw stuffed into some coarse sacking. A wooden chest against one wall displayed an arrangement of crude clay figures surrounding what looked like a small, round hand mirror.

Mr. Data drew his fingers over the mirror's surface,

then over the top of the chest. He studied the dust smearing his fingertips with close interest and began to pick up and examine the items on the chest one by one.

"Nothing's been touched since she was taken," V'kal piped up from the doorway. "That's why it's all so dirty in there. You mustn't think she kept it so. Always neat, she was. My mother said that it was a miracle she knew enough to keep a tidy house, growing up so wild as she—"

A loud slap rang out and V'kal's face disappeared from the doorway. "Don't you *dare* go spreading such lies about me, you worthless creature!" The entrance to Ma'adrys's hut filled with the stocky figure of a formidable older woman. "I never said one thing against holy Ma'adrys, so don't you try saying I did! Wasn't I always first to give her something decent to wear? Didn't I feed her at our very table more times than anyone?"

She stopped ranting long enough to peep into the hut and give the startled Away Team an ingratiating smile. "Your pardon, honored visitors. I was just looking for this ungrateful child of mine and Sekol told me he'd come up here to show you the blessed house where *she* once lived among us. I was so pleased to hear that he was turning his mind to holy things, I couldn't keep from following after to hear him speak to you of Kare'al's saintly daughter."

She glanced to one side, probably at her son, and the sunny smile ducked behind a black cloud. "And what do I hear? Blasphemy! Lies! Speaking ill of his own mother at the very doorstep of *her* house!" Her hand shot out of sight, but judging by V'kal's yelp of pain she had him by the ear, at best. "Everyone knows that Ma'adrys favors mothers, that even now she's laying all our prayers before the holy Six in Evramur. It's because her own mama was taken her from her at her birth."

She let go of her wayward son and clasped her hands together, the image of piety. "Poor woman, she wasn't in her right mind. That's the only explanation any of us could find for the way she talked, denying the gods, clamoring for someone to take her to see the Na'amOberyin, spouting nonsense. Begging your pardon, but I'd wager that even in the lowlands you wouldn't allow such license."

"Never." Counsellor Troi lowered her eyes.

"Oh! Did such a blasphemer come from *our* lowlands?" Ambassador Lelys looked devastated by the possibility. "We are shamed." She grabbed Data's hands away from the few pitiful objects atop the wooden chest and exclaimed, "We must do something to atone for it!"

"There, there, dear, don't take it to heart." V'kal's mother forced her way into the already crowded hut and put her arms around Lelys. "There's no saying where that poor woman came from. Stakis, that was her name. One day she was simply here, in Kare'al, dressed all peculiar and talking so very strange, ordering us to take her to the Na'amOberyin. Their holy place is only a day's journey from here, you know," she preened.

"Ordered you?" Lelys made a sound of disapproval. "The very idea! I cannot speak for all the lowlands, but in our village we do not conduct ourselves like that."

"Well, I never said you did." V'kal's mother sniffed and pointedly released Lelys from her embrace. "All we knew was that no self-respecting *mountain* woman would act so, so we just assumed she was from downslope, where the earth still shakes, sometimes. They say that when that happens, there's great cracks open up and evil vapors come out that leave people touched in the head. Anyway, no one would help her—we'd hardly go near her if we could avoid it—so she took off, swearing she'd find her own way there. Maybe she would've, too, if she hadn't taken a misstep on the road and broken her foot.

"It was N'mar found her, him as became Ma'adrys's father. He brought her back here, to his own house, and looked after her when no one else would, and listened to her ravings kindly. He was a gentle spirit, and he healed her of most of her madness. When they were wed, she went through all the rites just as quiet and biddable as if she'd been one of our own. A shame he died without ever seeing his daughter born. That was a hard winter; there was a lot of sickness in the village, and not enough healthy hands to bury the dead, let alone tend the ailing. N'mar said he would go over the mountain to ask the Na'amOberyin for aid, but his luck ran dry. He was caught in a snowslide, poor fellow. I remember how my good man heard the rumble and went out to see and found N'mar with both his legs broke under him but still with the living." She paused for breath and sighed.

"Mother, that's all ancient history," came V'kal's thin protest from outside. "Our visitors don't care about—"

"Hush!" his mother snapped. She looked Troi steadily in the eye and said, "Would you have me tell this through to the end or not? No offense taken if you say no, I swear it by the Lady of the Balance."

Counsellor Troi opened her mouth to answer. Of course she would say yes. The information this woman was giving both confirmed and supplemented what they already knew, clear evidence that Ma'adrys had not lied to them about her origins. Yet before she could reply, she sensed a strange presence at the borders of her mind, a faint but distinct force that seemed to *demand* that she say: "We would *love* to hear what you have to say more than anything."

Now where did that come from? Troi mused.

"There, you see?" V'kal's mother yelled triumphantly out the door. Having settled her son's hash to her satisfaction, she resumed her tale. "They brought N'mar home and set his legs, but there was an unclean spirit got into his body—one of Yaro's cursed children—and no healing came. I've seen the like many times, too many times." She shook her head sadly. "Mother Se'ar was summoned. She took one look at the darkened flesh and said what all of us already knew. Death came soon after."

"And Ma'drys's mother, Stakis, you say she died in childbirth?" Lelys asked.

"That she did," V'kal's mother said stoutly. "When her man died, her madness was reborn. She raged at everyone who'd listen, saying how he hadn't needed to die of his hurt, how where she came from they had the power to drive out the flesh-rot that took him. As if that were possible! All Iskir knows that every scrap of healing lore on this world is in the keeping of the Na'amOberyin. When N'mar had his accident, another man set out to finish his mercy errand and the Mothers blessed him with success. He brought back one of the Na'amOberyin who saw to the cure of our village sickness but who couldn't do a thing for N'mar. Later on, when Stakis died, there were some who said that it was a judgment on her for blaspheming the Balance, all that talk of how N'mar didn't need to die when the gods had decided he must.

Hmph! A bunch of laundry-day flapjaws, the lot of them. I'd like to be there when the Balance tilts *their* way, for speaking ill of the blessed Ma'adrys's mother like that."

"Dad says you will be," V'kal shouted from what sounded like a safe distance, "seeing as how you were the first to say it served Stakis right! And all because you thought he was casting eyes after her!"

"Yaro take you, you nasty little—" There was a great gust of air that rushed back into the hut as V'kal's mother took off after her unfilial child.

Commander Riker leaned against the doorjamb, watching them race away down the road. Misik, too, had fled, either for friendship's sake or because he knew that V'kal's mother wasn't too picky about who paid the price for her embarrassment before the visitors. The offerings great and small on the threshold had been trampled. "There's one woman I'd hate to have mad at me," he remarked. He turned to face the others in the hut. "There's no room for doubt now. The Ne'elatians lied about this planet. The question is, why?"

"The people of Ashkaar seem to have clung to the ideals of their ancestors," Lelys said. "They lead a simple life, farming, herding, some basic crafts and industries. Could it be that their existence is a living reproach to the Ne'elatians for having fallen short of their ancestors' dream? To speak of Ashkaar as it truly is would be to shame themselves."

"If that were true, then they would have concealed the existence of Bovridash as well," Mr. Data said. "According to Udar Kishrit, the members of that community also live in accordance with the ideals of the first Skerrian colonists and this did not seem to disturb him."

"Then what could the Ne'elatians possibly have to

gain by concealing these people from us?" Troi asked. "It is almost as if they were guarding a treasure."

"What treasure?" Lelys demanded, flinging her arms wide. "The Ne'elatians have better food, better clothing, better transportation, better medicine, everything better than the Ashkaarians! Why guard a secret treasurehouse when all the gold is already in your own pockets?"

Commander Riker folded his arms. "That's what we're going to find out, and I can't think of a better place to start looking for answers than back at the inn."

"Sir," interjected Mr. Data. "I may have found an answer already."

Riker raised one eyebrow quizzically. "You can explain why the Ne'elatians lied to us?"

"I did not say that I had *the* answer, sir. I merely said that I had *an* answer, although it is to a question that none of us has yet asked."

"And that question would be?"

"Where Ma'adrys's mother came from." The android held up the little circular hand mirror and turned it so that it caught the light from the smokehole. The silvery surface sparkled for an instant, then began to crackle. Riker and the rest stared in fascination as pinpoints of multicolored brilliance radiated out from the center of the disc. These joined into wavy lines as the crackling became a low, intense buzzing, then a deep hum. Data cupped his other hand over the mirror and the noise cut off dead. When he revealed it again, it was just a mirror.

"A partially solar-powered communication device of some sophistication," he said. "Unfortunately its alternate power source has been badly drained over the years. Naturally it did not activate without my intervention." He turned it over so that they could all see the designs decorating its reverse side. What looked like a wreath of many different flowers could also look like an array of delicately fashioned control keys to the properly trained eye.

Riker looked at Data. "Ne'elat?"

"Affirmative."

Chapter Seven

IN THE PRIVACY OF HIS CHAMBER above the taproom, Commander Riker touched his communicator and as quietly as possible said, "Riker to *Enterprise.*"

"Enterprise. Worf here."

"Lt. Worf, is the captain there? We've got a lot to report."

"Captain Picard is still on the surface of Ne'elat. His last message said that he and the Orakisan emissary Hara'el were making good time even though they were traveling by pack animal and that the last gateway before the community of Bovridash was already in sight."

"Can you relay our findings to him?"

"Negative, sir. At this point, he and Hara'el must have entered the last gateway, which means he has temporarily surrendered his communicator to the guards. According to Mr. La Forge, no high-tech artifacts are permitted beyond the last gateway and all travel from that point on must be on foot."

"Since when is Mr. La Forge an expert on Ne'elatian customs?"

"Before the captain left, he determined that it would look extremely suspicious if all of the *Enterprise*'s most prominent officers suddenly disappeared from the Ne'elatian government palace. Dr. Crusher and myself have taken it in turns to visit, but our duties aboard the *Enterprise* prevent us from spending much time on the planet's surface. In the absence of a crisis in Engineering, Mr. La Forge suggested that he would be the logical choice to accompany Legate Valdor as our permanent representative on Ne'elat."

"I'll bet he did." Riker smiled.

In the pause that followed, Riker could almost picture the perplexed look on Lt. Worf's face. The Klingon officer did not pay a lot of attention to the subtler clues of budding affection in others. "Anyway, let me tell you what we've learned here so far."

When Riker finished giving his report, Lt. Worf asked, "What about the plant the Orakisans need? Have you encountered any living samples of it there?"

"Negative," Riker said, glum. "Since this world was the original Skerrian settlement in this system, we had hopes, but it doesn't look good. N'vashal's not a staple crop; if they had it growing anywhere, they'd cultivate it in an herb garden. Ambassador Lelys has already made it her business to become friendly with the local women. You'd be surprised how much information you can gather about native plant life when you talk to the people who use it in their daily cooking."

"Yes, sir."

"Of course, Kare'al village is only one settlement,"

Riker went on. "And there's still the possibility that Captain Picard and Hara'el will have some luck in Bovridash. How soon do you think you might hear from them?"

"I do not know. I only hope it will be soon. The situation on Skerris IV is fast approaching critical."

Riker didn't want to ask but knew he had to: "Fatalities?"

"Yes, sir. Ambassador Lelys's brother was among them."

Riker was silent for a long, heavy moment, then said, "I'll tell her. Riker out."

He cut off transmission to the ship, and before hiding his communicator under his pilgrim's robes made sure that it was still adjusted to give silent notification of any incoming messages. No matter how convincing the Away Team's resemblance to native Ashkaarians was, one high-pitched beep from a concealed communicator would put an end to all their carefully devised disguises. Having taken care of this, he went downstairs to the taproom.

Here he found Mr. Data at one of the tables, the center of a small group of villagers—V'kal and Misik among them—who were watching avidly while the android played some sort of board game against a local challenger. The board and the gaming pieces were unfamiliar to Riker, but clearly it hadn't taken Data long to familiarize himself with them. As he watched, the android tipped over two of the pieces on the board, moved a blue wooden disc next to a red ceramic triangle, and announced, "Bikbik." His opponent stared at the board, sighed, and added another white pebble to the pile already standing at the android's elbow. The crowd cheered.

Riker took this opportunity to tap Data on the shoulder and ask, "Where are Troi and Lelys?"

"They are both outside near the well with the other women."

"Where'd you think they'd be, at this hour?" Misik joshed. "Come all this way on a pilgrimage and neglect the evening rites?"

Riker covered quickly. "I'm sorry, I must have lost track of the time. Will you excuse me?" He ducked out of the inn.

The well stood in the little walled courtyard just outside the stables. There were benches all around the walls, every one occupied by village children and elders. The women, including Troi and Lelys, ringed the well, all of them holding small ceramic cups. Thin wiggles of fragrant smoke rose from the cups to the night sky.

Bava, the innkeeper's wife, led the ritual. She was a fat, squat, homely woman, but a regal dignity clung to her as she intoned the ceremonial words. "We open the Gate of Evramur to prayer," she said solemnly, lifting up her cup of incense in both hands and slowly moving it from right to left.

"We open the Gate of Evramur to prayer," the other women repeated, their actions mirroring hers.

"We open the hearts of Iskir to peace." Now Bava moved the cup in a circle before her face.

"We open the hearts of Iskir to peace." Many circles were traced with sweet smoke while the children stared like owls and the elders sat nodding approval.

Commander Riker pressed himself against the stable wall, unwilling to disturb the rite, unsure whether or not his presence would offend. His love of Earth history was bound to a love of the old mythologies as well. More than a few of those were cautionary tales of men who had witnessed things they were not supposed to see, and who were destroyed in a variety of unpleasant ways for their daring.

The women were singing, their voices melding into alien harmonies. Riker watched with admiration as Troi and Lelys pretended to join in. At last the song ended and Bava made a sign to the others to follow her. She led them in single file to the courtyard trough where she stooped, took a handful of water, and poured it into her cup. The remaining incense died with a final burst of smoke and she placed the cup on a waiting tray held by one of the older girls present. The other women did likewise. When the last cup was extinguished, the gathering broke up into smaller groups, some going back into the taproom, some leaving the inn, some lingering for gossip and laughter.

The children, as if freed from a spell, broke from their benches and ran around like mad things, shouting and squabbling happily. Some of them crowded around Troi and Lelys, still fascinated by the sight of anyone new to the village, but in a very little while most of them drifted back over to one of the benches by the wall. It was a stone bench, unlike its wooden mates, and it was placed under a beautifully trained climbing vine. The old man who sat there had the most tranquil expression Riker had ever seen. He waited patiently for the little ones to settle at his feet.

The group of children that had formed around Troi and Lelys were plainly torn between the desire to join their playmates and the yearning to linger in the company of the visitors. The old man waved at them. "My stories are for all, good ladies," he said. "You would honor me by your presence."

Troi answered his invitation with a dazzling smile. "We'd love to!" She and Lelys hurried forward to take their places on the ground, but the old man patted the stone bench to either side of him, his eyes twinkling.

"I tell my stories to our children freely, but pretty ladies must pay the price of sitting beside me." His glance flashed across the courtyard to where Commander Riker lingered in the shadows. "You, too, may join us if you like, friend, but you'll have to find your own bench."

"That would be *my* honor," Riker said amiably, accepting.

When he was sure of his audience, the old man leaned back against the vine-draped wall and lifted one gnarled hand to the stars. "Long and long ago, in the times after the Lady of the Balances had poured out the stars from one pan and the children of the stars from the other, there came a day when she called all the children to her and said, 'There is strife among you. I have heard your shouts of anger and your cries of pain. Why do you quarrel? Why do you raise your hands against your brothers and sisters?'

"No one answered. They were afraid to speak. They knew they had done wrong, but even though they had fought among themselves and made the stars weep with their wickedness, they would do anything rather than lie before the Lady."

One of the smallest children there shyly touched the old man's knee. "But the Lady knows everything," the child said. "She'd know if someone lied to her. Is that why they didn't try?"

The old man patted the boy's head gently. "In those days the Lady walked with the children of the stars. They did not know that she was any different from them, only that she was more beautiful and that she could make wondrous things. They did not suspect that if they lied to her, she would know. They did not even try to lie to her because when she made them, she formed their bones of truth and their flesh of honor. To destroy the truth would be to destroy themselves."

Riker looked over and saw Lelys nodding approval. For her, at least, here was more proof of the Ashkaarians' kinship with Orakisa.

"After a time," the old man went on with his tale, "someone did speak. It was Rika'an, the first man, the one whose spirit the Lady first poured from the blessed Balances. He bowed before the Lady and he said, 'We fight because there are too many of us too close. We quarrel because we cannot take a step without treading on the feet of our neighbors.' Because, you see, in those times all the children of the stars inhabited only a single world."

"We still do," the boy spoke up. He had gained courage from his previous question and was no longer quite so shy.

"Yes, yes, *now*. But this was long ago, before the flames of Yaro made the stars weep for all their vanished children." The old man's eyes darkened when he spoke of this, and he made a warding-off sign over the child's head before going on with his story.

"Then the Lady laughed. 'Why do you all live like this, then?' she asked Rika'an. 'Why do you cling to one world when I have filled the sky with stars and wreathed the stars with worlds and formed the worlds with beauty?' So Rika'an called to the other children of the stars and they built great silver ships and set them upon the seas of night and sailed away——"

"—and came to Iskir!" the boy cried eagerly, bouncing in place.

"Very good." The old man was pleased, though some of the other children gave the child hard looks for putting himself forward so boldly. "But remember, it was only Rika'an's own ship that landed here. The others scattered to the farthest stars, never to be heard of any more. The good teachings say that Yaro, in his envy, sent fire after them and wiped them from the worlds and the stars and the sky. Only Rika'an's ship survived."

"Why didn't the Lady stop Yaro from—"

Before the boy could ask yet another question, the girl seated beside him gave him a hard shove and exclaimed, "Oh, shut *up,* Herri! I want to hear Grandfather's story, not your stupid questions."

Little Herri sprang to his feet, tears starting in his eyes. "I hate you, Shomia! You're mean! I wish you were *dead!*" He spun around and ran away, sobbing, but before he could go five steps, Lelys swept him up in her arms, seated him firmly on her lap, and dried his tears.

"You know that you do not mean such ill wishes, child," she crooned. "And I think that Shomia knows better than to speak so rudely to you when all you did was ask a question." She looked meaningfully at Shomia, who colored deeply and stared at her hands.

"The only foolish question is the one that is asked to shame another," the old man decreed. He turned to Riker and said, "Honored visitor, why don't you give the boy his answer?"

Me? A hard knot clenched in Riker's belly. *I don't know the answer. I don't know how their stories go. I don't—* Then he felt the tension leave him as realization dawned. *But it's the same question children have asked forever: Why does an all-powerful force for good allow evil to exist?*

He looked kindly at the sniffling child in Lelys's lap and said, "The Lady knows that sometimes bad things must happen along with good ones so that the Balances may stand even." He looked up at the old man and added, "I'm afraid I haven't explained it very well, but that's the way I was taught it."

"And well taught." The storyteller seemed satisfied. "When the children of the stars stepped out onto the good land," he went on, "they discovered that Yaro had been busy here as well. Though the land was rich and the harvests plentiful, Yaro set his blade deep in the rocks and made them shake and crack. Fire and smoke streamed from the earth, fields became valleys, valleys swallowed mountains, and everywhere the people were afraid. Many of them came to Rika'an and begged him to take them away in the silver ship, but he refused. 'This is the land where the Lady's hand has placed us,' he told them. 'We must stay here, so that if she seeks us, she will know where to find us.'"

"Um—" The little boy named Herri stirred in Lelys's lap. He looked as if he wanted to say something, but just then Shomia broke into a loud fit of coughing. Herri gave a start. "I wasn't going to say anything, Shomia, honest!" he cried.

Shomia paid no attention to him. Instead, she clambered to her feet, still coughing, and ran out of the courtyard.

"I thought she was going to tell me to shut up again," Herri said in a small voice.

"But she did not, see? Now go on, child," Lelys urged him. "You are free to speak."

"Well," he nibbled his lip, "I think Rika'an was wrong. The Lady knows everything, so why wouldn't she know where to find us even if we went all the way across the sky?"

"You're right, Herri," the old man said. "And Rika'an was right too, but for a different reason. This *is* the land where the Lady placed us, she who is mother to the Six Mothers and whose blessed Balances hold us all. She brought us here for a reason, though it is a reason we can never hope to know without being raised to the realm of the gods themselves. We must accept her wisdom even if we cannot understand it."

A warm, dry breeze stirred the vine leaves over the old man's head, bringing with it the last trace of the smoke from the vanished incense cups. He coughed as if a wisp of it had tickled his throat, then spoke on. "Even though Rika'an spoke well, the people were still afraid and still they begged him to take them away in the silver ship. At last he lost patience with them and said, 'Go, then! Take the silver ship and be gone!' And so they did go, more than half the people who first came to Iskir. They stepped into the silver ship and sailed away across the seas of night and were never seen again.

"When the true people who were faithful to the Lady's judgments came to ask Rika'an what had become of the silver ship, he told them, 'Wait until nightfall and I will show you.' And when the darkness came and the moons rose bright, he pointed to a new light in the sky, a blazing disc the color of hearthfire, and said, 'Yaro's fire has consumed the silver ship and all who sailed in her. See there where it burns eternally! That is their punishment for having denied the wisdom of the Lady.' But he was smiling when he said it, and his true thoughts were *That is their punishment for having ignored my words!* The people saw the fiery disc and feared it more than the shifting ground or the rumbling mountains."

The younger children, too, trembled with fear to hear this part of the tale, though the older ones did not, having heard it many times before. A little boy, far smaller than Herri, began to snivel. The sudden bleat of a sheep from a nearby pen startled him into full tears and he had to be taken away by his older brother. The old man clucked his tongue sympathetically, but he looked pleased that his words had had such effect.

"The Lady, who knows all things, knew what Rika'an had told her people and it troubled her," he said. "She worried that because of Rika'an's words, the true people would come to serve her out of fear, not out of love. So she herself stepped down onto a high place and there she birthed the Six Mothers, one by one, and one by one she told them, 'Heal my children of their fears.'

"The First Mother took the shape of fire and plunged into the cracks that Yaro had made in the world and tamed the rocks so that they would be more peaceable.

"The Second Mother took the shape of smoke and blew over the faces of the people and sent them into a deep sleep where there was no fear.

"The Third Mother took the shape of a dream and entered Rika'an's sleep and told him, 'Those who joy in the punishments of others will suffer a worse punishment. Teach your people to grieve and to pray for their lost kindred, as you will grieve and pray for them all the rest of your life.' "

A fresh cough shook the old man's shoulders, but he fought it down. "The Fourth Mother took the shape of many dreams and entered the sleep of all the people and told them, 'When you wake, you will no longer fear the fiery mouth in the sky. That is not the silver ship that carried away your kindred. It is the Gate of Evramur, a holy realm where their spirits live in peace and where your spirts will find them some day.'

"The Fifth Mother took the shape of Rika'an, the first man, and from that one shape made many, all alike. When the people woke up, there was a great darkness over the land. Their eyes could not see any farther ahead than a child can toss a rock. Then the many shapes of Rika'an said, 'I will lead you to a better place, where the soil is not as generous but where the ground lies still.' So the people all went in many different directions, in many different groups, each group believing that they alone were following the first man."

The old man stopped and took a dark red leaf out of the pouch at his belt. He rubbed it in a leisurely way across his few remaining teeth until they turned a pale pink. A scent like lemons filled the courtyard while the children fidgeted, waiting for him to resume his story.

Riker took notice of the red leaf. *Not n'vashal, that's for sure,* he thought, disappointed. He debated whether he wouldn't do better to go back into the taproom. Data might be wondering what had become of them. Even worse, Data might still be contentedly playing that alien board game and beating all comers. *I should've told him to lose once in a while. A winning streak that long isn't normal for anyone but him. It'll draw attention to us, and that's something we don't need.* He decided to go check on the android.

"Honored visitor, where are you going?" the old man asked. "I know that you've heard this tale many times, from childhood on, but I'd hoped you would find our mountain version different enough to amuse you."

"I'm sorry. It's not the story or how you're telling it. It's just that I remembered something important that I have to—"

"Won't you wait for the end?" The old man's eyes fixed themselves on Riker's.

"Of course I will," the commander heard himself

say, and he sat back down hard on the wooden bench, blinking as if someone had just roused him from a daydream.

The old man gave him a warm smile. "Now while all of this had been happening," he said, "the Sixth Mother was still suckling at the Lady's breast. She was the youngest, and the Lady did not want to let her go. 'All is well with my people,' she told the Sixth Mother. 'There is no healing left for you to bring them.'

"But the Sixth Mother watched the people of Iskir, and she saw that despite all that her sisters had done for them, they were still sick at heart for their lost kindred. There were even some of them who had banded together to build themselves a new silver ship, so that they could sail after their kindred and discover whether they were truly gone forever or only wandering lost over the seas of night.

"The Sixth Mother saw the silver ship that was being built at the bottom of the Great Break, which was the place where Yaro's blade had first cut open the heart of Iskir. She saw it and she knew what she must do if she was to save the true people.

"Then the Sixth Mother took the shape of a dark mist, ugly and foul smelling, the kind that seeps up out of the earth in the places where Yaro's blade marks have never fully healed. She drifted over the surface of the world, over all the sleeping people, and when they awoke they had forgotten very much. They had forgotten so much that to this day we do not know all that was forgotten, but this we know: They had forgotten the art of building the silver ship. They had even forgotten where it lay, for everyone knows that it lies at the bottom of the Great Break, but in all Iskir no one knows where the Great Break lies.

"So the darkness lay over us for many ages, until the Lady chose to lift us from our ignorance to all this!" The old man spread his arms wide, happily embracing his world. "For all these blessings, let us be content." He brought his hands together over his chest in what might have been Ma'adrys's dove sign but which his age-twisted fingers transformed into a spider.

The story was done, and done in time for the children to hear their mothers calling them home to bed. Little Herri slid off Lelys's lap, complaining bitterly, "That's *always* the way it happens! Doesn't matter what story Grandfather tells, it always takes the *whole time* between the end of the evening ritual and bed!"

"Oh my, it does?" Lelys and the old man exchanged a conspiratorial look over the top of the child's head.

The courtyard emptied out quickly after that. Mothers and fathers and older siblings came to claim the children too young to find their own way home in the dark. An elderly woman showed up, rubbed her cheek tenderly against the storyteller's, and the pair of them went off arm in arm. Soon the only people left behind were Troi, Riker, and Lelys.

Riker stared at the Orakisan ambassador, dreading the news he had to give her. *Better get it over with,* he thought. He started toward her, but Counsellor Troi intervened.

"What happened to you?" she asked.

"You're going to have to be more specific than that," he teased.

"You know what I mean. You wanted to leave before the old man had finished telling the story. Something was bothering you deeply, a thought that became an urgent reason for going back into the taproom."

"I'd left Data playing one of the local games. Winning, of course. I thought it'd be smart to step inside and suggest he throw a match or three, in the name of helping us all stay inconspicuous."

"Why didn't you do it, then?"

The simple question left Riker at a loss. *Yes, why didn't I?* "I . . . don't know. I wanted to hear the whole of the old man's story. After all, it's the Ashkaarians' own version of what happened when they settled this world. But you were here. You could've told me anything I missed."

"I had something similar happen to me when we visited Ma'adrys's old house," Troi said. "V'kal's mother was telling us about the girl's family history. She asked me whether I wanted to hear the rest of it and I said yes."

"Well, there's nothing strange about that. We all wanted that information."

"But I did not simply say yes. I *implored* her to go on. I spoke as if it were the most important thing in my life to hear what she had to say."

"Hmm." Riker stroked his beard. "I think I remember that. You were almost gushing at that woman."

"Not something I do, as a rule," Troi said crisply.

"No, it isn't." Her regarded her speculatively. "You think the Ashkaarians have some kind of psionic powers, then?"

Troi pursed her lips. "I am not sure. It was *there,* but it was so faint, I might be wrong."

"We both might be. Maybe it's nothing more than two very strong personalities at work, nothing psionic behind it at all. You know, my mother used to tell me about an uncle of hers. He liked to tell her long, pointless stories about his hunting trips. He told the same ones over and over and over again and somehow she always found herself sitting there and listening. She said that when she knew he was coming to visit, she'd make up a dozen plausible excuses to let her escape. Once she even fixed it so one of her friends would call to rescue her with some phony emergency, but it never worked. He'd start up the stories, she'd try one of her excuses, he'd listen to her politely, *he'd even tell her that he understood how it was with young people and it was fine with him if she went!* But she didn't go. Not once. Not even when her friend made the fake emergency call to help her out. She actually heard herself telling the friend one of the excuses she'd prepared to use on her uncle. Then she went right back, sat down, and listened to him tell the one about the possum that got away for, oh, maybe the fifty-third time." Riker wore a look of grudging admiration for the great-uncle he'd never known. "Now *that's* what I call a strong personality."

"What is a possum?" Lelys asked. The Orakisan had joined them in the course of Riker's story.

He looked at her without answering. He knew that there was no sense in putting off the bad news he had to tell her, though he wished with all his heart there were. *No, not putting it off,* he corrected himself. *Changing it. Turning back the clock, giving her brother a little more time if that would do any good, in the long run.*

"Ambassador Lelys, there's something I need to tell you."

Chapter Eight

THE PEACE OF THE ASHKAARIAN NIGHT was torn by the jagged sound of a woman's grief-stricken scream. The door of the inn flew open and a horde of people poured out, eyes wide, to hear the heartbroken wail. "Dead! Dead! Oh no, it can't be, please, *no!*"

"Dead?" Ambassador Lelys repeated softly. She stared at Commander Riker, tears trickling from her eyes, her word the echo of the unknown woman whose wild cries had roused the whole inn.

"I'm sorry." It was all he could say, all that anyone could ever say at such a time, and never enough. "If there's anything we can—"

She turned her back on him, pressing her hands together. "Not now. Not—" The anonymous Ashkaarian woman howled her grief into the night again, and Ambassador Lelys seized hold of the sound as a desperately needed diversion from her own sorrow. "Listen! Do you hear that cry? We had better go and see what it means." She started after the surging crowd, in a daze of sorrow, as if Riker had never told her that her brother was dead.

"Wait." Counsellor Troi laid restraining hands on her, drawing her back. "Go inside. Whatever is happening now, you are in no state to get involved."

"Let me go." The ambassador shook her head stubbornly. "I am all right. I will mourn my brother afterward." She broke away from Troi and raced after the people. Troi and Riker exchanged a look and followed her.

The woman whose screams had brought all the inn and most of the village out into the streets of Kare'al stood bathed in icy moonlight, her face turned to the sky. In her arms she held a blanket-wrapped bundle. A corner of the blanket fell away to reveal a thin face, pale in death.

Troi drew in a sharp breath. "Shomia."

Beside her, Ambassador Lelys was shaking her head again, rapidly, like a dog trying to get dry. "The girl— Impossible. We just saw her less than an hour ago, alive, well, running—"

The innkeeper himself approached the sobbing mother of the dead child. "What happened?" He touched the woman's shoulder carefully, as if a heavier touch would shatter her like glass.

"She went with me to the evening rites and stayed for the storytelling," Shomia's mother said, her voice hoarse and strange. "I couldn't stay. I had the mending waiting for me. I didn't want her to stay either. She had a cough these past three days—just a little dry one—and I was worried. But she pleaded so!" The woman cuddled her daughter's body close. "She loved the stories."

A man stepped out of the shadows leading a small boy by the hand and holding an even smaller girl on his shoulder. He looked haggard, his eyes burning. "She came home saying her head hurt," he said. "She wouldn't eat or drink. She said she only wanted to lie down. We didn't even notice when she climbed the ladder to the children's sleeping loft. When I took our son up to bed, I saw her lying on her mattress fully clothed. I wanted to wake her, to tell her to put on her nightgown, but—" He bit his lip to keep from saying the words, as if his silence would have the power to undo the dreadful thing that had happened tonight. His whole body began to shiver.

The little boy stared up at his father, more frightened by what he saw now than by his sister's death or his mother's screams. He wrenched his hand free of his father's grip and put it to his mouth. He looked as if he were about to cry, but he didn't.

He coughed.

Riker paced the length of his room in a cold, tightly contained rage. He could feel his insides being eaten up by anger, made worse by the certainty that there was absolutely nothing he could do about it. He was a Starfleet officer; he had seen many deaths. Most of them weren't half as peaceful as Shomia's. Her parents hadn't even been aware of the moment when she slipped away. Almost every people he'd encountered, with the exception of the Klingons, agreed that a peaceful death was a blessing.

He knew all this. None of it soothed his spirit, and so he paced the room, hagridden.

Well out of Riker's way, Mr. Data sat studying the Ne'elatian artifact that he had carried away with him from Ma'adrys's hut. With the aid of a few fine tools he had brought along, the android had no trouble persuading the antique device to yield up its secrets.

"Fascinating," he remarked.

"What?" Glad for any diversion, Riker was at the android's elbow in two strides.

"I believe I have repaired this device, sir," Data replied, holding the silvery disc at eye level. "Of course we cannot hope for it to be fully functional without its original power source, but that only affects its interplanetary communication capabilities."

"Interplanetary?"

"With a sufficiently strong self-contained power source augmented by the device's solar collector, this unit should in theory be able to transmit messages from Ashkaar to Ne'elat. It would definitely be able to transmit from the surface of Ashkaar to a vessel orbiting this world. That is its primary function, at any rate."

"I take it that it has others?" Now Riker was studying the object as intently as was the android.

"Without a doubt. The design and array of its interior components suggest that it could also transmit a strong distress signal as well as a heat ray of limited power. However, here is one function that I think you will find most interesting." He used one of his slenderest tools to flip open a minuscule panel on top of the disc, then tweaked a sliver of metal near the center of the opened device. Immediately the room crackled with the sound of a woman's voice.

". . . at heart. I do not know how we can justify what we have . . . these people. I have seen how they perform . . . rites with reverence, how . . . old tales and give the gods true worship. Father, if you hear this . . . why I can never come back to Ne'elat. I will not consent . . . drink their souls, lead them deeper into darkness . . . death . . . turn myself into an agent of lies!"

Data tweaked the sliver a second time and the voice stopped. "The quality of the recording has degenerated with time, but I think it can be salvaged."

"Is there more?" Riker asked.

"Quite probably. Shall I play it?"

"Any danger of losing the recording once it's played?"

"I do not believe so, but I can take the appropriate measures to capture and save the information. This is not a very sophisticated device. I would characterize it as part of an explorer's basic kit, suitable for field work in any of a number of the sciences, such as anthropology, for instance."

"You think the Ne'elatians have been sending their scientists to study the Ashkaarians in secret?"

"There is no doubt that any Ne'elatian presence here was intended to be secret," Data responded. "However, I do not yet have sufficient information to judge whether the purpose of such a presence was strictly academic. The young woman who made this recording speaks of drinking souls, leading others deeper into darkness, and being herself an agent of lies. None of this sounds particularly scientific to me."

"Come with me," Riker said, heading for the door. "I want the others to hear all of this."

Troi and Lelys sat on the edge of their bed staring at the device in Mr. Data's hand. Riker stood behind the android, leaning against the wall, jaw set, eyes steely. They had all just heard a ghost talk, bringing them a message from the past that had left them incapable of immediate speech. The stillness in the room was absolute.

Mr. Data calmly closed the little panel on the back

of the disc and asked, "Would you like me to play it again?"

Troi shook her head. "Not now, thank you." She still looked stunned by what she had heard. "All those years," she said, half to herself. "Incredible."

"They are *not* our kin." Ambassador Lelys spoke so abruptly, so fiercely, that all eyes snapped onto her. "They cannot be our kin. What are they, these Ne'elatian creatures who claim to be descended from the blood of S'ka'rys?" She hunched over, her hands in fists on her knees. "I wish we had never learned of their existence!"

Mr. Data regarded her inquisitively. "I fail to understand why this recording has provoked such strong reactions. It does not strike me as inflammatory, nor even particularly informative. Any facts it contains are obscured by the young woman's emotional outbursts."

Riker closed weary eyes and pinched the bridge of his nose. The hour was late, but apart from that he felt drained by the events of the night, not least of them the words he had just heard. "What we have here, Mr. Data, is a multifunctional device that belonged to the woman who the villagers here knew as Stakis but who identifies herself at the end of this message as Isata Kish of Ne'elat."

"That I understand. What I do not see is—"

"She didn't come here as a scientist or an emmissary or even just a curiosity seeker. She came as a spy. We've all heard the same story from different sources, all about how both these worlds came to be settled, how all contact between them was lost, if it ever existed in the first place. What we didn't know until now was what happened after Ne'elat rediscovered space travel and came back here."

"That is another thing I do not understand," the android said. "Both worlds were settled at the same time by the same people. Why did Ne'elat enjoy such accelerated technological progress while Ashkaar apparently stood still?"

"The answer may lie in the story we heard this evening," Troi suggested. "Do you remember the part about the Sixth Mother?"

"She became a foul-smelling mist that rose up out of the ground and stole the people's memories," Riker answered. "Probably a reference to the fumes they must have endured in the more geologically unstable areas."

"Prolonged exposure to the substances contained in certain cthonic emanations can cause extensive brain damage, which in turn could account for widespread memory loss in a given population, among other effects," Data observed. "That is the best evaluation I can make, given the fact that the sole source of pertinent information is folk tradition rather than scientific record."

"So, a time of darkness," Lelys reflected. "All the old arts and sciences stolen from their minds as if they had never existed. The Ashkaarians had to remake their world." Her eyes glittered angrily. "This only makes the sins of Ne'elat all the worse."

"Sins?" Mr. Data repeated.

"The Ne'elatians lost none of the old knowledge that had accompanied them here from Skerris IV," Troi said. "By their own admission, after they subdued the harsher environmental conditions of their new world, they were free to make as much technological progress as their own abilities allowed."

"In other words, no need to lose time reinventing the wheel," Riker put in. "The Ne'elatians remembered as much Skerrian technology as their parents and grandparents had brought with them, they just didn't have the means to reproduce it all right away."

"But there was another memory their ancestors brought along that the Ne'elatians did not want to reproduce," Troi said. "They were not aware of it immediately. They spent many generations simply trying to establish themselves on their new home-world, but in time, as their civilization made more and more rapid progress, someone must have remembered it."

"Remembered it in an accursed hour," Lelys said through gritted teeth. "It was their own fault that they had turned from the gods! You heard what Isata Kish said as well as I. The Ne'elatians worshipped only what they could see, touch, compel to make their lives more comfortable. And once they had their comfort, they wondered why their lives were barren." Bitterness twisted her mouth. "An evil hour, when they remembered how things had been on S'ka'rys and realized that they had remade their new world on the same cold model as the old."

"It would have been worse if they had not recognized their error," Troi said, seeking to ease Lelys's mind. "Otherwise Ne'elat might have come to the same violent end as Skerris IV."

"Better if they had," the Orakisan spat. Suddenly all her rage dissolved and she buried her face in her hands. "No, that is untrue. Oh, listen to how I speak, wishing destruction on them! They have sinned horribly against their Ashkaarian kindred, and I sin against them by my words. To desire the death of a whole world!"

Troi put one arm around the sobbing Orakisan. "The Ashkaarians worship the Lady of the Balances. It can be a very difficult thing for any people to balance the things of science against the things of the spirit, but it is necessary. The Ne'elatians realized this in time. Too many other peoples never do. It is only unfortunate that they reached this realization at the same time that they rediscovered their surviving kindred on Ashkaar. They had two choices: to remake their spiritual life by seeking it within themselves— not a thing quickly or easily done—or to take what was already there on Ashkaar. You spoke against them so fiercely just now because they chose the easier way, and because you fear that their choice reflects badly on you, their distant kin."

Ambassador Lelys first shook her head no, then paused and sighed. "I wish it were not so. I wish I had the power to change it."

"According to what you are saying, the Ne'elatians adopted the Ashkaarian's religious practices," Data said. "Why do you regard this as improper?"

"Because they did not adopt, they stole," Lelys exclaimed. "They came here in secret and took the trappings of this people's faith without the substance."

"The Ne'elatians go through the motions of Ashkaarian rites, but they don't really know much about the underlying beliefs," Riker added. "They've been playacting at something that's sacred to another people."

"This is offensive?" Data asked.

"This is *vile,*" Lelys said.

"Ah." The android did not seem to be convinced.

"Why do you doubt her, Mr. Data?" Troi asked him.

"The Ashkaarians are ignorant of the existence of the Ne'elatians. They are certainly ignorant of the fact that the Ne'elatians have appropriated their religious practices, whether frivolously or sincerely. If they do not know of the offense, how can they be offended?

And if they are not offended, what actual harm have the Ne'elatians done to them?"

"Aren't you forgetting something?" Riker nodded toward the silvery device still cradled in the android's palm. "Isata Kish wasn't sent here just to observe the Ashkaarians and borrow a few more rituals for her people." He reached over and touched the replay control. The device hummed briefly, then brought back Isata Kish's words:

"I have left the village where I was supposed . . . will *not* kidnap the man! I . . . seen his invention and . . . preliminary reports . . . correct. He *has* discovered . . . form of unrefined . . . or explosive. Even if we were seeking to intervene in the name . . . maintaining peace for . . . would still be wrong. I refuse. Let another of our agents tell . . . he is ascending to Evramur in the flesh! I . . . no longer. I would choke on the lie. Better . . . save what is left of your souls! Do you . . . —lieve that we can keep them ignorant forever? That we . . . stop progress by stealing away any . . . scientific minds among them?" The recording crackled with a scornful noise. "Why don't we bring them to Bovridash and breed them for religion . . . way we breed beasts for meat? But I would be afraid that you . . . the Masra'et would take my . . . seriously."

Riker touched the unit again, silencing it. "Now do you see?" he asked Data.

"I believe so. It would seem that the Ne'elatians have done the Ashkaarians significant harm after all."

"First they steal what they please of the Ashkaarians' beliefs, then they steal their brightest minds." Ambassador Lelys held herself stiff, fighting for self-control over rage. "They think that if the Ashkaarians make any technological progress, they will lose their faith, simply because that was how it happened on Ne'elat."

"Isata Kish was obviously one of the agents in place stationed here to be on the lookout for any natives who might turn out to be this world's answer to da Vinci, Pasteur, Galileo," Riker said. "Once a Ne'elatian agent spotted someone like that, it wasn't hard to whisk them away, and no one here would get suspicious. The first agents were probably the ones who planted all the stories about how these living saints were carried off to Evramur. Who'd ever question it?"

"None," Lelys said. "That would be blasphemy, and none would want to. The village that produces a saint gains fame, prestige, and attracts many pilgrims."

Troi sighed. "We can at least be thankful that the Ne'elatians did not simply kill the Ashkaarians they carried off. To someone born and raised here, Ne'elat must indeed look like paradise."

"I am unfamiliar with everything that the term paradise implies," Data said. "However I would suggest that a situation based on deliberate lies could not be a true paradise. A very attractive and comfortable prison, perhaps, but not a paradise."

Ambassador Lelys stood up, a dangerous light in her eyes. "This situation is an atrocity, an injustice that has gone on for far too long. It is intolerable. I will endure it no more." Her glance swept their faces. "I am well aware that as Starfleet officers you are restrained from direct intervention here as well as on Ne'elat. I am not. As soon as it has been determined whether or not these worlds have preserved the plant our colonists need so desperately, I will make all this public. More, I will lay the case before a Federation tribunal! I will—"

A commotion from the hallway reached them, the

sound of lumbering feet followed by a wild pounding at the door across the hall, Riker and Data's room. "Help, oh help us!" It was Sekol, the innkeeper, and he sounded like a man without hope.

Riker rushed to the door of the women's room and threw it open. "We're here. What is it?"

If the visitors had transgressed against any local custom by having both sexes closeted in one room, Sekol was past caring about such things. His pallor was one step removed from a dead man's. Sweat spangled his brow and his eyes were dark with terror. "There are more deaths," he gasped. "Old Maskan, who told the stories, he's gone, and his poor wife with him! B'ist the tanner, he and his two sons, all of them strong and healthy this morning, dead, and his wife sounds three breaths away from the grave herself! Not a house in all Kare'al but someone's fallen ill of this curse. Oh, honored guests, flee! Save yourselves! You did not make a pilgrimage to find your deaths." He leaned against the doorjamb, gasping.

Riker supported him, helped him into the room, lowered him to sit on the edge of the bed beside Troi. The Betazoid stroked the innkeeper's hand. "A pilgrimage is more than walking from one shrine to the next just to look at piles of stone," she said. "We will stay."

Chapter Nine

"THERE," SAID DR. CRUSHER, closing the wooden box. "That's the last of it."

Lt. Worf picked up the packed box and asked, "Did you make sure to remove anything that might look suspicious to the natives?"

"The only possible way the locals could catch on is if they don't use glass containers for medicines. Other than that, these supplies look as if they'd fit right into any healer's kit in a low-tech, agrarian civilization like Ashkaar."

"If the supplies you are sending to the Away Team are no different from what the Ashkaarians already have, what is the point?" the Klingon asked.

Dr. Crusher smiled. "I said they *look* like what they already have. I promise you, these medicines are much stronger and more effective than any native remedies."

Lt. Worf's expression grew even sterner than usual.

"I do not like this. Starfleet regulations clearly prohibit us from interfering with—"

"I obey the Prime Directive as scrupulously as anyone aboard this ship, Lt. Worf," Dr. Crusher cut in. "It's not the easiest thing in the world to do. Sometimes it goes contrary to all my instincts as a doctor, but I obey it. However in this case, I'm not the one performing direct medical intervention among the natives. Ambassador Lelys is the one who ordered this delivery. There's no reason for me to deny a special envoy access to what are fairly basic medical supplies. What she intends to do with them once she receives them—" Dr. Crusher shrugged.

"I do not approve of your reasoning, Dr. Crusher," Lt. Worf said severely. "It is clear that she intends to use them to help the Ashkaarians. If she needed medical attention herself, she could have returned to the ship."

"I did point that out to her when she first communicated her request via Commander Riker. She refused on the grounds that if we were to transport her aboard the *Enterprise* now, her abrupt departure would cast suspicion on the remaining members of the Away Team. That, in turn, would endanger their mission." Dr. Crusher made a gesture of helplessness that was purely for show. "What else could I do?"

"You are a resourceful person, Dr. Crusher," Worf responded. "You could have found any number of alternate solutions to this situation, if that had been what you wanted."

"You sound as if it annoys you that I didn't," Dr. Crusher said, giving him a canny look.

"It does not . . . annoy me," Worf replied in a way that as good as said that it did, but that he'd sooner die than admit it. "I merely think that such behavior sets a bad example."

"What sort of behavior? And for whom am I setting this bad example?" Dr. Crusher maintained a calm expression. "Your son, perhaps? Lt. Worf, this is *not* about Ashkaar, is it." It wasn't a question. She knew very well what was on the Klingon's mind. "We've been over this time and again. Look, if you don't want him to have that hamster, why don't you just take it away from him? Why keep *hinting* at the subject every time we speak? I already told you, I'm *not* going to go to Alexander and tell him that I've changed my mind and that I'm taking back his pet."

"Do you know what he named the beast?" Worf's eyes narrowed. *"Fido.* What sort of a name is that for a young Klingon warrior's companion?"

"Uh." Dr. Crusher swallowed her mirth. "A very good name, actually. It means faithful, but it isn't a name that's usually given to, um, hamsters. He didn't happen to get the idea from Mr. Data, by any chance?"

Worf stared at her. "How did you know?"

Dr. Crusher thought of the tabby-striped pet cat that the android had named Spot. "Oh, just a lucky guess."

"All the beast does is sleep and eat and run around in that accursed wire wheel. I have taken the wheel to Engineering for adjustment several times and it still squeaks."

"Well, there you are, then. That's a suitable lesson for a future Klingon warrior to learn. Owning a hamster will teach Alexander how to endure persistent mental torture," Dr. Crusher said brightly.

"A lesson that will only be of use to him should anyone ever give *his* son a hamster." Worf wheeled about and strode out of sickbay. Dr. Crusher did him the courtesy of waiting until the door hissed shut behind him before she gave way to laughter.

The shimmer of a transporter beam cut through the poorly thatched roof of Sekol's inn, depositing the wooden box of medical supplies at Ambassador Lelys's feet. The Orakisan flung herself on the package as soon as it was solid and began distributing the contents to Riker and Data. She had a reed basket beside her, which she filled with a double portion of the supplies before rising to her feet and straightening her pilgrim's robes.

"There. I will take these to Counsellor Troi in the village. You two would do well to slip your shares into the keeping of the healer downstairs."

Commander Riker looked doubtful. "Ambassador Lelys, your heart's in the right place, but this is too risky. The village healer doesn't have the training of the local oberyin, but she taught herself her skill by being observant. She probably knows what's in her own kit down to the last bottle, and besides, she'll notice that the color of some of these powders is radically different from what she's been using to try and bring down the fever."

"The fever, the cough, all the symptoms that are killing these people," Lelys muttered. "The sickness itself that keeps on killing them while their healer and their oberyin try in vain to stop it. With what? Herbs that give a little relief but do nothing more than make the dying easier—herbs and prayers."

"They do appear to take a great deal of comfort from their religious observances," Mr. Data remarked. "Their conception of the link between their world and the afterlife—"

"Evramur," Lelys said bitterly. "A promise of

paradise while their children die. Die needlessly! You yourself said that this disease could be prevented by a simple vaccine."

"It does bear a striking similarity to certain historic Earth ailments that were effectively eradicated by widespread innoculation programs," Data admitted.

"It bears an even more striking resemblance to Talossa fever," Lelys said. "A sickness that we on Orakisa know."

"I am not surprised to hear that," Data said. "Since Orakisans and Ashkaarians are in effect the same people, it is to be expected that your common ancestors would have transported the same microbes with them when they left Skerris IV."

"If you know this ailment for what it is, maybe you could help the local healer use the most effective means to cure it," Riker suggested.

"If I knew that, I would," Lelys replied. "But there is no one left on Orakisa who has ever had to treat Talossa fever. I was immunized against it when I was an infant; all our children are. Our scientists believe that soon it will be extinct." Her eyes blazed as she added, "Do you think the Ne'elatians allow *their* children to die of something so simply prevented?"

"I can't defend what the Ne'elatians have done here," Riker said. "They've held the progress of an entire culture hostage to their own wants."

"Then do not help them further by holding back something that might help their victims." Lelys jerked a small vial of medicine out of her basket and thrust it inches from Riker's face. "Say whatever you must to make the healer use this."

Riker took out one of the vials that he had already hidden inside his robes and contemplated it. "I suppose I could say that we brought our own medicines with us for our journey and that this is what they use for fevers in our home village."

"Good, good." Lelys nodded. Suddenly her whole face lit up. "Ah! But I have an idea that is even better. If it works, we will not even need to persuade the healer or the oberyin to use this." She turned the vial in her fingers. "They will not *dare* to refuse! Commander Riker, will you allow Mr. Data to accompany me?"

"Where are you going?"

"To make a miracle."

The downstairs portion of the inn was no longer the jolly taproom of only a few days ago. The trestle tables and even some of the benches had been converted to sickbeds, with a few set aside to hold the rudimentary equipment of those who tried to heal the sick, or at least attempted to bring some comfort to their dying.

Mr. Data noted the way in which the villagers had mobilized to deal with the illness. To judge by their methods—efficient in spite of how primitive they were—this was a situation that they had faced many times before. He was particularly impressed by their establishment of the makeshift hospital in Sekol's inn. They were doing their best to segregate the sick from the well. As for how effective this would be in the long run, he had his doubts. The illness had spread rapidly since Shomia's death. Few homes could boast that not one of their occupants had been touched by the disease. When he consulted his memory, it revealed that most other ailments analogous to Talossa fever were at their most communicable before symptoms manifested. The time to separate the sick from the well was *before* anyone seemed to be sick.

It was far too late for that now, even if the Ashkaarians could have diagnosed the disease before it manifested. Shomia had been one of many children crowded around the storyteller's feet that fateful night. The illness had gone home with every one of them.

As he and Lelys passed through the bustling taproom-turned-medical-ward, someone hailed him. It was the innkeeper's son, Kinryk. The lad stood at one end of a bench where a body lay very still, its face covered over with a square of blue cloth. "Hoi! Give us a hand. Got to get this one out of here. No more we can do for him."

"Certainly." The android turned to Lelys and said, "I will not be long."

"Hurry," she replied, and walked out of the inn.

Mr. Data was true to his word. It didn't take him long to help Kinryk remove the body to the large storeroom behind the bar. Like the taproom, this place, too, had been converted to another use. A table cut the room in half. Before the table stood four young men, their faces pinched and grave. They stepped aside to allow Kinryk and Data to place the body on the board, then one of them arranged six small clay figurines around it. These were the images of the Six Mothers, all lovingly made and glazed, their long, full skirts swept forward to form cups where mounds of incense now smoldered. The atmosphere in the storeroom was thick with fragrant smoke whose scent effectively masked the smell of death.

Behind the table stood a fifth man, hardly older than the others. He wore dark robes of blue and brown embroidered with silver thread, and in his left hand he held a ball that seemed to have been woven of brightly colored feathers. His right hand removed the blue cloth covering the face of the dead and dropped it into a brazier beside him. Between the heat of the brazier and the smoke of the six incense holders it was almost impossible to breathe in the storeroom. Sweat streaked the faces of the four attendants, but the man behind the table remained untouched, cool, focussed only on the task before him. He raised the feather ball and chanted for the dead. Throughout all the rite, Kinryk stood with his arms crossed over his chest and his head tilted back, eyes on the bare ceiling beams or perhaps on something beyond them. Mr. Data observed him and imitated his pose exactly.

When the chanting was done, the man set aside the feather ball, reached under the table into a basket, and produced a strip of white cloth with which he bound the dead man's eyes. This accomplished, he nodded to his four assistants, who carried the body out past Data and Kinryk. The innkeeper's son went up to the empty table and bowed.

"Your blessing, Bilik oberyin," he said.

"Given with joy." The village oberyin cupped Kinryk's face with his hands and released him. His expression did not match his words, but his lack of joy was more than understandable.

The blessing received, Kinryk ducked out of the storeroom as Mr. Data went up to the table. The android knew the value of maintaining the Away Team's masquerade. If he rushed off, back to the Ambassador, without doing as Kinryk had done, he risked discovery for them all. Lelys would have to wait a short while longer.

"Your blessing, Bilik oberyin," he said, mimicking Kinryk.

The oberyin took Data's face in his hands as he had done for the innkeeper's son, but he did not repeat the words of the blessing right away. Instead he gazed into the android's eyes and said, "You are one of the pilgrims. Be welcome. A hard welcome, I fear, but what the Lady holds in her sacred Balances is often hidden from our sight. They tell me that you and your friends have been helping us in this time of trial. For that you have our thanks and my special blessing, given with joy. May you have no cause to regret your goodness of heart." This said, he let Data go.

The android didn't know whether or not he was expected to thank the oberyin for his blessing. He settled for making a second bow before leaving the storeroom. Outside the inn, he found Lelys in deep conversation with the innkeeper's wife. The two women were seated on a bench set against the inn wall. Between them, his small body crumpled with misery, the child Herri wept.

"—*must* eat," the innkeeper's wife was saying. She tried to put her arm around the boy, but he jerked away.

"Yes, listen to Bava," Lelys urged. "You must not allow yourself to weaken. You will fall ill."

"I wish I would!" the child wailed. "I wish I'd get sick and die and be taken up to Evramur with Shomia! But I won't go there. I can't. Not even the Sixth Mother would speak for me. This is all my fault. I got mad at Shomia and I told her I wished she'd die, and she did, and now everyone else is dying too, and—and—and—" He broke into fresh sobs.

Lelys took the boy into her arms. "Hush, child, hush," she said, stroking his hair. "None of this is your doing. Was this the first time you ever ill-wished anyone? I do not think so. And yet no evil times came after those ill wishes, did they? Did they?" she insisted, making him look up at her.

"N—no," he admitted, gulping down the tears.

"There, then. You see? Not your fault at all. Now do not make a hard time harder by letting your strength go and falling ill too. We have enough sick ones to tend already. Eat something so that you can help the others to get well."

The boy stared into her face for a while, then nodded solemnly. He made Lelys a brief, awkward sign of respect and turned to the innkeeper's wife. "I'm sorry. I'll eat now."

"Good child." Beaming, the woman led him away. Lelys watched them go before addressing the patiently waiting android.

"Was it necessary for that poor boy to believe he was the cause of all this?" she demanded. "His mother is already among the dead, Bava told me, and his father is ailing. She has taken charge of him and his siblings until this is over, this—this epidemic of *stupidity!* He may survive, but his childhood is dead, lost forever. Needlessly!" She looked up into the sky with a scowl on her face that could kill. Though it was still daylight and the bright disc of Ne'elat was not visible, there was no question as to the object of her rage.

"If we wish to help these people, I would suggest that we implement whatever plan it is that you have in mind as soon as possible," Mr. Data said.

"Yes, of course." Lelys composed herself and picked up the basket that she had left under the bench. "Let us go." She led the way up the village street.

The path leading through the center of Kare'al to the upland slopes of the mountain was no longer the busy, lively route it had been just days ago, when V'kal and Misik first conducted the Away Team to Ma'adrys's old house. No housewives chatted with their neighbors while they peeled vegetables for the evening meal, no children played in the dirt, no doors stood open to welcome friends and release the rich scents of homely cooking. The street was deserted, the doors all shut, the only sounds the muffled echo of sobbing or prayer, the only scents the burning of incense and the sour reek of sickness.

"Now listen to me," Lelys told Data, anger driving any attempt at diplomacy out of her words. "When we get there, I want you to cause some sort of a distraction for me."

"I will do my best," the android replied. "But where is 'there'?"

"We are returning to the shrine these people have made of Ma'adrys's house," she replied. "If no one is nearby, I will not need you to do anything. But if someone is there, watch me closely and when I signal you, draw their attention away from me."

"Understood." Data saw no need to question Lelys further.

They continued up the track. Ma'adrys's house came into view, and with it the fence of crudely hacked saplings and thin rope that had sprung up around it. There was a narrow gap in the fence, guarded by a knot of three stone-eyed men. All of them were armed with cudgels and looked ready to pick a fight even if no one wanted one. Two more of their number walked along the inside of the fence, patrolling the newly established perimeter. Behind them, just inside the gateway, sat a man who looked as if his presence among so much brawn and sullenness was a mistake. He was garbed much like the lad that the Away Team had first encountered on the road to Kare'al, with the same bland, amiable, vacant expression. He sat with a shepherd's crook and a broad-brimmed hat on the grass beside him, playing happily as a child with a herd of carved wooden sheep.

The other men sat up and took notice as Lelys and Data approached. The Orakisan ambassador paused a little before the gateway, surveyed the fence, then tried to pass through as if there was nothing out of the ordinary going on. The largest of the men stepped directly into her path, his arms outstretched to bar her way.

Lelys's eyes flashed. "What does this mean?" she demanded. "Why is the way to holy Ma'adrys's shrine blocked?"

"Not blocked, honored visitor, not like that at all," the man said. He sounded sincerely apologetic, but he didn't move an inch.

"Indeed?" Mr. Data was perceptibly intrigued by this situation. "If that is so, perhaps you are not aware that you are blocking it at this very moment?"

"It's like this," the man said. "What with the sickness and all, folk have been flocking here half out of their minds with fear and worry. The hut was packed tight as a fleece bale for days until Bilik oberyin gave the word that we was to come up here and keep things, uh, orderly. Terrible things folk do when they're afraid. Terrible things." He shook his heavy head. "You realize that one of the people who came here to pray for holy Ma'adrys to save their family went and—"

A second man gave his comrade a hearty jab with his elbow and growled, "Don't you go talking like that before visitors about our own, M'kin. Could be there's another reason why it vanished."

Mr. Data opened his eyes wide in inquiry. "Why, what vanished?"

The second guard made a disgusted sound and gave the first man a dirty look. "That's done it. Might's well tell him." He glowered at Data. "Then you can go running back downslope to your own people and tell them that we're all a bunch of thieves in Kare'al village. You'd like that, wouldn't you?"

"No, I cannot say that I would," Data admitted honestly. "What has been stolen?"

"One of the relics," the guard named M'kin said. "A mirror that Ma'adrys had from her mother. That's what La'akel the herbwife said, anyhow. It was mostly her that tidied up the place after Ma'adrys was took up. She knew what was in there and what wasn't."

"Shame. Just a shame," a third man spoke up. "All the time since she's been gone off to Evramur and nothing of her's touched, except to keep the dust off. Free entry to her place for all. That's how it used to be, how it *ought* to be, and now this!"

By this time, one of the men walking the fence line had reached the gateway, overheard the conversation, and wanted to add his mite to it. "Well, could be whoever took it'll fetch it back after this hard time's over and done. Maybe it was a woman hoping that the touch of it would save her babies' lives. Can't really blame her for that." He continued on his way around the fence.

"So you see," M'kin concluded, "we're here to make sure no more of that sort of thing happens. If you want to visit the holy place, Avren there'll take you up. He's a shepherd, but there's no harm in him."

At the sound of his name, the childlike man looked up and waved at the visitors, then got to his feet and tried to make a present of one of his toy sheep to Mr. Data. The android accepted the gift and stood holding it as if it were about to bite him.

"There now, Avren, take back your toy," M'kin said in a kindly voice. He took the sheep from Mr.

Data and shoved it back into the shepherd's hands. "You know you'll only be crying after it if he keeps it."

"You can have one of my *real* sheep, if you want," Avren told the android. "Symo's watching 'em for me 'til I can go back up the mountain, then I'll watch his when it's his turn to help here. We're going to get a big bag of sweetcakes, after."

"Thank you, but I already have a pet," Mr. Data told him.

While this was going on, Lelys discreetly whispered in the second guard's ear, "Does he really take care of sheep?"

The man seemed nonplussed by her question. "Why shouldn't he? That's what we have our shepherds do."

"But he seems so—so helpless."

"I grant you, he's simpler than most of 'em, but he's not really one of our own. He come up over our mountain past Six Mothers' shrine from the seaward side years and years ago. He didn't have too big a herd with him when he come—it'd do your heart good to see how they've prospered since—and he said he didn't recollect his old village's name. Well, with shepherds that happens more'n you'd think, especially after the midsummer rites. They're simpleminded and memories run out of their minds like water through a sieve, but they do raise up the herds fine, and those of their sons who don't go through their initiation rites grow up the same in mind as you or I."

"Are they all like him?" Lelys stared at Avren, who was now trying to coax his toy sheep to graze on the cockade of brown, lacy, dried flowers pinned to his wide-brimmed hat.

The second guard nodded. "All. Some folk like to make sport of 'em, but they do their job and they can do other jobs as well if you explain the *how* of it to 'em plain enough. Bilik oberyin says that the shepherds are a living reminder of how it used to be for all of us, in the times of the Sixth Mother, and how we should be kind and grateful to 'em instead of teasing, but some people—" He shrugged. "My sister married a shepherd for her second husband and she's happier with him than she ever was with the first, and he was a merchant."

"You two go on ahead up to Ma'adrys's shrine with Avren," M'kin urged, standing aside to let Data and Lelys inside the fence. "He knows what's in the hut now down to the last spoon and he knows to tally up everything that's there after you've made your prayers and left. *Not* that I'm saying you're likely to take anything," he added quickly.

"I can promise you that we will take nothing that is there now," Mr. Data assured him as he fell into step behind their beaming shepherd guide.

When they were about halfway between the house and the gateway, Lelys scampered up the slope to tug at Mr. Data's sleeve. "This will be easier than I hoped," she said. "He can be our witness." She nodded at Avren, who was striding along ahead of them, singing a tuneless song at the top of his lungs and playing toss-and-catch with one of his toy sheep.

"Witness to what?" Data asked.

"The miracle I've got planned. He has taken a liking to you. All you will have to do once we are inside the house is start talking to him while I pretend to pray. The last time we were in there, I saw a basket in one corner of the room. That is where I will kneel and while you keep him occupied, I will drop the medicine vials from my basket into that one."

"Ah." Data nodded his comprehension. "You will then pretend to discover them there?"

"A miracle," Lelys affirmed. "A gift sent by Ma'adrys herself to her people in their time of need. No one will question it and no one will balk at using it."

"I see. What I do not understand is how what you are doing is so very different from what the Ne'elatians do."

"What?" There was no measuring Lelys's shocked indignation. She stopped stock still, staring open-mouthed at the android. "You dare compare me to them? To those—those soul-drinkers?"

"They pretend to follow the Ashkaarians' faith because they cannot spare the time to explore their own spirits, and they deceive them when it suits their ends. You are going to pray at this shrine as if you share the Ashkaarians' faith as well, and you will also deceive them because it suits your purposes."

"I will save their lives. The Ne'elatians do not care whether these people live or die."

"There does appear to be a difference in your motivations," Data admitted. "I hope I have not offended you. I only wished to have it made clear to me."

"Honored vistors?" Avren stood on the threshold of Ma'adrys's hut, gazing earnestly back at his charges. "Will you come?"

"Coming!" Lelys called to him. "There was a pebble in my shoe." As they hastened up the path and into the hut, she whispered to Data, "You I can forgive; the Ne'elatians, never." She cast a wary glance at Avren, but the shepherd seemed to be indifferent to the conference presently taking place between the two visitors. As soon as they had entered the hut, he sat himself down with his back to the doorjamb and began playing with his toy sheep once more.

"The daughterworlds of S'ka'rys are banding together to form a confederacy," Lelys went on in a low, intense voice. "Each newly rediscovered world is admitted on the word of the envoys sent to establish contact. I swear by all I hold holy, Ne'elat will *never* be admitted to the confederacy. Let them twist in the dark for what they have done here."

"What if Legate Valdor and Hara'el overrule your decision?" Data whispered.

"It will not matter. My people only acknowledge three voices together as binding, or voices grouped in threes. One vote over or under the chosen number can bar any action. And I say to you, my voice will bar Ne'elat forever."

"But suppose that Captain Picard and Hara'el—"

"—find n'vashal on Ne'elat? I will still refuse them entry. I will not contaminate our newly reunited sisters with their evil. And if they refuse to give us n'vashal unless we admit them, then I will recommend to my superiors that we come here and take—"

"This is for you, pretty guest." Avren was suddenly standing between them, smiling his vacant smile, offering one of his toys to Lelys. "If you can't think of how you want to pray, watch this sheep until you can. That's how I help myself remember the things I want to pray for: I watch my sheep until it all comes back into my mind."

"Thank you, Avren, but"—Lelys exchanged a look with Data—"I already have a pet too."

"Ohhhh. Well, I'll go sit over there, then, and you pray. Ma'adrys will listen. *I'm* here. She likes me. She went up to Evramur from *my* meadow," he finished proudly, and went back to his place in the doorway.

"He is very quiet when he wants to be," Mr. Data observed, eying the shepherd. "I did not hear him approach. Perhaps we would do better not to discuss your hostilities toward Ne'elat until we are back at the inn."

"No harm was done," Lelys declared. "Look at the poor thing. He would never guess what we are talking about. Now go to him and stand ready." She turned to the corner where Ma'adrys's abandoned basket stood and knelt before it.

"Congratulations, Ambassador Lelys," Commander Riker said. "Your plan was an unqualified success." He leaned back against the closed door of the women's room, pleased to be the bearer of good news. "The fever's broken in every case where the herbwife and the oberyin used the medicines you planted."

"Please, Commander Riker, I can't take credit for a miracle." The Orakisan ambassador returned his smile. She stretched her arms over her head and yawned. "Though I suppose we can all take credit for lending these people a hand in their time of need. When I return to Orakisa, I will commend you and the rest of the Away Team to my superiors for your humanitarian efforts here, among our distant kin."

"No need for that," Riker replied.

"And I will take full responsibility before Captain Picard for having introduced the medicines to the Ashkaarians."

"Thanks, but there's no need for that either. It's done. If there are any consequences to be accepted, I'll take them. It was in a good cause." He sighed wearily. "I'm glad we've broken the back of this epidemic so quickly. Now we can get back to our initial mission. I only hope—" He didn't finish the thought. Hope of finding n'vashal was too closely tied up with the possibility of failure. So many dead ends, and so many lives in the balance—

The Orakisan ambassador understood without his having to say another word. "Commander Riker, the Ashkaarians revere the Lady of the Balances, the keeper of harmony. They believe that in all deeds, there is weight to sway the Lady's scales for good or evil. What we have just done for them has dropped the balance of life in our favor. If prayers of thanksgiving for their lives and their children's lives carry any weight at all, this Lady of theirs must surely give us the lives of *my* people in payment, to restore the balance of the universe."

"You sound as ready as the Ne'elatians to adopt the Ashkaarians' faith," Riker remarked.

Lelys's face darkened. "If I do, I will do it from my heart, in truth, not merely for show."

"I meant no offense, Ambassador."

As suddenly as it had come, her scowl was gone. "None taken. I apologize, Commander. We are all tired, and fatigue often makes me short tempered. But with the sickness stemmed, we can resume our initial purpose here, as you say. Let us take our success against the fever as a favorable omen, one that promises us the swift, equally successful conclusion to our search."

"If I had a glass, I'd drink to that with you," Riker said affably.

"Why should we not go downstairs and see if Sekol can provide us with some refreshment, then?" Lelys suggested. "The inn is no longer a hospital ward; business is nearly back to normal."

Riker bowed and offered the Orakisan his arm. "At your service."

They left the room in high spirits, despite how tired they both felt. The heavy door closed behind them, sealing the chamber in silence for the space of half a dozen breaths. A scrabbling sound came at the window. The little casement, cracked open just enough to admit the fresh, cold mountain air, now swung back outwards on its hinges and a tall, thin body slipped inside.

Avren the shepherd stood in the space between the two narrow beds, breathing hard after his exertions and brushing off the plaster dust that still clung to his clothes. He no longer wore the bland, empty expression of a simpleton, and he had left his shepherd's hat and crook behind him on the small outthrust roof just under the chamber window where he had lain hidden, listening, all this time.

His eyes were keen and alert, sweeping over the little room with the cool, searching gaze of a hunting hawk. When he caught his breath after the wriggle and scramble through the little window, he flung himself down on his belly to ferret around under the beds, examining every stick of furniture and every corner of the room closely.

His search turned up nothing, but his disheartened look lasted only an instant. A slow smile spread itself across his features. He reached into the pouch at his belt and drew out a device that was almost identical to the mirror-like object of Ma'adrys's mother. "Udar Kishrit," he said, his voice low and terse. "Urgent. Immediate response required."

The device hummed briefly, then stilled. In the time it took to count to five, Udar Kishrit's voice emanated from the glimmering circle. "Yes, Avren. What is it? This isn't the agreed-on time for your report.'"

"I know that. I have information that I believe you'd do well to have immediately. I'm in one of their rooms at the inn and—"

"In one of their rooms?" The head of Ne'elat's council repeated the agent's words, stunned. "You fool, get out of there before you're discovered!"

Avren chuckled. "What would they discover? Just another poor, half-witted shepherd who wandered somewhere he wasn't supposed to be because he didn't know any better. I'm safe enough from *them.*" He didn't bother hiding his contempt.

"You're too smug by half, Avren. Too smug and too daring. One day someone is going to teach you the difference between courage and folly." Udar Kishrit sounded as if he would relish giving the agent a lesson or two himself. "All right, make your report. Quickly. If they walk in on you in communication with me, I doubt they'll still think of you as just another empty-headed shepherd."

Briefly and rapidly, Avren relayed all that he had witnessed and overheard: Lelys's ploy at the shrine to Ma'adrys, her conversation with Data, and the words she'd just exchanged with Riker. "In short," he concluded, "the Orakisan ambassador is not very kindly disposed to us at the moment, and her word will be enough to kill any chance we have of renewed contact and commerce beyond this star system."

"Through the Skerrian union, yes, but there would still be the Federation." Udar Kishrit mulled this over, then added, "But the Federation would never provide us with the full measure of technological aid we want. Some, yes, but what we desire they would view as undue interference in our culture."

"Even if we tell them that we don't see it that way?"

"The Federation has its paths and policies, and no doubt its reasons for them. I have been speaking with this Mr. La Forge on the subject, and his words confirm my suspicions. On the other hand, the union of Skerrian daughterworlds would be much more forthcoming about helping one of their long-lost sisters regain the stars."

"Not if Ambassador Lelys has her say," Avren commented.

"Which is why," Udar Kishrit said distinctly, "you must make sure that she does not."

Chapter Ten

GEORDI KNEW THAT HE WOULD find her in the garden. That was where he always found her, whenever he was able to absent himself from his duties as the *Enterprise*'s senior representative to the Ne'elatian government. As Captain Picard had told him, it was a purely ceremonial appointment. While the captain and Hara'el pursued the Orakisan delegation's quest for the elusive n'vashal plant in the settled hinterlands of this world, someone from the ship had to stay in the capital to show the flag. Besides, Geordi's presence had a secondary purpose. As long as someone of his rank from the ship was present at all the fetes and festivals the Ne'elatian government was staging in honor of their starfaring guests, it was unlikely that anyone would comment on the absence of certain others.

In other words, Geordi was a distraction, a sop to the Masra'et to prevent their wondering why they had not seen Commander Riker or Counsellor Troi or Ambassador Lelys lately. He knew this; it didn't bother him in the least. He couldn't have asked for an assignment that suited him more.

"Ma'adrys?" He knew her favorite spot in the gardens, the place where they always contrived to meet at least once a day. It was one of the smaller enclosed spaces, a bower where a narrow stream trickled over smooth brown stones, where only the most fragrant native plants bloomed between high walls of prickly hedge. At the head of the stream, presiding over the heap of stones from which the waters bubbled up, was a statue of a robed and crowned woman holding a pair of scales. Unlike the old Earth images of Justice, this lady did not carry her balances by the centerpiece, but supported the pans of the scales in her cupped hands. The power to tilt them one way or the other didn't depend on the weights tossed into either pan, but solely on her will.

This was where Ma'adrys waited always for him, sitting on the tender grass beside the stream's source, flowers in her hair. This was where he found her today also, yet seeing her there, her face greeting him with joy, was just as sweet a shock to his heart as it had been the first time they had met in this little garden.

Why does it always surprise me? he wondered. *I ought to know by now that she's going to be here. She's always here for me. She knows my agenda of official appearances before I do, sometimes, and adjusts her own schedule accordingly. Why can't I take it for granted that she'll be here waiting every time I come seeking her?*

And in the instant before she raced into his arms and kissed him, he knew the answer. This was love, and love was something he could never take for granted, never accept as anything less than a constantly renewing miracle.

They lingered in each other's embrace for a time, then reluctantly parted. Although they had never yet been surprised by any interloper stumbling across one of their trysts, they were both conscious of that possibility. The gardens were open to all who lived or worked within the governmental palace, and to any visitors who could thread the maze of paths and hedge-lined walkways. While it was true that they might enjoy perfect privacy if they met at the old tower, there was too great a chance that someone would notice them going to the ruin daily. People would talk. They both agreed that it was better, safer in the long run, to keep this sweet place for their meetings.

"I missed you," Geordi told Ma'adrys, smiling.

"Truly? It has been less than a day. Did you not see me this morning at the rite to awaken the dawnlight? I was graciously permitted to carry the basin of rainwater." There was more than a little tang of bitterness to her words when she spoke of her part in the ceremony, and Geordi noticed.

"What's wrong?" He brushed a lock of her bright hair away from her face tenderly.

"On Ashkaar, the dawnlight awakening is for maidens only, and for boys who have not yet received their knot of manhood. The girls perform the rite on the days of earth, the boys on the days of water. But here—" She made a disgusted face. "Here they *all* take part—boys and girls, men and women. They mix the words of the earth-day chants with the water-day songs. They give the leader's part to anyone they wish to honor, as if it were a—a prize at a wrestling bout instead of a holy thing. Today was an earth day, but the rite was led by an ancient husk of a man. I know him; he is one of the most prosperous, powerful businessmen in the city. The rumors say he has been using his power to speak out against a new tax the Masra'et wishes to establish, so they called on him to lead the dawnlight ritual, hoping that the honor of it would soften him. They have taken what should be an offering to the gods and turned it into a bribe."

"I—I'm sorry. Maybe they don't know any better. Maybe if you asked to speak with Udar Kishrit—" Geordi wanted to soothe her, to charm that hard look from her eyes. He tried to take her back into his arms, but she pushed him away.

"And tell him what? That I know what he and all the rest like him have been doing to my people, to my world? He would only laugh. I have no power to harm him, and if I persist enough to annoy him, what do you think would become of me then?"

Geordi pulled her to him and held her close. "I won't let anyone hurt you."

If he hoped his assurances would make everything all right, he was wrong. Ma'adrys tensed in his embrace, then shrugged free. "Do you think I fear only for my own safety? That is unimportant. I would sacrifice it in an instant if I thought it would put an end to what these people have been doing to my world, my home! When I think of how they deceived me—" Her face darkened with anger, her hands became fists.

Geordi's hands closed over hers. "What the Ne'elatians did to you—what they've been doing to your people—that can't be changed. It's past. We can only hope to change the future."

"Will we?" Her expression became one of eagerness, of hope. "Oh Geordi, what you've told me of your world, of all the worlds you've seen, of the Federation—so many wonders, so much power." She grew thoughtful. Her gaze strayed from his face to the softly chuckling garden stream. "The power to right so many wrongs. Surely once we tell them what has been happening here, the Federation will do something to punish Udar Kishrit and the rest. They will not allow this injustice to continue. They will send more of your starships here to enforce a righteous judgment against Ne'elat!"

Geordi took a deep breath, on the verge of explaining the limitations binding all Starfleet interventions. He let it out again, the words unsaid. Why try? Not now. Now was not the time. Ma'adrys would never understand. It wasn't that she lacked the intelligence to understand; she was exceptionally bright. That same keen mind he had come to admire was the reason she had been stolen away from her people. Such a mind might carry within it the seeds of technological advancement for Ashkaar, and that was something the Ne'elatians wanted to prevent. No, there was no question that Ma'adrys was capable of understanding anything he chose to explain to her. It was her potential reaction to the Prime Directive that made him apprehensive and hesitant.

She wants to hear that her people will get justice, he thought. *She won't care about Starfleet rules and regulations. There's nothing she can do to change them, any more than she could hope to change the way the Ne'elatians have been robbing her people all this time, so why add to her frustration?*

And so he took another breath instead, drawing the sweet scent of the bower greenery deep into his lungs, and said, "Some day I'd like to show you all the worlds I've seen. The Ne'elatians took you from your home against your will, but—but do you think you could ever leave Ashkaar willingly? With me?"

Now Ma'adrys put her arms around his neck and smiled up at him. "More than willingly, my love."

Counsellor Troi did not sleep well that night. Something was troubling her, an impression that clung to the shadows on the far side of conscious thought. It was only a vague impression, nothing she could pinpoint or put a name to, yet its presence nagged at her and refused to be set aside. It was a feeling that had been with her almost from the moment the Away Team had come among the Ashkaarians of this village, a feeling that there was *something* about these people.

Something . . . but what? she pondered. The specifics eluded her abilities, like a mysterious shape glimpsed out of the corner of one eye that vanished when you tried to look at it directly. It left her feeling somehow off balance, a sensation she didn't relish at all. For a time she had been able to put her discomfort aside, in the frantic days of the sickness sweeping the village, but now that the crisis had been dealt with, the disturbing sensation was back again, stronger than ever.

I must rest, she told herself, turning over on the coarse mattress covering, hearing the dried grasses inside the ticking rustling and crunching under her. *I can focus on this properly in the morning, but not if I am exhausted.* She willed herself to relax and soon it seemed as though sleep would come.

Just as she was drifting off, she thought she heard footsteps in the room she shared with Ambassador Lelys. She sat up in bed suddenly, peering all around her into the dark. The door was open, and in the meager light she saw first, two shapes outlined in the doorway, then that the Orakisan ambassador was also awake and alarmed by this unlooked-for intrusion.

"Who is there?" Lelys demanded angrily. "What is the meaning—"

One of the shapes raised a hand and the words died on Lelys's lips. Troi started up from her bed, but the hand now swept toward her and she felt a wall of complete blackness slam against her eyes. She crumpled back against the mattress and knew nothing more until she awoke to daylight and Commander Riker's concerned face.

"—you all right?" he was asking. She nodded. Her head felt strangely heavy; any movement came with effort. She wanted to tell him what had happened, even though she could find no explanation for it, but her tongue was like wood and the words jerked from her mouth. Little by little she shook off the sensation of fetters, words and movement returning to her own command more and more easily. It was only then that her eyes fell on the other bed in the room.

"Where is the ambassador?" she asked.

"We were hoping you could tell us that," Riker replied. "You said there were two intruders here last night, but if they kidnapped her, there's no sign of a struggle."

"Perhaps she was asleep at the time of her abduction," Mr. Data suggested.

Troi shook her head. "No, she was awake. She was the one who challenged them." She got up and went over to the foot of the other bed where a many-layered rectangle of cloth lay. When she picked it up, it unfurled in her hands. "This is her nightdress," she said. "It seems as if she not only changed into her day clothes but even took the time to fold this."

"So, not exactly an abduction after all," Riker

remarked. He turned to the android. "The question is, where is she now?"

"That will not be too difficult to answer." Mr. Data reached into his robe and consulted his tricorder. "Her vital signs are clear and easily traceable. She appears to have left the village, but she has not gone far. I believe we will find her in the grazing meadows just above Ma'adrys's abandoned house."

"But why?" Troi asked. "Why would she go willingly with whomever it was who came into our room last night?"

"That will not be too difficult to answer either, once we find her," Data replied.

He was wrong.

"Ambassador Lelys?" Troi was the first to spot her. The tricorder had functioned perfectly, leading the Away Team out of the village and up the mountainside to an isolated clump of trees. Here they found a little stream bubbling over smooth stones, threading its way down to the village, and here too they found the Orakisan ambassador. She sat on the green bank, dabbling her bare feet in the water. She was singing to herself happily and seemed to be completely oblivious to their approach. *"Ambassador!"*

Lelys turned her head lazily at the sound of Troi's shout. A slow, dreamy smile edged across her face. "Look what I found," she said, holding out her hand. A bright gold leaf rested on her palm. She bent over and set it on the surface of the water, sending it sailing down the stream. She clapped her hands and laughed out loud to watch it twirl and bob on the swift current.

Troi sank to her knees beside the Orakisan and seized her shoulders. "Ambassador, what is wrong?"

Lelys only laughed again and shrugged free of Troi's grasp. "Nothing is wrong. I am so happy. So many

165

children, so many daughters of our beloved mother-world S'ka'rys! Each blooms with beauty, each returns to our mother in peace, and the most beautiful of these is Ne'elat. Soon we will all be reunited in love."

"Ne'elat?" Troi echoed. "But you were angry with the Ne'elatians for what they have done to Ashkaar. You said you would oppose—"

A frown flitted over the ambassador's face as she glanced at Troi, a look as poisonous as it was brief. "What is a family divided? I will oppose nothing. Ne'elat must become one of our confederacy. I will give all my effort to this cause."

Troi stood up and drew Riker aside. Lelys paid no attention to their private conference, gladly returning her attention to sending a fresh armada of leaves sailing down the stream. "Something is *very* wrong," Troi murmured.

"No argument. I'd almost say she's been brainwashed, only how? This world doesn't have any devices capable of turning out results this complete this fast."

"Devices . . . I wonder—" Troi cut short her musings to declare: "We must return to the ship. Dr. Crusher should examine her."

"Agreed."

They went back to the stream. By now Lelys was sprawled on her belly, avidly watching Mr. Data fold the fallen leaves into more seaworthy shapes before he sent them on their way for her amusement.

"Ambassador—" Riker extended one hand, meaning to help the Orakisan to her feet. The other hand slipped inside his robe to touch his communicator. "Riker to *Enterprise*. Stand by to beam up a party of—"

"No!" Lelys rolled onto her back and lashed out at Riker's shin with her foot. Reflexively he jumped out of range just as she leaped up and dashed deeper into the shelter of the little grove. Troi pursued her.

"Ambassador, please. We *must* go back to the ship," she insisted. "Something happened to you last night. Something that has affected your mind. You must come with us. Dr. Crusher can help you." She groped for Lelys's arm.

The ambassador slapped her hand away, scowling ferociously. "Do not touch me! Demons! *Demons!* Keep away from me! Help me, someone! *Help* me!" Her voice rose to a shriek as she pressed her back protectively against the trunk of a great tree.

All at once the grove seemed to teem with people. A group of five men armed with heavy wooden staffs and a few sharp-edged farming tools burst through the trees behind Lelys as a second, larger crowd came swarming up the mountain. The shepherd Avren and the village oberyin Bilik were in the lead.

"See? See?" Avren gestured wildly at the Away Team. "It is so. It is just like what the holy Ma'adrys told me in my dream! See? They are the ones, the evil ones who brought the sickness to us. Even one of their own accuses them! They are not travelers, they are demons, the living spirits of sickness. Only *that* one is safe"—he pointed at Lelys—"because holy Ma'adrys has made her her voice and saved her. If we do not capture them, the sickness will return and we will all die!"

The men didn't need a second telling. They charged the Away Team from both sides. Mr. Data calmly stepped into the path of the upslope group. He reached up into the trees overhead and tore off a heavy limb to use against the assault of their staffs. He fought with that mechanical precision peculiar to him, a cool and efficient style of combat completely free of any emotion except the need to get the job done. With the first blow he struck, he disarmed his attacker and with the second rendered the man unconscious. Stooping under the wildly aimed swing of the next man's staff, he picked up his initial opponent's abandoned weapon.

"Commander? Here," he called crisply as he tossed Riker the staff.

"Thanks, Data." Riker snatched it in midair and set himself ready to meet the mob from below. He fought with a little less detachment than the android. Jaw sct, he went into a waiting stance, ready to hold his ground or leap forward to meet the first man to come against him. His eyes narrowed, evaluating the onrushing crowd. They were making a lot of noise and there was no question that they outnumbered the Away Team, but they were farmers, not fighters, and some of them were drained from the recent illness in the village. He took a step forward, muttering the old saw, "The best defense . . ."

He was right. They were no fighters. The first man to reach him carried a hoe and flailed it at Riker as if the commander were a cat that needed shooing off a table. Riker stepped under the sweep of the hoe handle, came up too close for the man to take another swing at him, and drove his elbow hard into his opponent's side. The man's breath left him in a rush and he staggered. Riker had no trouble knocking the sense from him with a light tap of his staff. He went down.

Upslope, Data was almost free of his attackers. The village men lay sprawled at his feet, unconscious or groaning, except for one who had watched his comrades meet their fate and was now hanging back, reluctant to test his own questionable battle skills against the android's.

Mr. Data regarded him with that alert, speculative expression he always wore when confronting new phenomena and said, "I wish you would come closer. Then I could eliminate you from this part of the combat and be of greater help elsewhere."

"Ah." The man nodded once, then turned on his heel and ran away as fast as his feet and the slope would allow. Mr. Data observed his retreat, bemused, then shrugged it off for future analysis and went to Commander Riker's aid.

Throughout the battle, Counsellor Troi had not been idle. Her hands were full elsewhere, trying to lay hold of and restrain Ambassador Lelys. The Orakisan tried to elude her, slipping between the trees, backtracking, always trying to break away and reach the spot where Bilik and Avren stood waiting. The oberyin and the shepherd did not take part in the fight, but watched its progress closely. From the corner of her eye, Troi thought she glimpsed a sly, gloating look on Avren's face, an expression completely at odds with the shepherd's supposed simplemindedness.

A mask, she thought as she placed herself between Lelys and those two for what felt like the fiftieth time. *A carefully cultivated illusion. But why?*

She had no chance to think more about it. At that moment, the remnants of the group harrying the Away Team seemed to reach the same conclusion as the lone villager who had fled combat with Data alone. They were falling back, slowly at first, then more and more decisively. Avren saw this, and his hand closed convulsively on the oberyin's wrist. He whispered urgently in Bilik's ear.

Bilik nodded and shook off the shepherd's grip. With all the dignity of his office around him, he strode majestically up the slope to face Riker. He carried no visible weapon and his hands were extended, palms forward, in what might have been a gesture of peace.

When he was no more than five paces away from Riker, he brought his hands together in a clap that echoed up and down the mountain. Riker's mouth gaped, the staff fell from his hands and rolled away down the hill. A dull film crept across his eyes and he stood immobile, as if that one crisp sound had been some sort of magic spell to turn a man to stone.

That is it! Troi thought, staring at Riker's frozen body. *That is what I have been sensing here, among these people: Compulsion! That is their power. Not too strong in most of them, but in the oberyin, oh yes, it is strong in that one. I would not be surprised to learn it is strong in all like him. And yet, it is not boundless. I sense some limits. Still, a useful power for a leader.* Her exultation in having at last put a name to the problem that had troubled her so long was muted by her horror at what had befallen Riker.

Even as she came to understand Bilik's power, the oberyin was giving orders to the villagers to seize the helpless Starfleet officer. Seeing their spiritual leader in apparent control of the situation gave them new zeal. Those still standing rushed to obey, and those who had been only stunned in combat revived amazingly and surged to their feet to aid their fellows.

Mr. Data fought on, holding them off. It was only a matter of time before their numbers overwhelmed him, but this did not seem to suit either Avren or Bilik. Again the shepherd tugged at the oberyin's robes and again the oberyin stepped forward, hands raised in that deceptively peaceable gesture. The villagers fell away, giving him a clear path to Data. He was smiling as he brought his hands together in that limb-freezing clap.

His smile vanished when his intended victim stood unaffected by what must be the most impressive weapon in the oberyin's weird arsenal. "De—demon!" Bilik's voice trembled as he pointed one shaking finger at the impassive android. "These *are* demons!" He backed off quickly.

"Mr. Data, get us out of here," Troi called. She pounced on the elusive ambassador and held her firmly. She was fleetingly surprised when Lelys did not struggle, but the immediate need for escape didn't let her dwell on this too long.

"A strategic retreat might be in our best interest," Data agreed. The villagers had been just as shocked as their spiritual leader by his apparent immunity to the oberyin's power of compulsion, but this same power still affected them. Bilik was shouting orders, and the men were bound to obey, despite their fears. Some laid hands on Riker, others closed in on Troi and Lelys. In the confusion, the Orakisan ambassador broke away from Troi. There was something in her hand, something she flung far into the trees.

Data was not concerned with this. There was no need for Counsellor Troi to keep hold of Ambassador Lelys in order to effect their return to the ship. He held his ground, keeping his own assailants at bay while he pulled out his communicator and crisply said, "Data to *Enterprise*. Four to beam up. Use communicators to determine our coordinates and energize on my signal. Energize."

Troi heard him give the order. She saw his body waver as the transporter beam locked onto it. Riker's figure, too, shimmered and was gone, leaving an empty space where a small knot of horrified and astounded village men clustered, dumbstruck.

Four to beam up . . . and she was still here.

"Demon!"

She turned to see Ambassador Lelys leering at her in triumph. Her hand darted inside her robe, to the place where she had hidden her communicator. It was gone. There was no need to wonder what had become of it. The ambassador was still here as well, despite the orders Data had given the ship. It was an easy thing to tear off a communicator and throw it away. Lelys had done it while pretending surrender.

As the villagers closed in to take her prisoner, Troi heard Avren laugh.

Chapter Eleven

FOR THE FIRST TIME in her career as one of Starfleet's most promising young Security officers, Ensign Lori Wolf was at a loss for how to handle a situation. When Lt. Worf had summoned her to his quarters, she had assumed it was something to do with the mission currently staging on Ashkaar. She counted it as a favorable sign—perhaps an unofficial recognition of her accomplishments—that she was one of the few lower ranking shipboard personnel informed of the Away Team's purpose. Perhaps the summons to Lt. Worf's quarters meant that she was to be dispatched to the planet's surface as well and her superior officer wished to relay the command as discreetly as possible. As Lt. Worf had often instructed his people, discretion was a major part of Security, and Ensign Wolf had a formidable reputation for discretion.

She was going to need it, as she discovered when Lt.

Worf told her the real reason why he had invited her to his quarters.

"Um," she remarked. Under the circumstances, *um* was pretty much about all she could think of to say. That is, it was all she could think of to say and still maintain her reputation for discretion. In her most private thoughts she knew that what she really wanted to say—and discretion be damned—was more along the lines of: "Have you gone completely out of your *mind?* Sir."

"What did you say, Ensign Wolf?" the Klingon demanded. His words boomed so loudly that for an instant Lori wondered whether she'd actually been indiscreet (to say nothing of suicidal) enough to have voiced her true feelings aloud.

"Um, I believe I said um, sir." She tried to maintain eye contact, but every one of her finely trained survival instincts urged her to put her eyes to better use elsewhere, seek an escape route from the room and *use* it ASAP. Unfortunately, Lt. Worf and a large table stood between her and the only available exit.

"Is that all you have to say for yourself?" Worf asked. As a rule, it was hard to tell when a Klingon was scowling, but somehow he managed to convey the impression that his brow was even more seamed and furrowed than usual.

"Well—well, I do want to thank you for this—this, er, honor, but I can't accept."

"Of course you can!" Lt. Worf would stand for no contradiction.

"It's just that I don't—I don't see what—" She took a deep breath and blurted out, "I don't see what I've done to deserve *this.*" And she pointed to the tank on the large table between them where Alexander's hamster lay curled up in its nest, peacefully asleep.

"Ensign Wolf, you surprise me." (Lori realized that her superior officer was now trying to sound *jolly*. It was not the sort of emotion that Klingons wore well.) "Your record is stainless, exemplary! You are an inspiration to us all. Official recognition of your efforts is all very well and good, but meritorious performance should be rewarded by more tangible means as well. You have more than earned an honor of this magnitude."

To Ensign Wolf's ears, Lt. Worf's words made it sound as if this unlooked-for gift originated with Starfleet. "Are you sure, sir? That is, maybe it's supposed to be for you. You've done *much* more than I have to deserve this award." She eyed the tank askance and added, "Wolf, Worf, you can see how easy it would be to confuse our names, especially at the bureaucratic level. I honestly think that—"

Lt. Worf rested his knuckles on the tabletop, leaned across the hamster's tank, and thrust his face less than an inch from Lori's. "Take the beast away. Take it away now, and I will see to it that you receive a commendation."

"But—"

"And extra shore leave."

"But—"

"But *what?*" he roared. "Do you *dare* to want more?"

"I want—I want to return to my post, sir," the much-beleaguered ensign replied.

Lt. Worf sighed and backed off. "Ensign Wolf, I wish you would rethink your decision. This creature was given to my son Alexander by Dr. Crusher in a moment of improperly considered generosity. I have attempted to make her see that it is not a suitable companion for the boy, but she can be . . . stubborn. She will not take it back. If you will take this beast for your own pet then I will be in your debt always. This is not something I promise lightly. A warrior's honor demands that he hold fast to all his obligations."

Ensign Wolf could hardly believe what she was hearing. *Lt. Worf in my debt? That does call for a second thought. Or three. Still . . .*

Lori had heard all the ancient "red shirt" jokes, the old jibes about how easily expendable Security personnel were, and she didn't think they were funny. She hadn't reached her present position by leaping first and looking afterwards. Surely Lt. Worf would never give her a *dangerous* animal, but there was no harm in asking a few preliminary questions. She examined the creature in the tank. Born and raised on Alamo Station at the very fringes of the Beta Quadrant, she had never seen a hamster before, so of course her first question was:

"It's a tribble, isn't it, sir?"

Lt. Worf quickly corrected that understandable misconception.

"A hamster, sir? What, precisely, is hamming and what action, if any, should I take if the animal starts to do it?"

The Klingon took a deep, slow breath and explained a few more details of Fido's natural history, gleaned from Alexander's impromptu lectures on the subject. The boy was delighted with his exotic pet and had set himself to absorb all available information that the ship's computer could provide about the beast. Not for the first time, Worf felt a pang of conscience over how his son would react when he found the animal gone.

I am doing what is best for my son, in the long run, he reminded himself. *That is never an easy task, but it is a necessary one.* With this reassurance in mind, he renewed his attention to Ensign Wolf. "Well? Will you take it?"

"Sir, it may not be my place to ask this but . . . does your son know you're doing this?"

That infernal question again! He could not lie. "No, he does not. However, that is of no consequence. I have made the decision: The animal goes. All that remains to be settled is whether you will take it or if I must find someone else to perform this service for me. Well?" Again the impression of a scowl, a very fierce one.

Lori was neither a coward nor a fool. Although the sight of an angry, impatient Klingon was enough to give her a momentary start, she quickly recovered enough to think over her options with a calm mind. While the notion of having her superior officer in her debt was appealing, her own sense of honor rebelled at the idea of taking away a child's pet without the child's knowledge or consent.

When you were with Security, there was one lesson you learned in a hurry: Try to find more than one way out of a tight spot or become the punchline to yet *another* joke about Security personnel. Lori Wolf wasn't about to sacrifice either her principles or her superior's good will. She saw a another way out and she took it.

"Sir, I'll be happy to take this animal—"

"Ah!"

"—as soon as I can determine beyond the shadow of a doubt that it's harmless."

Worf glowered at her.

"Sir, perhaps you've forgotten I don't live alone. I have a family. I'm certainly not afraid for myself, but I can't ask them to share living space with an alien creature that for all we know might be—"

"But this creature is innocuous!" Worf protested. "I have seen Rigelian *narf*-puddings with more spunk! Why do you think I do not want my son to keep such a thing? All aspects of the life of a young warrior must present some sort of challenge. What manner of challenge is there in owning this—this—" He groped for a word of sufficient scope to convey the utterly peaceful, unaggressive, bland, and boringly safe nature of the hamster. He couldn't find one, and so instead he flipped away the top of the tank and scooped up the creature itself, intending to persuade Ensign Wolf by way of solid evidence.

"Gnnnnggghh!"

The evidence was not solid but the hamster's teeth were. Rudely roused from sleep, swooped down upon from above, lifted high into the air, all of the little creature's instincts for self-preservation kicked in at once, along with a good portion of its nasty temper. A gnawer by nature, the hamster had formidable, chisel-like incisors in both upper and lower jaws, and it knew how to use them. It bit deep, it bit hard, and it bit for keeps.

The hamster had a vicious bite, but Lt. Worf could bear pain as well as any Klingon warrior. Gritting his teeth, he tried to remove the beast by flicking it from his impaled finger, only to encounter yet another unguessed quality of Alexander's pet: It knew how to hold on. Though Worf whipped his assaulted hand sharply back and forth, the hamster set its teeth still more firmly in the Klingon's flesh, closed its eyes, and refused to let go.

"Hold still, sir. I'll help you!" Ensign Wolf shouted. For an instant her hand dropped to her phaser until she realized just how ridiculous a solution that would be.

"Father!"

Worf froze in mid-fling. His son Alexander stood in the doorway to their quarters, staring at him with a mixture of surprise and horror. The boy rushed forward and cupped his hands around the determined hamster. Perhaps it was the familiar scent of its master, perhaps it was the promise of the immediate feeding which always seemed to follow its master's arrival, or perhaps it was just the conviction—held even by hamsters—that enough was enough. For whatever reason, the little creature released its hold on Worf's finger and dropped docilely into Alexander's hands.

"What were you doing with Fido?" Alexander demanded.

"Er, if you'll excuse me, sir—" Ensign Wolf decided that this would be her golden opportunity to leave. Domestic incidents were touchy things, even for a trained Starfleet Security officer, but when it was a domestic incident within a *Klingon* family, in that case, the best place to be was far, far away.

"Ensign Wolf!" The sound of Lt. Worf barking her name had the same effect as if someone had yanked her back by an invisible rope. She stopped dead in her tracks and turned around slowly. Her superior officer was standing beside his son, studying his savaged finger. Fido had done a thorough job of minor mayhem. The finger was bleeding profusely and was already beginning to swell up. The Klingon's face betrayed not even the shadow of pain, though the wounded finger must have been throbbing. Instead he regarded it with an expression that could only be described as . . .

Bemused? Lori pursed her lips. *I don't think I've ever seen a* Klingon *looking bemused. And I don't think I ever want to do it again.*

"Yes, sir?" she responded.

"Ensign Wolf, you will tell my son why I asked you to come here."

"Sir, are you—"

"Tell him." There was no mistaking that tone. It implied that nothing but the whole truth would be acceptable. Taking a deep breath, Lori informed Alexander of Lt. Worf's failed attempt to give her the hamster. There was no describing the expression on the boy's face when he turned to his father.

"Did you?" Alexander asked. "Did you really try to give away Fido?"

"Do not question the honor of Ensign Wolf; she does not lie. I did all that she reports I did." Worf had a few basic first aid supplies in his quarters. During Lori's explanation he had brought these out and was now applying a bandage to his bleeding finger, one that would do well enough until he could get himself to sickbay. "I had my reasons. I did not believe that this . . . *hamster* was a fit companion for you. It seemed to be meek and lazy, a bad example." He tied off the bandage and added, "I was wrong. It is my duty to raise you in the way of the warrior, but I betray that duty by acting behind your back. I sought to avoid the unpleasantness of a confrontation with you over possession of the animal. One who tries to hide from small disputes may fight bravely in great battles, but such actions diminish his honor. The size of the conflict does not determine the true warrior."

"Neither does the size of the warrior," Ensign Wolf remarked to herself.

"What did you say, Ensign?" Worf demanded, his eyes flashing.

"I only meant, well—" She gestured at the hamster, now happily creeping from one of Alexander's hands to the other, whiskers twitching and small pink nose wiggling avidly. "It may be pretty small, but pound for pound that's *some* fighter you've got there, Alexander," she said.

"It is brave, spirited, strong, and ferocious, a warrior beast," Lt. Worf agreed. "And as such, it is a more than suitable companion for my son. I regret having underestimated it."

"You know what they say, sir," Lori reminded him. "Appearances can be deceiving."

"Then it is our duty to make certain that no one else is ever deceived as to the true worth of this creature," Worf declared. "We will give it a more fitting name than"—he made a face—"Fido. It is a warrior beast and it shall bear a warrior's name! I call it *batlh-ghobbogh-yIH.*" He made an elegant gesture over the hamster's head with his uninjured hand, then announced, "Now I will go to sickbay."

Ensign Wolf looked at Alexander. "What kind of name is that for a hamster? It's bigger than the whole animal."

"It means Tribble-who-battles-with-honor," Alexander explained, stroking his pet's tiny head with his thumb. "I liked Fido better, but at least Father won't mind my keeping him any more."

Tribble-who-battles-with-honor gave a happy little sigh, then burped.

When Lt. Worf arrived in sickbay he learned that his injured finger would have to wait.

"Ah. You are here already, sir. Very good." Mr. Data stepped forward to intercept the Klingon. "Has Dr. Crusher explained the situation or did she merely urge you to come as quickly as possible?"

"What situation?" Worf demanded, the hamster's bite immediately forgotten. "What are you doing back aboard? Where is the rest of the Away Team?" His eyes swept sickbay, spied Riker's body stretched out at one of the diagnostic stations. Dr. Crusher was working over him, her face a study in tension and perplexity. "What has happened to the commander?"

In his usually concise manner, Mr. Data explained the fate that had befallen the Away Team on Ashkaar. In conclusion he remarked, "I would theorize that there is some level of psionic capability in the native population, more strongly developed in a few select individuals than in the general population."

"Psionics?" Worf repeated. He had encountered numerous examples of mental powers both in his studies at the Academy as well as firsthand, during his career with Starfleet. Yet in spite of his familiarity with such phenomena, he still found them disquieting and, somehow unnatural, even in those close to him. "What kind? Do the Ashkaarians possess broad-spectrum psionic abilities or—"

"I do not think that they do, sir," Mr. Data replied. "From what I have observed, I would say that their capabilities are limited but effective, and concentrated in the field of mental compulsion. You can see for yourself the effects of this power at its most potent in Commander Riker. He is still immobilized under the influence of a psychic attack, despite the fact that our encounter took place some time ago."

Lt. Worf studied the face of his felled shipmate. Riker's eyes stared up into nothingness, his expression blank. The Klingon tried to lift one of Riker's arms, expecting it to be limp, and instead encountered a good deal of resistance. His eyes met Dr. Crusher's. "What is your prognosis?"

"He'll recover," she replied. "Unfortunately I can't give you any estimate of how long that will take. His mind has received the equivalent of a substantial physical blow. I can't gauge the strength of it any more than I can estimate his own ability to recuperate from this type of assault."

"And the others?" Worf looked back to Data. "Are they, too, in this state?"

"I have reason to believe that Counsellor Troi has not been similarly affected, but that would be only because the Ashkaarians saw no need for it, already having Ambassador Lelys well under their control."

"Yes, you told me how she aided them." Lt. Worf was grim. "Captain Picard must be notified and I feel it is my responsibility to do so. Permission requested to beam down to the planet." The android nodded. "Permission granted Mr. Worf." Without another word, the Klingon strode from the room.

The gardens of Bovridash were lovely, a refuge from the world's clamor, an inspiration to the poets of a dozen generations of Ne'elat. His body freed from the constraints of a Starfleet officer's uniform, clad in the loose, flowing robes of the bovereem, Captain Picard admired his surroundings. As he walked the gardens' winding paths of crushed stone and shell, breathing in their thousand perfumes, he wished that he could have come here to enjoy their beauty in peace, without the spectre of a dying world hovering at his back.

So much beauty . . . and so useless. He and young Hara'el had searched the library of the great spiritual center, questioned the bovereem—as the local priesthood styled themselves—searched the sanctuary grounds plant by plant, all with as little success. A few of the older bovereem had heard of n'vashal—that was something—but Picard knew that many people back on Earth had also heard of the philosopher's stone, the fountain of youth, and pixie dust. They told him old folktales—some brought all the way from Skerris IV—in which the poor farmer's clever daughter tucked a sprig of n'vashal into her bosom for luck and went on to make her fortune, but the plant itself remained elusive.

Picard picked a cluster of lacy orange flowers from a bush and let their spicy fragrance fill his mind. Such a little thing, a single plant. Fertile worlds like Ne'elat and Orakisa and Earth all teemed with green growth of infinite variety. What did it matter if one lone kind were destroyed or allowed to perish? What would be the harm?

What would be the harm? Let them ask the dying colonists of Skerris IV.

"Captain Picard?"

He wheeled around at the sound of his name, startled out of his joyless contemplation. "Hara'el, I didn't hear you come up behind me."

The young Orakisan looked sheepish. "I apologize. I have been practising walking the way the bovereem do. They do not make a sound, even when they're walking over gravel. They call it drinking silence from the earth."

Picard could not help but smile. He had come to know the junior ambassador better since their arrival in Bovridash, and he genuinely liked him. Hara'el was dedicated and hardworking. He regarded every dead end in their search for some trace of n'vashal as a personal defeat. Given how quiet and meek he acted when in his father's presence aboard the *Enterprise,* it was surprising to find so much fire and determination in the young Orakisan. "What will they teach you next?" Picard asked him jovially. "The power of invisibility?"

It was a lighthearted jest, but Hara'el's face fell. "That is something I could teach them. There have been many times during this mission, Captain Picard, when I have wondered whether I exist at all, so thoroughly have I been ignored."

"What do you mean?" Picard was concerned. "If their has been a problem with one of my crew . . ."

"Not any of your people," Hara'el answered. "Mine. My father told me before we undertook this mission that I was to remember my place and expect no preferential treatment from him. He has kept true to his word." There was a fugitive note of bitterness in the young Orakisan's voice. "I was prepared to tolerate that. But Ambassador Lelys—It is as if I were not even a part of our mission in her eyes. I may not have her level of professional experience, but I would not even be here if our superiors did not feel I had mastered the diplomat's art. What will it take to make her see that?" He sighed.

He wants more than her professional notice, Picard thought, regarding Hara'el's slumped shoulders. He turned his right hand palm upward, took the little spray of blossom he had picked, wedged it between his fingers, and held it out so that the sun shone full and bright upon it. "Hara'el, what do you see in my hand?"

"What did you say?" The Orakisan was bewildered.

"What do you see in my hand?" Picard repeated patiently.

"I see . . . that orange flower. I think the bovereem call it va'n'kast, but perhaps I am not remembering it correctly."

"Is that all you see?"

"I . . . yes?" Hara'el no longer sounded sure.

"Then what is this?" Picard pointed to where the feathery blossom cast an equally feathery shadow against the lined skin of his palm.

"But that—that is only the plant's shadow."

"And what are you and all your diplomatic training when you stand with your father?" Picard asked gently. "If you can't see this flower's shadow, how can you expect Ambassador Lelys to see you?"

Hara'el frowned. "You insult me, Captain Picard."

"I tell you what I've observed. No insult is meant. Perhaps I shouldn't speak so frankly, but this place seems to be conducive to washing away all the layers of protocol, leaving nothing but honesty behind. I've seen how you act when you're with your father. I've heard you agree with him or keep silent rather than contradict him, and I've wondered whether two adults could be in such perfect accord on every possible point under discussion."

"I do not always echo my father!"

"Don't you?" It was not said as a challenge, but as an invitation for the young man to look inward and find an honest answer.

Hara'el opened his mouth to snap back a reply, but none came. A thread of thoughtfulness crossed his brow. He brought his lips together and stood there for a few breaths, considering what Picard had said. At last he spoke. "Is that it? Is that truly why she treats me so?"

"I can't say so for sure, but I wouldn't be surprised. Hara'el, I'm not telling you to attract her attention by deliberately contradicting Legate Valdor. That would be as foolish and as childish as always agreeing with him. I'm asking you to remember your own principles—yours, not your father's—to find your own standards, to know your own boundaries and then to take a stand only when they need to be defended. No, on second thought I'm not asking this of you, I'm only suggesting it."

Hara'el nodded slowly. "As you . . . suggest, Captain Picard, I will do. Do you know that when I was at school I was a noteworthy debater? Do not think me vain, but I not only won awards, often I brought my opponents around to share my point of view. Then I entered the diplomatic service and was placed under my father and everything changed. I was no longer the champion of my class; I was only a little boy again, with Father always there to point out the countless mistakes I made on every case assigned me. It never mattered whether the outcome of our mission was favorable—he never mentioned that—only the errors I had made that *might* have cost us success."

"Sometimes it's difficult for a parent to see his child grow up," Picard said. "It's even more difficult when that child has chosen the parent's career for his own and might someday outshine him. It makes him afraid, and frightened people strike out at what frightens them even if it's something that they love."

"Do you think that is why my father treats me so?" Hara'el asked earnestly. "Because he is afraid of me?" He sounded as if he could never believe such a thing.

"Whatever his actions, whatever his reasons, he can't treat you as less than you are unless you submit to it. If you speak—"

"Captain! Captain!"

Picard and Hara'el turned their heads sharply at the summons and saw one of the bovereem hastening toward them on the path. He was a portly man, above middle age, and he puffed audibly as he neared them, a piece of paper clutched in his fist. When he reached them he was panting too hard to speak, and so he handed over the paper without explanation.

Picard read the message, his face rapidly tightening with anger. "When did you receive this?" he demanded.

"No more than a day ago," the Ne'elatian replied, still catching his breath. "It was urgent, they said, so it was sent here from the final gateway by our fastest couriers. Is there—" The sight of Captain Picard's grim expression gave him pause. "Is there to be any answer?"

Picard said nothing, the message a wad of utterly crushed paper in his hand. With a curt bow, he marched toward the main sanctuary building where his Starfleet uniform awaited.

The Ne'elatian watched him go, then looked at Hara'el and said, "No answer, then?"

"I think he is going to deliver it himself," the Orakisan replied, a trifle uneasily, and hurried to join him.

Chapter Twelve

GEORDI LET OUT A LOW, long whistle of astonishment. "Psionic powers?" he asked, echoing the portion of Mr. Data's report he had just heard. Beside him at the briefing room conference table, Legate Valdor and his son exchanged a look of surprise and speculation.

"Apparently so," Lt. Worf commented. "In ordinary circumstances it would be easy to rescue Counsellor Troi and Ambassador Lelys in a straightforward manner, but given this new factor, I would recommend a well considered strategy. We do not know the extent of the Ashkaarians' mental capabilities. We would not wish to give them more hostages than they presently control."

At the head of the conference table, Captain Picard rose to his feet. "Your point is well taken, Mr. Worf, but I strongly dislike the idea of remaining here, doing nothing, knowing nothing of what has happened to our people on Ashkaar."

"So do I," Hara'el put in, a bit more loudly than usual. "We must act immediately for Ambassador Lelys's safety." He might have said more, but a scowl from his father made his face color brightly and he subsided.

"Sir, personally I would also most certainly prefer a course of immediate action, but it would be irresponsible of me to recommend it," Worf said. "Commander Riker is still in sickbay, his condition unchanged. We are not dealing with a minor threat as far as the Ashkaarians' powers are concerned. We must not act rashly."

"If only Counsellor Troi still had her communicator." Picard smacked his palm with his fist. "Mr. La Forge, do you think you could get a reading on their life-signs and use that for a transporter fix?"

"With respect, sir, I tried that as soon as I found out why I'd been recalled to the *Enterprise*. The readings I've picked up from the planet's surface are indistinct. Either there are disruptive atmospheric factors at work or this is some sort of mental static linked to the Ashkaarian population, sort of a psionic smokescreen effect."

"A deliberate one?" Legate Valdor asked.

Geordi shook his head. "Highly unlikely, sir. If it were deliberate it would come from a focussed source, one I could pinpoint. As I said, it could just be atmospheric."

"So much we don't know," Picard muttered. "So much we *must* know before we can do anything."

"Permission to speak, sir," Data said. Picard nodded curtly. "The chief source of conflict lies in the relations between Ashkaar and Ne'elat. These two worlds have been existing in a kind of spiritual parasitism for ages. We have proof that the Ne'elatians have been keeping the Ashkaarians in an artificially backward state for their own purposes. As a result of this enforced primitivism, the Ashkaarians view all aliens as either angels or, in the case of the Away Team, demons. If we can reestablish normal relations between the sisterworlds, the Ashkaarians will learn that the Ne'elatians are no more angels than Counsellor Troi and Ambassador Lelys are demons, and will release them accordingly."

"An interesting plan, Mr. Data," Captain Picard said, resuming his seat and leaning forward intently. "Unfortunately it is also an unacceptable one under the terms of the Prime Directive."

"Is it, sir?" Geordi said. "If we reveal the Ne'elatians' role in controlling the history of Ashkaar, that would be a violation of the Prime Directive, but if the Ne'elatians themselves decide to make amends, it would violate the Prime Directive if we tried to stop them."

Legate Valdor made a disgusted sound. "This is futile. Why would the Ne'elatians want to change a system that has served them well for so long?"

"Sometimes you do not know what you truly want until someone else suggests it," Lt. Worf said in a voice that vouched for the Klingon's special powers of persuasion.

"And how would you propose we initiate this course of action?" Picard asked the table in general. "I needn't remind you that we haven't got an unlimited amount of time."

"Confrontation, sir," Geordi said. "Immediate confrontation. The Ne'elatians have been able to exploit the Ashkaarians without a second thought because they don't have to face the people they're hurting. There's a girl on Ne'elat—" He paused, feeling the sweet catch at his heart that was always there whenever he thought of Ma'adrys. "You know her—the Ashkaarian who was stolen from her people because she had the potential to help them advance beyond the point where the Ne'elatians wanted them to stay. There've been others like her over the years, but she's the first who *knows* she hasn't been carried off to paradise. Bring her aboard and have her testify before the Masra'et. When your actions only produce a mass of faceless victims, it's easy to pretend they don't exist. That all changes when you've got to look into the eyes of an individual you've wronged."

"Let's hope it changes things for the better, Mr. La Forge," Captain Picard remarked. He was older than Geordi and unable to share the engineer's optimism fully. Still, it would be worth a try. "But why have the confrontation take place here? Why not on Ne'elat, as long as all parties concerned are already there?"

Geordi's smile was anything but naive. "The *Enterprise* is neutral ground. More important, the Ne'elatians have never seen anything like it. They've been controlling the Ashkaarians for ages by virtue of their technological superiority. They understand power, they respect it, and they'll be more likely to pay attention to any . . . suggestions we might have to offer concerning their future relations with Ashkaar."

Captain Picard nodded, then said, "Make it so."

Ma'adrys gazed around the transporter room as she permitted Geordi to help her off the pad. "The wonder is still here, my love," she said, smiling. "It does not matter that I have seen these marvels before; they are forever fresh to me."

"You'll grow used to them in time," Geordi said. "After you've lived here while—" He stopped, taken aback by his own audacity. It was the first time he had ever spoken to Ma'adrys about what was in his heart for their future.

To his relief he saw that his words had pleased her. "Could such things come to be?" she asked softly. "It would give me so much joy, so very much if—" She bit her lower lip and looked away from him. "But no. I will not hope. I will not dream. I knew dreams when I was young, and they were all snatched away from me."

"When you were young?" Geordi laughed and took her into his arms. "You're not exactly a crone, Ma'adrys, and I promise you, this is one dream that won't be taken from you if I have anything to say about it." He kissed her, briefly but tenderly, then said, "Come. They'll be waiting for you."

She hung back a little. "What must I say? What must I tell them?"

"Tell the Masra'et what you know of your home-world, of your life, of how their interference affected you and all your family, your neighbors, your friends. By now they've heard Mr. Data's report about what the Away Team discovered of life on Ashkaar, but your words will more than confirm his. They need a good dose of truth, Ma'adrys. Give it to them."

"Yes." The uncertainty was gone from her face. Her eyes reflected a sudden, hard look of determination. "Yes, they do."

The members of the Masra'et were all ranged along one side of the conference table when Geordi brought Ma'adrys in. They looked grim, and more than a few of them were giving Mr. Data hard stares. The android was just completing his report of conditions on Ashkaar with the capture of Troi and Lelys, making special mention of the shepherd Avren's role in the proceedings. Data was never one to color the facts. The Ne'elatians could no longer pretend that their interference there was a harmless thing, yet they did not appear to feel remorse, only resentment.

The Masra'et were not the only ones at the conference table. Legate Valdor was seated to Udar Kishrit's right, his son Hara'el beside him. He was deep in whispered conversation with the Ne'elatian headman, a close counsel that he broke off abruptly when Geordi and Ma'adrys entered. Captain Picard headed the table as always, Mr. Data at the far end of the board, with Lt. Worf standing ready to oversee that the proceedings remained orderly, if not civil.

Is it my imagination or did Udar Kishrit just do a double take when he saw Ma'adrys? Geordi wondered. He tried to focus on the Ne'elatian's face, but the moment had passed, if it had ever happened at all. He shrugged it off, escorted Ma'adrys to the lone seat opposite the Orakisan embassy and the Masra'et, and took his place behind her. He was confident that once his beloved spoke, telling firsthand of all the harm that Ne'elat's misguided use of Ashkaar had done, her revelations would so move the Masra'et that they would immediately move to right the old wrongs. *They might be able to convince themselves to doubt Data's word, but they won't be able to put hers aside so easily.* He caught himself smiling over how simple it would be.

He was a man in love; all problems seemed to have a simple answer for him. But Udar Kishrit and the Masra'et were not in love with Ma'adrys, as Geordi soon discovered.

"—think this means anything to *us?*" Udar Kishrit's lip curled. If Ma'adrys's appearance had ever had any unsettling effect on him, it was well and truly gone now. He regarded the Ashkaarian girl with disdain.

"Are you denying any of what she has said?" Captain Picard asked.

"No," Udar Kishrit replied. "Why should we? The Ashkaarians are barbarians—"

"The Ashkaarians have had no other choice."

"Bah!" Udar Kishrit waved Picard's statement aside. "It is in their nature. The volcanic activity on their planet releases atmospheric gasses that forever bridle their mental development."

"Those conditions no longer apply," Picard countered. "I've had my chief medical officer examine this woman." He gestured at Ma'adrys. "She found her intelligence to be equal to that of any of our own people."

"That does not speak very highly of your people, then, does it?" Udar Kishrit drawled. His fellow counsellors chuckled.

Captain Picard took a deep breath. "I must remind you that what you have done to the Ashkaarians will be made known," he said carefully. "Any aspirations your world has for joining the Federation will be considered accordingly."

For an instant, Udar Kishrit blanched. Then he recovered himself and gave a short, dry laugh. "You may work to exclude us from the Federation if you like. You have that power. But you have no say over how we choose to conduct our lives. How we have always conducted them and how we will continue to conduct them," he added deliberately, showing his teeth in what should have been a smile.

Picard met him glare for glare. "You have seen the *Enterprise*," he said. "Are you so certain that we have no say?"

The other members of the Masra'et drew in their breath and began to chatter anxiously among themselves. They had indeed seen much of the *Enterprise*—Picard had taken pains to offer them a tour of the ship's most impressive features while the rest of the crew still stationed on Ne'elat were being transported home again—and they knew that here was power not to be trifled with. They had no way of knowing that the Prime Directive—

"—forbids you to do *anything*," Udar Kishrit said triumphantly. To Worf's consternation, the Ne'elatian laughed aloud and added, "My good friend and brother, Legate Valdor, has told me much. If you bar us from your Federation, we shall simply have to content ourselves with membership among the union of Skerrian daughterworlds."

"Legate Valdor?" Captain Picard turned a blazing look on Hara'el's father. "Haven't you been listening to Mr. Data's report, to this young woman's testimony? How can you approve of what these people have done? How can you willingly admit them to the Skerrian union? Your own Ambassador Lelys would never—"

"What Ambassador Lelys would and would not do concerning Ne'elat no longer matters at all." Valdor cut him off coldly. "I *have* been listening, Captain Picard. Have you? Your own man reports that Ambassador Lelys has undergone a sudden and complete behavioral change. In plain terms, she has lost her mind, become incompetent to carry out her official duties."

"I beg your pardon, Legate Valdor," Mr. Data spoke up. "To the best of my knowledge, Ambassador Lelys's condition is not permanent and was brought about by the Ashkaarians'—"

"Impossible." Valdor folded his arms. "The honorable leader of the Masra'et himself has just said that the Ashkaarians are mere barbarians. How could they even dream of exerting mind control over our ambassador?"

"You have the testimony of a Starfleet officer," Picard said.

"I prefer the opinion of one of my own lost brothers," Valdor replied. He reached into his tunic and took out a small device which he placed on the table and covered with his palm. "I hereby record on behalf of the Orakisan mission that Ambassador Lelys having become mentally unfit, as witnessed by Commander Data of the *Enterprise,* she is to be declared incompetent and her vote in any subsequent ambassadorial decisions to be rendered null and void. The requisite vote of three will be therefore reduced to a vote of two, according to emergency procedures. In approval of which I and our junior representative in the field, Hara'el, do here give our—"

A younger hand slammed down atop the recording device. Hara'el's voice shook only slightly as he said, "I give nothing."

"Do you *dare?*" Valdor's thundered out, filling the conference room. "Do you dare to defy *me?*" By reflex, Hara'el quailed and looked away. As he averted his eyes from his father's outraged stare, the younger Orakisan glanced toward the head of the table. Picard caught his eye. Very subtly the captain of the *Enterprise* turned one hand palm upwards on the table and with the other mimed the plucking of a flower's shadow.

Hara'el's spine stiffened. He looked his father in the eye and decreed, "If you make this statement part of our official record for this mission, I swear that I will use my vote to block any decision of yours, first of all this move to disenfranchise Ambassador Lelys. I say that we must see her condition for ourselves."

"And how will we do that?" Valdor snapped.

"That will be our job," Captain Picard said, rising to his feet. "Gentlemen of the Masra'et, if you will follow Mr. La Forge to the transporter room, you will be returned to your own world as soon as—"

"Not so fast, Captain Picard." Udar Kishrit, too, was on his feet. "My people and I have some unfinished business to discuss with Legate Valdor. That is, if you do not propose to interfere?" He raised one eyebrow in a manner intended to provoke.

Picard did not react to the taunt. "Naturally you are welcome to remain aboard the *Enterprise,* Udar Kishrit. In fact, I would prefer it if you did. When we recover Ambassador Lelys, perhaps her testimony will help you change your mind about Ne'elat's continued role in Ashkaarian life."

"If it pleases you to think so." Udar Kishrit inclined his head slightly, then he and the rest of the Masra'et accompanied Legate Valdor from the room, Hara'el trailing reluctantly after.

As soon as they had gone, Picard swung into action. "Mr. Data, you will head the rescue mission to Ashkaar. You are familiar with the territory and you seem to be proof against their mental powers."

"Indeed, sir," the android agreed. "I believe that they found my resistance to be most disconcerting. Shall I select the rest of the mission personnel?"

Before Picard could give his approval, Ma'adrys spoke up. "My lord Captain Picard, let me go with him."

"Young woman, that must be out of the question," Picard said gently. "This is a Starfleet mission. Only Starfleet personnel can—"

"But *I* know the territory far better than anyone," she protested. "Kare'al is—was—my home. Besides, you do not wish to save your people by violence, do you?"

"I would prefer to avoid an armed confrontation, if possible," Picard admitted.

"Then you must send me! I heard the last part of his report." She pointed at Data. "There is something important that I know, something that will turn the villagers from blindly following the word of the shepherd Avren. He is no shepherd. He is not even one of our own. I should have realized it long ago. He never took part in the sh'vala, the shepherds' rite, with our village herders. He claimed that in his native village the shepherds performed sh'vala privately, so no one ever saw him do it. For all we knew, he never—"

"He never did what?" Picard broke in, puzzled. "Why is this sh'vala so significant?"

"Because it is a religious rite *all* shepherds perform to consecrate the safety of their flocks to the Mothers," Ma'adrys said. "They gather together and drink a special herbal brew, a sacred drink that makes them—Well, there are certain jokes we have always made about shepherds, how slow of wit they are, how thick headed, but they never mind. They have chosen their state—it comes from drinking the sacred brew—as an act of faith in the Mothers. By making themselves like children, they give over the welfare of their flocks to the Mothers' own keeping, a sacred trust. That was why I was even more awestruck when it was he who told me I had been chosen to ascend to Evramur. Simple Avren, no longer speaking like a halfwit, but like a holy messenger! Oh, no wonder I went meekly with him," she finished bitterly.

"I think I follow you," Picard said. "So because this Avren was never seen to share the sacred drink with the other shepherds of your village—"

"—my fellow villagers will more readily believe it when I tell them he is not what he says, but a deceiver of the worst sort. They will couple what I tell them to what they themselves know of him and—"

"Sir, permission to accompany Mr. Data and Ma'adrys," Geordi said.

"Mr. La Forge, I have not yet given permission to *Ma'adrys* to accompany Mr. Data, let alone the pair of you," Picard pointed out.

"With all due respect, sir, Ma'adrys's presence on this mission is vital. It's the one way left to recover Counsellor Troi and Ambassador Lelys without our resorting to a showdown. Imagine the effect it will have on the Ashkaarians when they see Ma'adrys again. You heard Mr. Data: She's a legend among them, one who's ascended to paradise alive! They wouldn't dare *not* listen to her."

"A compelling argument for her presence. But as for yours—"

"Sir, I'm willing to bet that they've never seen one of these." Geordi grinned and tapped his visor. "Plus, I can scare up a few high-tech tricks that'll convince them to cooperate. You know, like the old Earth adventure stories where the explorer flashes a cigarette lighter and the locals think it's magic? Smoke and mirrors, sir, good old smoke and mirrors."

Captain Picard was both impressed and a little bemused by Geordi's idea. "There are times, Mr. La Forge, when I wonder whether you've missed your calling. With your flair for the dramatic, perhaps you should have been an actor rather than an engineer."

"There's only one thing wrong with that arrangement, sir," Geordi replied. "There's not much call for actors on the *Enterprise.*"

Chapter Thirteen

THE CAVE WHERE TROI AND LELYS were kept prisoner
was dry, which was about all that could be said for it.
Otherwise it was chilly and reeked of sheep-tallow
candles. When their guards kindled a fire nearer to the
entrance to keep off the night cold, more than half the
smoke seemed to flood the cave and almost none of
the heat.

Even the daylight hours were cold this far up the
mountain. Troi wrapped a thin blanket more snugly
around Lelys's shoulders, then sighed when it slipped
off because the Orakisan ambassador made no move
to hold onto it. Lelys sat leaning against the cave
wall, just as the false shepherd Avren had left her
when the women had first been brought to this cell.
Sometimes, when sunlight stole into the cave, she
pointed in childish delight at the play of shadows over
the rock, but mostly she sat there in silence, smiling at
nothing.

From time to time, Troi tried to rouse the ambassador from her abstracted state, but all attempts at contact, physical or mental, failed. Still Troi persisted, talking to Lelys even though she knew better than to expect a rational answer.

"Here, *hold* this," she directed, kneeling to replace the blanket. "You will catch cold if you do not—" A sudden commotion from the cave mouth caught her ear. She glanced at the guards. They were alert, wary. They must have heard it too. She straightened, her bones aching from the cold, and took a few tentative steps toward the light.

Always when she had approached the cave mouth before this, the guards had met her while she still stood within the shadows of the entryway and urged her back with terse commands and the more solid arguments of their weapons. They carried the Ashkaarian equivalent of pitchforks, and the long, sharp tines were a glittering threat that Troi wisely chose to heed. This time, though, some strange spell had fallen over her warders. They stood like slabs of marble, their faces a study in dumb amazement and heart-shaking fear. They made no move to block her when she passed between them and out into the sunshine.

A crowd of Ashkaarians was trekking up the mountain, singing, shouting, and waving makeshift banners, but that wasn't the sight that had paralyzed the guards. Troi herself gasped aloud when she saw who was leading the mob. Torrents of red sparks leaping from the palm of one hand, Geordi La Forge tossed whirling silver pinwheels from the other. They arced above his head and linked themselves together to create the shape of a laughing girl wearing wings that were flowers. Her grass-green hair streamed out and tumbled down over the crowd, becoming a waterfall where fish leaped and jewel-eyed insects danced above the spray.

Immediately behind him walked the girl Ma'adrys and Mr. Data. The spray from the illusory waterfall wafted over Ma'adrys's head like a luminous canopy. She still wore her simple green robes from Ne'elat, but now there was an otherworldly glow about them. Tiny lights like captive fireflies winked here and there in her hair, and the silver netting gave off random rays of piercing brightness.

Watching carefully, Troi noticed how the glow and the lights faded in and out depending on how near or far the girl was from Geordi. *A holo-clip!* Troi realized. *He must have a miniature holo-clip projector hidden on him somewhere.*

The image of the flower-winged girl reappeared and came to rest before the cave mouth where it made a pretty curtsey to Troi. The guards took one last look, dropped their weapons, and dashed away farther up the mountain. Troi walked past the projection of the sylph and greeted Geordi with a sotto voce, "Nice touch. Where is it?"

"Up my sleeve." he replied just as softly. "Not a very original hiding place, but—" He shrugged and smiled briefly, for her eyes alone.

Ma'adrys touched his arm. "Is all well?" she asked urgently.

"Sshhh," he cautioned. "Don't let them see you looking anxious." He nodded to where the villagers, led by Bilik oberyin, stood a respectful and prudent distance from Ma'adrys and her otherworldly escort. "Remember: You're in command. You're supposed to make *them* feel uneasy. Ask—no—*demand* to have the other captive brought to you."

Ma'adrys nodded and followed Geordi's lead. The

girl carried herself as if she'd been born to give orders. The villagers scurried to obey, rushing into the cave and bringing Lelys out to join the others. The Orakisan ambassador looked all around her, smiling like a happy child on holiday.

"The captives have been returned to us, as the starlords decreed it must be. The Balance stands ready to be restored. Now, let justice be served!" Ma'adrys cried.

"Justice or vengeance?" Bilik asked. The oberyin glowered at Ma'adrys, who returned his hard look proudly, without flinching.

"Do you question me, Bilik oberyin?" she challenged. "Or do you question the teachings of holy Evramur itself?" Her words sent the villagers into a panic of renewed songs and prayers. Some of the brawnier men in the crowd began muttering among themselves, giving the oberyin dark looks that promised whose side they'd take in a confrontation between him and Ma'adrys. Bilik noted this, pursed his lips, bowed his submission to the girl, and led the way back down the mountain without another word.

Leadership, intelligence, and *courage,* Troi mused. *No wonder the Ne'elatians spirited her away. She could be very dangerous to them. And she is.*

The oberyin conducted the crowd to a modest house that stood well removed from any other habitation, even the rough hillside huts of the shepherds. Even at a distance, Troi could hear the sounds of a struggle coming from within the little dwelling.

"Sounds like Houdini's still safe," Geordi remarked. "'These people know how to tie knots that stay."

"Who?" Troi asked.

"Avren, the so-called shepherd. When we first

showed up, he tried to turn the people against us the way he did with your group. He might've succeeded too, if Bilik had helped him."

"Bilik was ready enough to attack us," Troi said. "Why did he refuse this time?"

"He didn't refuse, he didn't do anything. One look at Ma'adrys and it was like he'd had his own mental powers turned back against himself. He froze. That gave us time to throw the whole fireworks show, and time for Ma'adrys to make the villagers believe that the *real* 'evil spirit' among them is Avren. When Ma'adrys gave the word they grabbed him, hogtied him, and left him tucked away safe in Bilik's house there while we came to fetch you and Ambassador Lelys."

They were nearer the oberyin's house now, and Troi noted a change in the temper of the crowd. Their first flush of religious awe was fading, replaced by a darker, more dangerous emotion. There was a cold, angry purpose impelling them toward the sound of Avren's useless struggles against his bonds. She knew what it meant and she was afraid.

"Geordi." She clutched his arm urgently. "We must hold them back, we must do something. They'll kill—"

Even as she spoke, the crowd was gathering fury. Bilik, too, noticed this and redoubled his pace so that he was the first to reach the door. "Wait!" he commanded, spreading his arms wide to bar the way. "This man is not yours to touch."

"So *you* say," came a sarcastic voice from the crowd. "Why's that?"

"In with him, are you?" came another.

"Yes, why else would you stand up for him!"

"Evil spirits are known for their fine promises.

What'd he promise you, Bilik oberyin? That you'd get your girl back? Well, there she stands, but not in any state for the likes of you to touch!"

"Lead us wrong, make us lay hands on innocent folk. If the judgment of Evramur falls on our backs it'll be all your doing! You and your pacts with Yaro's own!"

"Stop!" Ma'adrys stepped forward to place herself between Bilik and the snarling mob. "Have you learned nothing?" she demanded of her fellow villagers. "Does the Lady of the Balances look kindly on killing?"

"That one in there has violated the sacred balance!" someone in the crowd shouted. "To destroy him is to restore it! To kill him is to serve the Lady!"

"To kill him is to destroy yourselves!" Ma'adrys shouted back. "You speak from ignorance and fear. I speak from knowledge. Have I not walked the white ways of Evramur? Have I not learned the true nature of that place you call holy?" The crowd fell back a little, muttering.

Troi tapped Data's wrist discreetly and whispered, "What *has* she told them of Ne'elat?"

"She has not yet revealed to them that it is merely their sisterworld," Data replied. "However, neither has she confirmed that it is the spirit-home they believe it to be."

"I have returned to help you, my people," Ma'adrys continued. "I cannot allow you to do that which will harm your souls beyond hope. Avren has deceived us for a long time. Yes, he must be punished for it, but there are many punishments. Give him to us and go in peace to your homes." Her gesture included Geordi and Data. "I promise that he will receive true justice."

The villagers conferred together, then ebbed back down the mountainside toward Kare'al. They went reluctantly, with many backward glances. Geordi surreptitiously touched the cuff of his uniform and a wall of fiery thorns sprang up to veil Bilik's house and encourage them on their way. It worked. One look at this fresh illusion and they ran like startled sheep.

"Now what, Ma'adrys?" the oberyin asked wearily. "Will you punish me along with Avren, you and your starlords?"

"Is that how well you know me, Bilik?" Ma'adrys replied. "We were once to be paired."

Troi's eyes widened in surprise. Then she heard Geordi suck in his breath sharply. *So I am not the only one to whom this is news. Ma'adrys and Bilik.* She couldn't help giving Geordi a sympathetic look. If he saw it, he didn't acknowledge it at all.

"We were," Bilik was saying. "Until you let foolish thoughts touch you!"

"How foolish was it of me to want to become an oberyin like you? You were the fool, Bilik. You could not allow me to make a trial of my powers before the Na'amOberyin, to stand or fall on my own merits. You had to speak against me to them so that you could have me to yourself." She looked at him with eyes that held more sorrow than anger. "What do you have of me now?"

He turned away from her. "He told me I might have you back again," he said. "He swore that if I helped him overcome the evil ones in our midst"—he cast a guilty glance at Troi and Lelys—"you would return to me from Evramur. And you have come back, but not to me." He dared to look back at her with the ghost of hope in his eyes. "Have you?"

Geordi took a step forward and rested his arm on

Ma'adrys's shoulder. The oberyin saw how matters stood even before Ma'adrys told him, "No, Bilik. Not to you."

Bilik's face twisted into a look of naked rage that he turned toward the house where Avren still waited. "This is *his* fault. You can speak to the others of the divine judgment he will face in Evramur, but I will not listen! If I cannot have you, I no longer care what becomes of me, body *or* soul. If I have lost you, he will lose his life!"

Bilik spun around and plunged into his house. Moving even before the others could react, Mr. Data dashed after him. Counsellor Troi burst in just in time to see the android wresting a knife from the oberyin's hand while a bound and helpless Avren squirmed on the floor between them.

Even disarmed, Bilik refused to surrender. He threw himself on the false shepherd and grabbed the man by the throat, roaring accusations and shaking him so violently that for a moment Troi couldn't tell whether he wanted to kill Avren by strangulation or by snapping his neck.

Data broke Bilik's grip easily and pulled the panting oberyin to his feet. "Given the circumstances, I believe it would be wise to remove the prisoner from the premises," he remarked, keeping Bilik a safe distance away from Avren.

Avren was more than ready to agree. "Get me out of here *now*," he begged. "He's gone crazy."

"And where do you suggest we take you?" Troi asked. "Back to the village?"

"By the Fathers, not that! They're ready to skin me alive."

"No more than you deserve," Bilik spat. "What a fool I was to heed you, Avren! All that I want—all that I ever wanted—was to have Ma'adrys for my wife. I have lost any chance of that, all because of you and your foul trickeries. Illusions, all. Illusions that led me to believe you were a messenger of the gods! And now my beloved, my faith, perhaps my soul as well are all lost, thanks to you." He leaned against the stone wall and slumped down, beaten and broken.

"Bilik." Ma'adrys was kneeling beside him, her arms around him. It was a simple gesture, such as one friend might offer another in need, but Troi saw that it struck Geordi like a blow to the heart.

"Let's get him out of here," the engineer said tersely, nodding at Avren. He didn't wait for the others to help, but slit the ropes binding his feet, set one hand under his elbow, and hustled the Ne'elatian agent out of the oberyin's house.

"Thanks," Avren said when they were in the free air.

"You can thank me best by explaining what you've been doing here on Ashkaar for—how many years?"

"What, just me? Or the rest of us?"

"Your record will do for a start."

"And for whose benefit will I be making this explanation?"

"Your own. They say confession's good for the soul."

"The soul." Avren shook his head. "I never cared much about all that. Leave it to the bovereem, that's what I always said. Still, a job's a job, and I'm damned good at this one. You won't find a better agent on Ashkaar than me. I was the one who came up with the shepherd dodge. Before that, we mostly had to do our observations from hiding. That's a pretty lonely life. No wonder so many of us went—well, crazy."

"What do you mean?" Troi asked. She was seated with Ambassador Lelys on a stone bench built right into the side of the oberyin's house. The Orakisan held a leaf in her hand and was tracing its outline against her palm over and over again.

"What would you call it when an agent throws over his life's work, gives up the game cold, takes to the land just as if he was born one of these Ashkaarian savages, and his last message to the Masra'et isn't fit to be repeated? Crazy, that's what."

"And what your people have been doing to the Ashkaarians is sane?" Geordi asked severely. "Maybe the Masra'et could do with a few more honest messages from agents who've come to their senses."

Avren snorted. "Honest death sentence, you mean." He saw Troi's inquiring look and added, "Well, what do you think they do when one of their agents goes native on them? Just let them run off free? Oh, yes! *That* makes sense."

Mr. Data cocked his head. "Sarcasm. Interesting, but unenlightening."

"Oh, it's *enlightenment* you want?" Avren drawled. "When I was sent here to replace the last agent that went over the lip, my first assignment was to find her and take her out of the picture before she said anything that could hurt our operations. I'll say this much for the Masra'et, they don't play favorites. It didn't matter whose daughter she was, she was dangerous and she needed to be eliminated."

"So you killed her," Geordi said, biting off the words.

Avren gave him an uneasy look, as if his response might bring reprisal. "No," he said carefully. "I didn't need to bother. By the time I caught up with her, she was dead already. Childbirth. Talk about going native! No need for her to die of something like that if she'd had the sense to stay Ne'elatian, but that didn't suit *her*. Not old Udar Kishrit's girl, no. Just as stubborn as her father, she was, and look where it got her!"

"Udar Kishrit's—" Geordi's lips moved over Avren's words. "Mr. Data, can I see you a moment?" He walked briskly away from the bound Ne'elatian agent and didn't stop until he was well up the mountain. Data and Troi traded a baffled look before the android went after him.

Geordi stood with his back to a lone tree, tall and prickle-branched as an Earth pine, when Data overtook him. "She's been telling me things, Data," he said.

"She?"

"Ma'adrys. Ever since I met her on Ne'elat, lots of things. But this was one thing she never told me."

"I do not believe that she was aware of this, Geordi," Data said.

"Not aware? Not aware that she and Bilik were going to be . . . paired?"

"Ah. I thought that you were referring to the fact that she is the grandchild of the head of the Masra'et. The timing is certainly right."

"Time." Geordi drew the word out. "Too much time. Too many years of injustice. It's got to end, Data."

"I am in agreement with you in theory, Geordi, although I admit I am not very sanguine as to any immediate change taking place. Of course the optimum modification in the status quo would be for the Ne'elatians to admit their past faults and take the first steps toward establishing cultural equality with their sisterworld."

"Wouldn't that be nice," Geordi muttered. "Starting with some simple medical help."

"Indeed." Data had learned to perceive sarcasm,

but he still failed to pick up on the subtle shadings of voice that denoted cynicism. "But it will not happen. The Ne'elatians have no reason to end the present state of affairs. Even if Ma'adrys succeeds in making her people understand how they have been used by Ne'elat, the situation will not improve. The Ashkaarians may decline to share their spiritual goods with the Ne'elatians, but a boycott of that nature will not in any way harm the Ne'elatians."

"How can a whole world claim to hunger after things of the spirit and refuse to see that what they're doing to get them is simply wrong?" Geordi drove his fist back against the tree trunk. A light sprinkling of needles showered over the two officers.

"I do not know," Data said, brushing the spicy foliage from his shoulders. "Perhaps not all Ne'elatians are to blame. They may not be aware of what their leaders have been doing."

"Maybe we should make them aware of it, then. If enough of them object, the Masra'et will have no choice but to—"

"That, too, is not a very practical solution, Geordi," Data said. "For one thing, the uncertainty of effective results is too great. For another, it would be impossible for us to undertake such a project without violating the Prime Directive."

"I know, I know." Geordi's sigh blended with the mountain breeze that stirred the branches overhead. He glanced back toward the house. "They're still inside. I wonder what they're saying." A bittersweet smile pulled up one corner of his mouth. "Does eavesdropping violate the Prime Directive, Data?"

The android's head made a tiny, speculative jerk to one side. "A joke?"

"Yes, a joke." Geordi slumped a bit against the tree.

"I guess it's always easier to go through the motions of a hundred rituals instead of just doing what's right."

"Very few groups of sentient beings in the known universe agree on what is the right thing to do, in the moral or ethical sense," Data remarked. "Fewer still are willing to do the so-called right thing for its own sake. They are generally motivated by some form of personal reward, real or implied, actual or spiritual."

The android's forthright analysis jolted Geordi out of his dispirited state. "Don't tell me you're turning into a cynic, Data."

"I am merely presenting my personal observations," Data replied. "The Ferengi are motivated to action by profit, the Klingons by honor, but the Ne'elatians have nothing to motivate them to correct their past offenses against Ashkaar. They do not even view their actions as offensive, since offense can only occur between equals. They have made it quite clear that they find the Ashkaarians so technologically and culturally backward that there is not the remotest chance of equality between the two worlds."

Geordi's chin lifted. "That's *it!*" he cried, snapping his fingers.

"Is it?" Data inquired mildly.

"Equality—no—*superiority!* The one thing the Ashkaarians have that the Ne'elatians don't! And it's something the Masra'et will understand right away: Power."

"Geordi, I do not see what sort of military advantage the Ashkaarians have over the Ne'elatians. They have not even recovered the technology to manufacture simple firearms."

"They don't need to." Geordi glanced back at the

oberyin's house. Bilik and Ma'adrys were just coming out. The oberyin looked downcast but resigned, even though the girl held his hand. Geordi was so caught up in his own revelation that he forgot to feel the least twinge of jealousy. He ran toward them, happily shouting Ma'adrys's name.

Chapter Fourteen

"No," Ma'adrys said, her eyes burning. And again, louder, "*No*. I refuse to obey what I do not understand. I have been deceived too often. I am no longer a fool who goes blindly where others command."

"Ma'adrys, please, you know I'd never ask you to do anything wrong, anything that would hurt you," Geordi pleaded. He stood with her on the far side of Bilik's house, out of earshot of the oberyin and the others. "I thought you trusted me."

"And I thought you respected me," Ma'adrys shot back. "To tell me that I must do this thing—or anything!—and ask no questions, that is not respect. Am I still a child? Am I still ignorant in your eyes?" She wrapped her arms around herself and bitterly added, "Not even Bilik ever spoke to me so when he tried to turn me from becoming an oberyin. This is not love."

"Ma'adrys!" Geordi tried to take her into his arms,

but she shrugged him off and turned her back on him. "Ma'adrys, please, hear me out. I've found a way to make everything right between your world and Ne'elat, a plan that will force the Ne'elatians to see that the Ashkaarians are worthy of treatment as equals."

"Force?" she echoed hopefully. "Then all that you have told me of the law your people follow, the one that prevents you from interfering in the ways of other worlds, it can be set aside?"

Geordi grasped her shoulders and compelled her to look at him. "All right, maybe force isn't the right word. It can't be. I'm a Starfleet officer. I can't intervene in relations between Ashkaar and Ne'elat, but that doesn't mean I don't see that something has to be done to reestablish equality of your worlds, if only so that Ashkaar can benefit from Ne'elatian medical knowledge. If my plan succeeds, the sister-worlds will come together on their own."

"But why all this secrecy?" Ma'adrys demanded. "Why do you not suspend this law of yours only for a little while, until all is set right between Iskir and the false ones, and *act?* I have seen your ship. You have great power. You could make the false ones undo the evil of ages instantly, easily!"

"It wouldn't be easy, Ma'adrys," Geordi said. "It would be impossible. Don't you think I want to better things for your people as quickly as can be? But if I— if any Starfleet officer ever did use the power of Federation technology at will, where would it end? We can't remake the universe to suit our personal ideas of right and wrong. If we did, we'd soon be no better than Ne'elat."

Her look was as cold as the wind that suddenly swept down the mountainside. "So you choose the path of deceit instead."

"I choose the path of guidance. The Masra'et of Ne'elat have seen how superior our technology is to theirs. We *could* force them to treat your people the way we think they should be treated, but for how long? We couldn't stay here playing moral watchdog forever. The Ne'elatians would always resent us, and they'd soon find a way to take it out on Ashkaar. But if they choose to change on their own, without ever suspecting our role in that decision, it can only profit everyone concerned. That is why the need for secrecy, my love."

"Lies," Ma'adrys said sullenly, lowering her head. "I am tired of so many lies. I heard the wise ones teach of blessed Evramur, only to discover it was all a lie. I heard you speak of love to me, then hear you say that you cannot trust my discretion."

"That's not what I said and you know it." Geordi raised her chin and kissed her tenderly, quickly, before she could jerk away. "My love for you is no lie, and neither is Evramur, not if you believe. The lie is that *Ne'elat* is Evramur. Do you see the difference?"

"I see that it is a fine plan, to make Ne'elat treat us as equals, when *you* refuse to treat *me* with any measure of equality," Ma'adrys replied, shrugging him off. "Do you even consider doing so? You are no starlord, but you come from worlds as far advanced above Ne'elat as Ne'elat dreams itself above Iskir. If we are barbarians to Ne'elat, how much less we—*I* must be to you!" She walked away from him, up the slope to where a small patch of white flowers starred the grass.

Geordi sighed and followed, his feet crushing fragrance from the tiny blossoms until he overtook her and laid hold of her arm. "If you won't listen, how can you understand? Look, Ma'adrys, the members of the Masra'et are on board the *Enterprise* right now, but I don't know how much longer they'll stay there. Bilik and Data have to travel overland to the seat of the Na'amOberyin—less than a day's journey, but it still takes time. For my plan to succeed, we need to bring the Masra'et and the Na'amOberyin face to face, the sooner the better. Can't you be satisfied with that for an explanation? Won't you go back to Bilik and tell him that you no longer object, that he should—that he *must* do what I've asked him?"

Ma'adrys's face turned stony. A second time she cast off his touch. "Your explanation is next to none," she told him. "Perhaps you do not know how great a thing it is that you have asked Bilik to do for you, for your . . . plan. Once and only once in a lifetime, each oberyin of Iskir may appear before the Na'amOberyin and ask that they—the nine most powerful oberyin of Iskir—grant a request, with no questions asked and no explanation given."

"I know," Geordi said. "I know because you told me all about it. Why do you imagine I thought to ask it of Bilik?"

"But what have you asked of him? What *exactly?*" Ma'adrys insisted. "Is it worth squandering the one unconditional request he can ever make of them?"

"I think it is."

"And that must be enough for me as well, eh?" For the first time since Geordi had known her, Ma'adrys spoke to him harshly, her sweet face twisted into a sneer. "Very well. I will give you what you ask of me, *starlord*. How can a simple savage of Iskir ever hope to fathom wisdom such as yours? I will urge Bilik to follow your commands and never ask why."

"Ma'adrys, you're overreact—" It was no good trying to make her see reason; she did not stay to hear. She was gone, vanished back around the house to where the others waited. By the time Geordi caught up to her, she was telling Bilik in no uncertain terms that he must follow the starlord's instructions to the letter.

Bilik did not look ready to comply, despite the new awe he felt in Ma'adrys's presence. He looked from Ma'adrys, whose bared teeth looked a little too fierce to be called a smile, to Geordi, and there were a hundred unspoken doubts in that single look. "Do you know what you ask of me, starlord?" he said slowly. "The Na'amOberyin possess such powers that when they unite their minds they can compel whole cities to march into the sea! The a'dyem—the boon we lesser oberyin may have from our supreme council only once while we live—was set in place to be an everlasting reminder to them that they are still the servants of the people, for all their power."

"Fascinating," Data remarked. "If the Na'amOberyin are masters of so much mental power, why do they submit to the a'dyem at all?"

Bilik stared at Data as though the android had begun to bark like a dog. "They do so because they must." He reached into his robes and pulled out a small gray medallion on a length of braided leather. "At the testing that takes place whenever one of the Na'amOberyin dies and a new one must be chosen, the winner of the competition fills a token like this with a measure of his own power. On his ascension, the disc is then melded to his brow, to be a sign of his perpetual service to the people. All oberyin carry one until the day we seek the a'dyem, but for the Na'amOberyin this token becomes part of them until the day they die."

"May I?" Counsellor Troi extended a hand for the medallion. Bilik passed it to her with some misgiving.

She studied it for a time, then returned it to him and said, "Interesting. It feels almost like a kind of . . . storage battery. The Na'amOberyin answer to each lesser oberyin because they must, and they must because they placed some of their own superior power of compulsion in these tokens."

"I think I understand," Geordi said. "If the Na'amOberyin combine their powers, they're too strong for anyone but themselves to control, but to be *allowed* to be a part of that united power they first have to surrender a little of that self-control to the other oberyin. Checks and balances."

Bilik frowned. "I do not know what you are saying, lord, but if you mock us—"

"Not at all," Geordi reassured him. "We respect you, Bilik oberyin, and we want to understand your ways."

"Then do you understand what it is you ask of me?" he countered. "To call upon *my* a'dyem!"

"Maybe the Na'amOberyin won't see it that way," Geordi said. "All I want is for you to take my comrade here"—he indicated Mr. Data—"to the Na'amOberyin and have them grant him an audience. I only want you to call in the a'dyem if there's no other way to get their cooperation."

"It does not *seem* to be so great a thing," Bilik admitted, stroking his chin. "And yet, his appearance is such that—" He shook his head. "How shall I explain him to my betters? Will they see him as a messenger of great good or greater evil?"

"The only important thing is that they *see* him," Geordi stressed. "Tell them—tell them he's a goodwill ambassador from—"

"Goodwill," Bilik interrupted. "But whose? Ma'adrys told me much about you, lord. I no longer know what to believe. What are you, in truth? Or is the truth something I will ever know? So much has changed, so much I once believed in. Evramur. After Ma'adrys was taken from us, I used to comfort myself with the thought that even though her going tore my heart, at least she was happy, blessed to walk the holy ways of paradise. Now she has told me that the refuge of all departed spirits is only another ball of dirt and stone. Is this message the goodwill your ambassador will offer the Na'amOberyin?"

Geordi saw the very real spiritual anguish in Bilik's eyes and it called up an answering pang in his own spirit. Faith could move mountains, but doubt could send them crumbling down into a handful of sand. He searched himself for answers he might offer Bilik and found none. The oberyin would have to find his own answers. All that he could say was, "Trust me." It was feeble, but it was the best he had.

Bilik gave him a hard, measuring look. Then, without another word, he gestured for Data to follow him and set his feet on the uphill path. Before the android could fall into step behind, Geordi detained him and whispered, "When you get there and Bilik's presented you to the council, I want you to excuse yourself for just a little while. Find somewhere private, signal the ship, then stand by."

"For further instructions?"

"For a package." Geordi smiled faintly. "Special delivery. It wouldn't be a goodwill mission without a few gifts for your hosts, now would it?"

"If you say so, I will assume that is the case." With that, Data turned and set out to catch up with Bilik.

"Gifts?" Troi asked. "What gifts?"

But Geordi had already touched his comm badge and told the ship that there were four to beam up. The air shimmered around them and they were gone.

* * *

"Feeling better, Ambassador?" Lt. Riker leaned over the med station where Lelys lay blinking as if she had just awoken from a deep sleep.

The Orakisan touched her temples gingerly with her fingertips. "What . . . happened to me?"

Dr. Crusher came to stand on the other side of the ambassador's bed. "The simplest way I can describe it for you is that you were the victim of a series of neural overrides from an external source, although we're still working on an explanation for how they were transmitted."

"Please, do not bother on my account." Lelys closed her eyes and looked pained. "It makes my head ache."

"That's the normal aftereffect of the stimulant I administered," the doctor said. "It took some time for me to find one that would remove the overrides without adversely affecting your normal mental processes."

"Good thing for you she had a guinea pig to test it out on first." Riker grinned.

"I remember everything." Lelys sounded surprised by her own admission. "It was terrible. It was as if I had no control over myself. They made me into a child again, a helpless child!"

"You're lucky they didn't just immobilize you," Riker said. "I felt like I was turned to wood, trapped in my own body."

The ambassador sat up slowly and turned her head as if working kinks out of her neck. "Better to be trapped in the body than in the mind. There will be grave consequences when I confront the ones responsible for this outrage."

"I'm afraid that you'll need to put aside your own grievances for the moment," Riker said. "You're wanted in the briefing room." He slipped one hand under the ambassador's elbow and helped her stand, then escorted her out of sickbay and through the corridors of the *Enterprise*.

"Ambassador Lelys! I am so pleased to see you well once more." Hara'el hurried forward to greet his superior, but there was more than a colleague's concern in his manner. He took her hand in both of his, a gesture that took her by surprise. "Are you fully recovered?" he asked.

"I am." It was his turn to be surprised when she did not pull her hand out of his gentle hold. She nodded toward the closed door of the briefing room. "Who is in there? The Masra'et? I have some words for them."

"They are there, and my father too." Hara'el's joy in seeing Lelys once more faded as he added, "We have had more news from S'ka'rys. More dead and more near death."

"We have failed them," Lelys said, but with more heat than sorrow. "There is nothing we can do for our kin on S'ka'rys. We cannot create a plant that has vanished from the universe. But we will do *some* good here before we return home." Her eyes darted to the briefing room. "Is the witness within?"

"Witness?" It was clear that Hara'el had no idea what Lelys meant.

Just then a low murmur of voices came from farther down the corridor and Geordi appeared, accompanied by Ma'adrys and Avren. The Ne'elatian agent looked decidedly uneasy, ready to jump out of his shabby shepherd's garb at the slightest sound. His hands were no longer bound, and he clutched and fidgeted with the wide brim of his hat so energetically that he was leaving a faint trail of dust behind him from the cockade of dried flowers in the band.

"Sorry we're late," Geordi said to the ambassador. "We wanted to be sure you were fully recovered and able to see this. Avren here has agreed to testify."

"Has he?" Lelys was openly skeptical. "Does it not strike you as strange that this person, who worked so hard to maintain the evil on Ashkaar, is now so willing to help end it?"

"I'm not up to any dirty tricks, if that's what's bothering you," Avren said.

"So noble, so suddenly?" Lelys mocked him.

He shrugged off her scorn. "I never pretended to be doing anything but my job. That's over now. So much for my disguise. I got off Ashkaar with my skin in one piece, I'm not fool enough to risk it a second time, but what about my comrades? Just because the Ashkaarians are savages doesn't mean they're stupid. They've got the wind up now, and they'll be looking for spies. The Masra'et's got to withdraw us all now."

"Will they?"

"Ha! Not likely, left to themselves. It's not *their* reverend necks that're at risk. Well, I'm not trusting the lives of my friends to luck and the mercy of the Masra'et. I'm doing my part now so that those old birds don't have any choice but to recall every Ne'elatian agent on Ashkaar." He jammed his hat down hard on his head, releasing another sprinkling of dust and dried flowers. "Let's do this."

Geordi stepped to one side of the door. "After you, Madam Ambassador," he told Lelys with a courtly bow. The Orakisan ambassador and Hara'el entered, followed by Ma'adrys and Avren. Geordi heard the sharp, startled gasps that welcomed the Ne'elatian agent, and smiled.

"It's working," he murmured to himself. *It's got to work,* he thought.

Just as he was about to go into the briefing room, his comm badge beeped. "La Forge here."

Lt. Worf's voice hailed him. "Mr. La Forge, we have just received a communication from Mr. Data on Ashkaar. It was extremely short. He said that he had arrived and was awaiting further instructions and the . . . special delivery. When I attempted to question him he only said that he did not have the time for a lengthy interview and that you would know what he meant."

"Thank you, Mr. Worf, I do. La Forge out."

In the transporter room Geordi set the previously prepared package on the pad, then touched his comm badge. "La Forge to Data."

"Data here." The android's voice came through hardly louder than a whisper. "Where is the package?"

"Coming. Where are you?"

"Just outside the chamber where the Na'amOberyin hold their audiences. This is not a very large building, Geordi. The audience chamber *is* the building, in effect. I have managed to find what appears to be a closet, but I cannot stay hidden here long. I suggest we proceed."

"Right. I'm beaming down the package to your coordinates. When it gets there I want you to open it and distribute the contents to the Na'amOberyin and Bilik."

"What are the contents?"

"Comm badges. Tell them whatever it takes, as long as they put them on, then signal me when it's done."

There was a short silence on Mr. Data's end of the conversation, and then: "Is it your intent to transport the entire Na'amOberyin aboard the *Enterprise?*"

"Yes."

"Ah. For what purpose?"

"To confront the Masra'et. Each is the supreme political body on their respective worlds. They have to meet if this is ever going to be settled."

"I do not know if this is a wise course of action at the present moment, Geordi," Data said. "When Bilik brought me into the presence of the council, he did not limit his remarks to my introduction. He has repeated everything that Ma'adrys told him about the true nature of the world they call Evramur."

"And they believed him?"

"He prefaced his recital with what I assume to be a sacred oath of inviolable honesty. To judge by the reactions of the Na'amOberyin, they accept everything he tells them as the unquestionable truth, and they are not happy. I do not think it prudent to bring aboard so significant a number of angered and hostile individuals. It is difficult to gauge any danger they might present. They all wear loose-fitting robes that make it impossible to determine whether or not they are carrying weapons."

"They're angry at Ne'elat, not us."

"They are angry at Ne'elat and you," Data corrected him.

"Me?"

"Bilik spoke rather eloquently of the manner in which Ashkaar has been deceived for so long by off-world agents. He made no attempt to differentiate between the Ne'elatians and us, you in particular."

"Yes, it would be me in particular," Geordi muttered, thinking of Ma'adrys and what she had once meant to Bilik.

"When I left the audience chamber, I overheard two of the council members pondering whether my intentions, too, were to be trusted."

"You'd better do what you can to bring them

around. We need them to trust you just long enough to put on those comm badges. Signal when it's done and I'll beam you aboard first. La Forge out." He pulled the transporter switch, watched as the package of comm badges flickered away, then settled back to wait.

In the briefing room, things were not going well. No matter where Captain Picard looked, he saw faces contorted by fury. Only his crewmembers—Counsellor Troi, Commander Riker, and Mr. Data—seemed immune to the storm of rage whirling through the room. Regarding Data, Picard idly wished that the android had been present from the beginning of this confrontation. Mr. Data could never be anything but the voice of pure reason, and that sometimes had a calming effect on more emotional beings.

But Data had arrived uncharacteristically late, and he left no time for Picard to request an explanation. By then the hostilities were well out into the open. The air crackled with the ranting voices of Ne'elatians, Orakisans, and the sole Ashkaarian, Ma'adrys, each trying to shout down the others. It was no use trying to restore order at this point. Tempers had risen too high, too many hard truths had been spoken. The disputants had not yet resorted to physical violence, but from where Picard sat it looked as if it were only a matter of time. He touched his badge. "Security to the briefing room, on the double."

Mr. Worf responded to the summons personally, accompanied by two of his staff. They entered just as Udar Kishrit was about to lunge across the table for Avren's throat. The Ne'elatian agent backed away fast and bumped into the Klingon. It was rather like stumbling into a solidly mortared brick wall.

"Ow!" Avren's hat was knocked to the floor. He

stood there rubbing the back of his head and glowering at Worf.

Worf had no time for apologies. His eyes swept the tumult and he thundered out a single word: *"Sit!"* One look at the Klingon and they sat. Quickly.

However, even with the contenders under some control, it didn't take them long to start bellowing at each other again.

"Lies!" Udar Kishrit pounded the table with his fist. "We are brought here to be assaulted by lies! Who is this fraud you have dug out of the muck to insult us?" He jabbed his finger at Avren.

The false shepherd ignored the slur. "You were glad enough to see me when I first came in," he said. "It was only when I opened my mouth and told the truth that you wanted to pretend you'd never laid eyes on me before. Well, it won't work. I can prove you know me." He reached into his pouch and brought out the same small device with which he had contacted the Masra'et about the problem of the Away Team's presence on Ashkaar. "There are more than a few recordings of your voice and image right here. I always keep copies of communications. That way no one can make me take the blame for executing orders you would prefer to deny later."

"Your lies have nothing to do with any orders we ever gave you," Udar Kishrit growled. "They have all been uttered here, before these witnesses. To accuse my daughter of disloyalty! To claim she turned against her own people! She was proud and honored to serve Ne'elat. She gave her life for us! May you pay forever for hurling such filth against a dead girl's reputation. Isata Kish was twice the agent you will ever be, a hero among heroes. Her loss will always tear my heart. I am consoled only by the knowledge that she died in the performance of her duty to Ne'elat."

"She died in childbirth," Avren shot back. "The child herself is here." He pointed at Ma'adrys. "Don't you have eyes? Or don't you remember your own daughter's face? I knew Isata Kish when we were both in training, and the resemblance—"

"Bah."

"Udar Kishrit," Counsellor Troi said softly, "The Away Team discovered certain artifacts in Ma'adrys's house that were of Ne'elatian origin. She said that they had belonged to her mother. One was a communications device. We have every reason to believe that this young woman is your grandchild."

"Your beliefs are your own," he replied haughtily. "Keep them to yourselves."

"What is the use of all this?" Legate Valdor broke in. "Why do you harass these people with such nonsense? What does it matter if this girl is anything to Udar Kishrit?"

"It matters to me," Udar Kishrit said, his voice cold. "The very idea that my daughter could lower herself to breed with an Ashkaarian! Savages and primitives, all of them."

"And who keeps us so?" Ma'adrys cried, springing from her chair. "It offends you to believe that your daughter took my father for her mate? I find it a worse affront that my father, an honest man, ever mingled his blood with one of you—you heshkatti!"

Udar Kishrit's upper lip curled. "And what would that happen to be?"

Mr. Data was quick to provide the answer. "The Ashkaarian heshkatti is a mythological creature, rather like a cross between two legendary monsters from Earth, the vampire and the harpy. It drinks the dreams of its sleeping victims and fouls their homes with its droppings."

"How *dare* you!" Udar Kishrit bellowed.

"Mr. Data," Captain Picard murmured, "I don't think Udar Kishrit actually wanted to know that."

"But sir, he did ask—" the puzzled android began.

"I will bear no more of this," Udar Kishrit announced, rising to his feet. *"We* will bear no more. Captain Picard, we wish to return to Ne'elat at once."

"Then go!" Ambassador Lelys spat. "The sooner we see the last of you, the better. Does it shame you to acknowledge Ma'adrys as your daughter's child? It shames us a hundred times more to claim you as any relation to Orakisa! You will never be a part of our sisterworld alliance while I have a voice. Ne'elat will remain the blighted backwater of the galaxy that it deserves to be."

"Speak for yourself, Ambassador," Legate Valdor snarled. "Would you cast aside a whole world of our kin for petty spite?"

"Spite! You are a fine one to lecture me on spite, Valdor," she retorted. "I have heard how you connived against me."

"You are mad." Valdor sniffed as if Lelys's anger were a trifle to be disregarded. "Your mind has been affected by your captivity among the Ashkaarian savages. I will report this unfortunate lapse to our superiors when we return to Orakisa. It may be that they will take it into account when they evaluate the reasons why this mission has failed so dismally, but if not—"

"Settle your quarrels on your own time," Udar Kishrit snapped at his onetime ally. "We will not be delayed here any longer. Captain Picard!"

"Yes, yes." Picard rose from the table slowly. He had weathered enough unfriendly parleys in the course of his career to know when it was useless to try forcing the issue at hand. Despite the fact that the Masra'et had been made to hear damning testimony not only from Ma'adrys but from one of their own agents in place, they refused to admit themselves or their ancestors guilty of any wrongdoing on Ashkaar. "We will transport you back to Ne'elat at once." He touched his comm badge. "Transporter room, prepare to—"

The briefing room door hissed open. Udar Kishrit and the rest of the Masra'et gasped and backed away as nine fiery-eyed men, their long, dark robes as wildly disarrayed as their beards, poured into the already crowded chamber.

"They have come!" Ma'adrys exclaimed, half in fear, half in awe. She arranged her hands in a gesture of deepest reverence and bowed low. "Gracious masters, be welcome to our—"

The words of greeting died on her lips. While she had been speaking, the door had opened a second time.

"Geordi!" she cried.

Even with his arms pinioned behind him and Bilik's dagger at his throat, Geordi managed a sheepish smile. "Hello, Ma'adrys. This isn't going the way I planned it at all."

Chapter Fifteen

LT. WORF ACTED WITH the speed of a Klingon warrior and the skill of one of Starfleet's most highly trained Security officers. Bilik might have his dagger to Geordi's throat, but Worf was confident that even unarmed he could deflect the blade and free his crewmate before the oberyin knew what hit him. He leaped into action—

—and turned into ice.

"Exactly like what happened to me," Commander Riker murmured to a stunned Captain Picard.

"Enough power to immobilize a Klingon," Picard marveled under his breath.

"I don't think our friend with the dagger's doing it alone," Riker observed. He nodded discreetly at the nine members of the Na'amOberyin who were staring at Worf with intense concentration. "If they can hold Worf, we'd better not make any sudden moves or they'll do the same to us."

"Agreed." Picard raised his voice and addressed the invaders. "Whoever you are, I promise you that you are in no danger here if you have come in peace."

"It was not our idea to come here," Bilik replied, his jaw set. "We were swept from our world unwillingly, just as so many of our own people were stolen by *those* children of Yaro before this." He shot a venomous look at the trembling Ne'elatians.

"It was not my idea to bring you here, either," Picard said. "But since you are here, I give you my word as a Starfleet officer that while you are on board the *Enterprise,* you have nothing to fear from us. Release my men and I will see that you are returned to your homeworld immediately."

Bilik made no move to lower the dagger. "We know nothing of the worth of your word. Why should we trust you?"

"I assure you—" Without thinking, Picard rose from his seat, intending to approach the hostile oberyin peaceably. He had taken perhaps three steps toward Bilik when he felt his limbs begin to go numb. He took the hint. "There is no need for that," he remarked softly. When he backtracked and sat down again, the shadow of paralysis left him. "We can talk like this, at a distance, if that is what you prefer."

"What is this nonsense?" Udar Kishrit's voice boomed. He gave Picard a contemptuous look. "Is your Federation made of such spineless stuff that you treat savages as if they were civilized beings?" He started for Bilik, and whether his hand was raised to deal the oberyin a blow or merely in a dramatic gesture, only he knew.

"Hold them, my masters!" Bilik cried. "Hold them all!" At those words, a shiver seemed to run through every non-Ashkaarian in the briefing room. This was a different sort of immobility than that which held Worf fast.

"My legs! What have they done to my legs?" one panic-stricken member of the Masra'et cried.

"And mine, curse you!" another shouted at the Ashkaarians. "Release us at once, or—" He reached for the flimsy dagger at his belt. It was a poor cousin to the businesslike blade Bilik held under Geordi's chin, most likely intended just for show and ceremony, but the Ashkaarians did not see it that way. To them, the intent of attack was as good as the act. One of them raised his hand and the belligerent Ne'elatian suddenly found his arms made as useless as his legs.

As for Udar Kishrit, he appeared to be struggling with an invisible assailant, one who first pushed his arms down to his sides, then forced him back into his place by inches, the Ne'elatian headman bawling his indignation all the while.

As further bellows of outrage arose from Legate Valdor and the members of the Masra'et, it became apparent that their vocal capabilities remained untouched by the power of the Na'amOberyin. It was, Picard reflected, like being held captive in a wizard's lair, surrounded by semi-animate statues. *Loud* ones.

The one exception to the selective paralysis upon them was Mr. Data. Whether it was Bilik alone or the powers of the nine combined with his, the android remained unaffected. However, when he attempted to rise from his place at the conference table, Bilik uttered a warning hiss and twitched his dagger ever so slightly against Geordi's skin, just enough to draw a thin trickle of blood.

"Bilik, *no!*" Ma'adrys cried, and stretched out her hands.

"Stay back," Bilik commanded. "For the safety of your own spirit, Ma'adrys, keep away from this demon. You have been led astray by these false ones for too long. You are too tender hearted, and Yaro's children speak with words of honey and voices of sweet song."

"Geordi is no demon," Ma'adrys said staunchly. "It is you who have been led astray by Yaro if you think that. How much farther down the dark road will you follow?"

"*Is* such precaution necessary, Bilik oberyin?" asked one of the other nine dark-robed Ashkaarians, eying Geordi. His beard was copiously streaked with gray and covered most of his chest. A silver sigil pinned to his robe marked him out among his peers. "If it is as Ma'adrys says, can you not release this captive?"

"I would not trust him, Nish na'am," Bilik snarled. "He is deceit itself."

"Nish na'am!" Captain Picard's powerful voice drew every eye to him. "Mr. La Forge is a Starfleet officer and I am his commander. Have Bilik oberyin release him and you have my word as well as his that he will offer you no opposition."

Nish na'am appeared to consider the captain's words. "Perhaps this one is right, Bilik oberyin," he said. "This chamber is already thick with the nets of holding and can contain precious little more. Trust is well named as the fifth moral treasure. A word well given can restrain an army. Besides," he peered closely at the immobilized Klingon, "you, too, know how strong this one was to resist us. Even now—"

"They are all the children of lies, Nish na'am," Bilik said hastily. "We can not be too careful. What do they know or care about the six moral treasures? Trust none of them."

"Not even me, Bilik?" Ma'adrys glared at him. "Not even when I speak hari'imash in his name?"

The alien word brought a great silence down upon the Ashkaarians in the room. The color fled from Bilik's face and the hand holding the knife to Geordi's throat slowly fell to his side, though Geordi himself still remained unable to take a single step away from his captor. "Do you, Ma'adrys?" Bilik asked in a voice hardly louder than a whisper.

"Willingly."

"But I never intended to kill—"

"Silence." Nish na'am raised his hands. The silver sigil on his robes seemed to glow with his power to command. "Intentions are blown seed pods. She has spoken hari'imash and spoken it willingly. The sacrifice is offered, made, accepted. So let it be. Release him."

Reluctantly, Bilik stepped away from his prisoner. Geordi shook himself like a wet dog, as if casting off the remnants of some old spell out of ancient fairy tales. Ma'adrys gave a glad little cry and rushed into his arms. She took a piece of folded cloth from her sleeve and used it to dab the slim cut Bilik's knife had left in Geordi's flesh. Watching her tenderness, the oberyin turned away, shamefaced.

"Bilik oberyin! Attend us!" Nish na'am spoke sharply. "Your inattention robs us all of our present advantage." The graybeard turned a piercing look on Captain Picard. "You are the one who rules here? Are you starlord or child of Yaro?"

"I am Jean-Luc Picard, captain of this ship," Picard replied evenly. "And that is all."

His response left the na'am somewhat puzzled. He made another try. "Do you side with the Balance or against it?"

"We side with a peaceful resolution of differences."

"Differences," the graybeard repeated. "And atrocities? Are these, too, merely differences to you? Bilik oberyin came before us to speak of many secrets, long buried. Injustice has been done to our people. What do you know of this? Much? Little? Nothing?"

"We know as much and more than you about the situation that has developed between Ashkaar and Ne'elat, Nish na'am," Picard said. "We would rejoice to see things made right between the two worlds."

"And our dead? The loved ones we have lost so needlessly for so long. Where is their rejoicing?"

Counsellor Troi spoke up, her voice soft and persuasive. "We cannot hope to undo the past, Nish na'am. Act for the sake of the living, not the dead, and look to the future."

"The future will be no different from the past, *can* be no different, unless these deceivers admit their offenses against us," the na'am said coldly.

"When the sun falls," Udar Kishrit snarled.

"Udar Kishrit, think about what you're saying," Picard said. "I have walked in the sacred precincts of Bovridash and heard your bovereem expound the teachings. If you worship the holy beauty of the Balance, how can you leave a debt unpaid?"

"What debt? I pay all my debts, Captain Picard. You insult me," Udar Kishrit replied, his mouth hard.

"Not this debt. For centuries the spiritual health of your people has flourished at the expense of the physical well-being of the Ashkaarians, your kindred. For ages you've chosen to take from them, but now you face a glorious opportunity, the chance to *give*, to pay back some small measure of all that you've—"

"Enough!" Udar Kishrit's face was livid. "What is this talk of debts to be repaid? Debts are contracted between equals! Hear me now and hear me well, Captain Picard: If we have taken the teachings of these savages for our own, it is because the gods *gave* us that power. Will you challenge the wisdom of the gods? If we had not done so, Ne'elat might have become like the old homeworld, lost because its people could worship nothing that was not the work of their hands."

"Do you hear your own words, Udar Kishrit?" Counsellor Troi asked softly. "If you think of the Ashkaarians as savages, why do you come to them for spiritual guidance?"

Udar Kishrit made an impatient sound. "You twist my words. I know only one truth, that if we have saved and preserved the advances of Ne'elat at the price of a dozen Ashkaars, we have done well."

"Saved the advances of Ne'elat, but for whom?" Troi murmured.

"Not for such as they, if that is what you mean." Udar Kishrit lifted his head proudly.

"You *are* such as they, you fool!" Ambassador Lelys shouted. "One stem, many flowers, but all sprung from the same seed."

"I might say the same of your people and mine as well," the head of the Masra'et returned coldly. "Yet you would turn your back on us too, without a second thought. You would deny us the stars."

Lelys's gesture embraced the Ashkaarians. "You would deny these people, your brothers, life itself!"

"And you, shiplord?" Nish na'am studied Captain Picard's face. "In your eyes, that have seen much, are we savages?"

"No," Picard replied. "By no means."

"Why do you say so when this . . . illspeaker"—he nodded at Udar Kishrit—"seems so convinced that we are? What makes a savage, shiplord? Blind selfishness? Casual brutality? Indifference to anyone whose life is not linked to his own closely enough? Or even"—With icy determination and a gaze whose meaning could not be mistaken, he looked deliberately from Udar Kishrit to Ma'adrys and back again—"to one whose is?"

"How *dare* you!" Udar Kishrit struggled against the invisible bonds that held him. Nish na'am's eyes narrowed, and the gaze of every member of the Na'amOberyin focussed on the enraged leader of the Masra'et. Udar Kishrit's eyes went wide as he tried to force more words of indignation from his mouth and could not. Nish na'am allowed himself a small, satisfied smile.

Suddenly, a guttural sound escaped Lt. Worf's lips. The Klingon's outstretched hand flexed ever so slightly. The Na'amOberyin wheeled as if their bodies were controlled by a single puppeteer, their faces transformed to masks of almost incandescent intensity. If Worf had been turned to ice before, now he was stone.

Not so Udar Kishrit. In the instant that the Na'amOberyin reclaimed control over Worf, he sprang back to full mobility. The ceremonial dagger at his belt flashed up as he drew it and threw himself at the nearest of the Ashkaarians.

"So." Nish na'am touched his silver sigil and laughed. "It has teeth, this many-headed monster." He spoke slowly, like a man with all the time in the world. Indeed, it seemed as if at his word time had slowed to the oozing pace of honey dripping heavy from the comb.

Udar Kishrit still moved, but sluggishly, his feet too weighty to carry him forward, his body swaying in an eerie dance. His free hand rose to meet the hand holding the dagger above his head until he grasped the blade with both. Then gradually, oh so very languidly, the blade descended, subtly changing course as it drifted down, until the leader of the Masra'et stared helplessly as he himself stood ready to plunge the glittering point into his own trembling belly.

At once, the other members of the Masra'et were siezed by the same uncanny power of animation and drew their daggers. Some laid the edges to their throats, some aimed the blades for their hearts, one terrified elder looked down the length of steel that awaited only another unspoken command so that it might jab deep into his eye.

"Nish na'am, stop this! Stop it at once!" Captain Picard slammed his fists against the tabletop. "Release these men immediately!"

"They will be released when they, too, have spoken hari'imash," Nish n'am said grimly. "They will utter their most sacred bond to give our people all the knowledge, all the wonders that they now hoard from us, to give us back lives for the lives that have—"

"Never," Udar Kishrit rasped. "Do you think you frighten us with these tricks, these cheap deceptions? You want us to believe that you have unlimited power? I see through such lies. You cannot hold us forever! There are limits to your power, I feel them, and I swear that when your hold over me slips, your life will end."

"If"—Nish na'am held up one monitory finger—"your life has not ended first." He slashed his finger left, then right, and Udar Kishrit's dagger darted away from his belly only to fly back again.

"What do they hope to gain by this?" Avren wondered aloud. "I know the Masra'et. Even if they do give their word to share out our knowledge with Ashkaar, what's to stop 'em from reneging once their skins are safe?"

"But if they speak hari'imash—" Ma'adrys began,

her eyes wide. "To break that oath is to court utter destruction, soul and heart!"

Avren dismissed her words with a snort. "Maybe we're one blood, but we're still two worlds. Your holiest vow is just words to them." He indicated the captive members of the Masra'et. "They'll mouth it and forget it, and how will you folk enforce any promises they make if they don't decide to keep 'em? Grow wings and fly to Evramur?"

Ma'adrys lowered her head and clenched her hands. "Do not profane what is still holy to us just to prove how witty you are, Avren. Ne'elat is not Evramur. It is as far removed from paradise as mud from wine."

"Is what this one says true?" Nish na'am inquired, leaning near. "Are these children of Yaro so debased that they would break their sacred word?"

"Do not fear that we will break any promises we make to you," Udar Kishrit rumbled, breathing hard. "We would sooner give our word to the lowest worm that creeps through garden mold than to you. If you will kill us for it, then do so and be done!"

"If that is what you desire." Nish na'am's eyes turned to slits of stone. He raised his hand.

"Nish na'am, *no.*" Having submitted to the Na'amOberyin earlier, Captain Picard was not now restrained by any measure of their coercive power. He was on his feet, one hand on the na'am's arm, before anyone could stop him. As he tightened his grip, he thought he felt a vague probing in his mind, and for an instant his hold slackened, but only for an instant. The tentative mental intruder pulled back, leaving him untouched.

Almost as if it's already got more than it can handle, he thought.

Aloud he said, "If you kill these men, you will be no better than they. You will have destroyed not only your sacred Balance but all hope of ever seeing it restored between your two worlds."

"And what would you have us do then, shiplord?" Nish na'am spoke bitterly. "Let them go free of debt, free of blame? Return to our world and watch our people's lives be blown away like ash whenever a sickness strikes, even when it is a sickness that these illspeakers could have cured or prevented? No, shiplord. We have tasted enough of our own deaths. Let us share this much with them even if they refuse to share with them." He twisted his arm from Picard's grasp and raised his hand once more.

"Stop!" Ma'adrys stood with her arms wrapped tightly around Udar Kishrit, her body wedged between his and the dagger. "Kill him and you kill me."

"Ma'adrys, what are you doing?" Bilik exclaimed. "Get out of the way!"

"No!" Ma'adrys was adamant. "On Iskir, we defend our own. He is blood of my blood, even if he will deny it. I cannot allow him to die."

"Girl, do not be a fool," Udar Kishrit hissed. "Look at their eyes. They will not hesitate to kill you if they want to kill me."

"Then so be it!" Ma'adrys tossed back her head and looked him in the eye. "I am not afraid to face death if it is for the sake of my family."

"Stubborn," Avren murmured. "Just like her grandfather. If that doesn't convince the old man—"

"Step aside, Ma'adrys," Nish na'am commanded. "The illspeaker speaks truly, for once. The Ne'elatians have run up a tally of needless death for our people. It is past time we began to even the score."

"He *is* one of my people," Ma'adrys maintained. "And what you seek to do here to him, to all of them, is wrong. It is as the shiplord says, it makes you no better than they!"

"This does not concern any but we of Iskir," Nish na'am said, his voice like steel. "You have chosen, Ma'adrys. Live with your choice and die with it." He raised his hand to the silver sigil.

"No!" Bilik's cry rocked the briefing chamber. Picard thought he felt something, something invisible, intangible yet present. As to what that something might be—

With a war shout in his own tongue, Lt. Worf sprang forward, free of the unseen bonds that the combined forces of Bilik and the Na'amOberyin had laid upon him. One open-handed blow and Nish na'am sprawled on the floor, stunned. The removal of the Na'amOberyin's most powerful member effectively hamstrung the others. Without Nish na'am they could no more hope to retain control over the Masra'et and the rest than they could keep Worf their prisoner without Bilik's help. A communal sigh of relief swept through the chamber as the Masra'et regained self-mastery and let their daggers drop.

As Mr. Data hastened to remove the dazed Nish na'am from the room—and so from any further possibility that the Na'amOberyin would take radical action against the Ne'elatians—Worf and his Security people saw to the others. Without their leader, the Na'amOberyin seemed harmless.

Harmless . . . or only dazed for the moment by what's happened here, Captain Picard thought. *If they recover and regroup—*

He gave Lt. Worf a significant look. The Klingon nodded and barked orders to his subordinates who drew phasers, set them on stun, and covered their prisoners.

"Think that'll do any real good if they decide to

make a fight of it, sir?" Commander Riker whispered. "Any one of them could freeze Worf's people in a wink."

"Agreed, but not Worf. I don't think they relish the thought of angering him any further," Picard replied. Riker looked at the fearful way that the remaining Na'amOberyin kept glancing at the Klingon and had to concede that his commanding officer was right. The situation was under control . . . so far.

Legate Valdor observed the proceedings with a smug demeanor. "Good. At least we are done with *that* rabble."

"This is not over, Valdor," Lelys said vehemently. "Nothing is settled."

"Nothing needs to be settled," he replied disdainfully. "You have been given a firsthand demonstration of the vindictive, uncivilized behavior of the Ashkaarians, yet you still expect the Ne'elatians to change their minds and deal with them as if they were rational, sensible—"

"Rational?" Udar Kishrit repeated thoughtfully. "Sensible?" He looked at Ma'adrys. "How sensible was what you did for me, child?"

The girl shrugged. "I cannot say. I do not know."

"No, you would not know, would you." The leader of the Masra'et fell into pensive silence for a little while, then slowly extended his hand to Ma'adrys. Gently he placed his arm around her shoulder. The girl gazed up at him, misgiving in her eyes, but his warm smile reassured her. Tentatively she returned his embrace. "Since I have been brought aboard this ship, I have seen and heard much in a very little time," he said. "So many new things that even now I find difficult to comprehend, to accept, and yet—"

"Why do you need to accept anything but what you

have just seen?" Legate Valdor cut in. "These savages—"

"Are they?" Udar Kishrit spoke like a man newly woken from a dream that carried the appearance of reality. "I don't think I can believe that any more, but—but I hardly know what to believe beyond what I have just experienced." He hugged Ma'adrys tighter. "Of all those here present today, this child has the greatest account to settle with us for what our treatment of her world has cost her. She should have placed her hand on the hilt of the dagger and driven it deep. Instead she placed her own life between the blade and mine. Was that the act of a barbarian? Of a vengeful savage?" His features set with a new resolve. "I say no."

"You say that because she is your grandchild!" one of the other members of the Masra'et challenged.

"I do not, Rak Ti'ask." Udar Kishrit drew himself up tall and wrapped his dignity around himself and Ma'adrys. "She is my daughter's child, I admit it now before you all, but that was never enough to sway me. She is more than the blood that bore her. Can a world that raises up such people be called uncivilized? Perhaps its people lack the technology we possess, the knowledge that might have been theirs but for our repeated intervention, but that can change. That *must* change, and we must help it."

A great muttering went up from almost every alien delegation in the briefing room. Robbed of his former ally, Legate Valdor smoldered. Among the Ne'elatians, Rak Ti'ask continued to voice his objections to any accord with Ashkaar. Other members of the Masra'et questioned Ma'adrys closely, some evidently pleased by her responses, others less so.

One of the latter spoke up: "Even if we are to offer

Ashkaar technological equality, *how* are we to do it? I am willing to grant that they are not savages, but are they ready to master all we have to teach them?"

"Some are," Ma'adrys said, speaking more out of blind conviction than hard facts.

"Are they?" Hara'el asked. "And what about the rest?"

"Are you still only your father's echo, Hara'el?" Lelys accused him. "Do you, too, believe these people are no more than ignorant savages?"

A marked change came over Hara'el's otherwise pleasant features. He scowled so intently at Lelys that she paled. "With respect, my lady ambassador, that was unworthy of you. You wrong me. I speak of a very real possibility, that immediate technological equality would be the destruction, not the salvation of Ashkaar."

Valdor snorted. "What nonsense!"

"On the contrary, Hara'el has a valid point, Legate Valdor, Ambassador Lelys," Captain Picard said. "On Earth we have a saying that equates technology with magic, if that technology is far enough beyond the understanding or experience of ordinary people. I myself have seen more than one old story where an explorer, captured by primitive tribesmen, becomes their god by showing them the great magic he can perform with something as simple as a cigarette lighter."

"A what?" Counsellor Troi inquired.

Picard smiled briefly. "An antique fire-making device, small enough to conceal in the palm of your hand. Think of what that must have looked like to people for whom fire-making was long, hard labor! How will the devices Ne'elat brings to Ashkaar be received if not as miracle machines? And then, what if some unprincipled person—Ne'elatian or perhaps an

Ashkaarian who proves to be a quick study—chooses to take advantage of the people's fear? No, the Ashkaarians will only be comfortable with higher technology if they are able to develop it for themselves, not have it handed to them."

"And how are we to do that, shiplord?" one of the Na'amOberyin demanded. "I have not seen the world these illspeakers come from, yet I can imagine the wonders they command. See, before us stands one of their number who walked among us for years!" He pointed at Avren, who had recovered his fallen hat and was once more twiddling the brim. "How did he come to our world if not by one of their own vessels? If even now they can sail from world to world, how can we ever hope to equal their accomplishments on our own?" His fellow council members set up a hum of angry agreement.

"Their accomplishments stem from the same root as will your own," Hara'el said confidently. "You are no less intelligent than they, and some among you are capable of greatness."

"That's for certain," Avren said. "Those were the ones we plucked away." The glares of the Masra'et compelled him to add, "Well, it's true! If *she* had had a head full of air instead of a mind full of curiosity, I'd never have stolen her off to Evr—Ne'elat." He indicated Ma'adrys.

"Maybe that's the answer," Geordi mused aloud.

"What did you say, Mr. La Forge?" Picard asked.

"I was just thinking, the Ashkaarians who are still on Ne'elat—they've seen Ne'elatian technology up close, grown accustomed to it. If we could repatriate them, no one on Ashkaar would be all that surprised if they brought back a few . . . souvenirs."

"And what's to stop them from setting themselves up as their people's new gods?"

"You know, sir, no one who's handled a magician's props ever sees his show with quite the same degree of belief afterward," Riker remarked.

"I trust you'll explain that, Commander?"

"My suggestion is that we make sure the Ashkaarians see where their new technology comes from, or will come from once they develop it for themselves. Their repatriated friends and relatives are a start, but remember, we're not making them an outright gift. We're going to give them"—His boyish grin lit up his face—"a kit. Build your own advanced technology, some assembly required."

"A kit?" Geordi repeated.

"A kit that's a clue. The Ashkaarians and the Ne'elatians came here together, one people on one starship. That was the same ship that kept up communications between the two worlds until it was lost. What do you think would happen if somehow the wreckage of that starship could be 'found' on Ashkaar?"

"Commander, are you proposing that we *create* this convenient wreckage? Starfleet regulations—"

"We wouldn't create it," Riker said. *"They* would." He smiled at the massed members of the Masra'et.

"It might work," Udar Kishrit admitted. He looked at Ma'adrys. "And with you and the others there to help your people see that these devices are no great magic, my child, but things that they can come to understand, re-create, build for themselves, then given time—"

"But my people cannot wait to reinvent all the work of your healers, Grandfather," Ma'adrys said. *"That* help we need now."

"And if the healers we send use their skills to make your people worship them? Child, we are all frail beings, too ready to take the easy way. I confess my own guilt there. I have offended against your people because I despised them, thought them lesser beings than myself. It is a fault for which I will atone with what power I have in the years left me. I have harmed Ashkaar; I cannot allow others to do the same."

"Harm? I think not. Not if you recruit your healers from one source." Captain Picard steepled his fingers. "Bovridash."

"The holy place?" Rak Ti'ask feigned laughter. "Are you suggesting we send our blessed bovereem into the Ashkaarian wilderness? For what?"

"For healing," Picard answered mildly. "All manner of healing. Who better to make amends than the bovereem, who have devoted their lives to the pursuit of righteousness? Who better to pass on the medical knowledge of Ne'elat than they? They could begin by teaching the oberyin new skills, instruct them in the making of new remedies and preventatives. The oberyin could in turn pass this on to the people of Ashkaar."

"Do you think it worth the risk?" Udar Kishrit asked, clearly interested.

"I spent time in Bovridash, Udar Kishrit," Picard said, "and I came to know many of the bovereem. I think that their integrity is strong, and I know that they regard justice as a holy duty, linked to the keeping of the Balance. I also realize that they are as fallible as any of us, but if you were careful about screening the ones who were picked to travel to Ashkaar, you would have no worries about their presence doing any harm."

"Then that is a risk worth taking," Ma'adrys maintained.

"That is a risk you *must* take, Udar Kishrit," Ambassador Lelys declared. "We came here on a mission to save lives. We have failed our own colonists, but I will not stand by and let more lives be lost over the vague possibility of Ne'elatian healers setting themselves up as false gods."

"Do not trouble yourself over that, Ambassador," Rak Ti'ask said. "It will never happen because we will never consent to it."

"Speak for yourself, Rak Ti'ask," Udar Kishrit spat.

"I do," the younger man responded with an ugly gleam in his eye. "For myself and for enough votes to forbid this absurdity from ever coming to pass."

"Turn your backs on Ashkaar and we turn our backs on you," Lelys cried.

"Exclude us from your union if you will," Rak Ti'ask said. "It would have been sweet to regain the secret of interstellar flight as a gift, but with enough time we can discover it on our own. When that day comes, we will come after you and *take* our rightful place among our sisterworlds. And I assure you, we will come with long memories."

"Are you threatening us?" Lelys demanded, and with that the room erupted into warring camps, everyone arguing at once, at the top of their lungs. Some members of the Masra'et sided with Udar Kishrit, others with Rak Ti'ask, others still tried to garner further information from what had become a shouting match rather than a reasoned discussion. Some of the Na'amOberyin let it be known that they would have nothing to do with anything that came from Ne'elat, others argued that their chief duty was the welfare of their people. Threats flew, and harsh names. It was only with the greatest difficulty that Captain Picard—with much help from Lt. Worf—reasserted control.

"In the circumstances" he boomed, then realized

that he had raised his voice to be heard over an argument that was no longer going on. In more tranquil tones he repeated, "In the circumstances I believe it would be better if the Ne'elatian delegation retired to reach some sort of internal accord before we proceed any farther."

"That seems . . . reasonable," Rak Ti'ask said, almost reluctantly.

"Very much so," Udar Kishrit concurred.

"Shiplord, I think it would be a good idea if the honored Na'amOberyin might also have some time apart," Ma'adrys said. "I wish to speak with them, if they will permit it, so that they may begin to understand the true nature of Ne'elat."

"Sir," Counsellor Troi put in before Picard could reply, "I, too, think this would be wise. I am willing to accompany them as facilitator, and to reintroduce Nish na'am into the group."

"By all means, Counsellor," Picard said.

"We, too, should be part of these discussions," Ambassador Lelys said. "Legate Valdor, I think it would be best if you were our representative among the Ne'elatians. I will attend the Ashkaarians, and as for Hara'el—"

"I will accompany my father," Hara'el spoke up. There was no mistaking his intention to stand with his father as equal, not shadow, in the counsels of Ne'elat.

"Then that's settled." Picard stood up. "Commander Riker, please conduct the Masra'et to an appropriate meeting room. Counsellor Troi, do the same for the Na'amOberyin. Report your progress to me within two hours, when it is my sincere hope we can reconvene this meeting under more civil conditions. Dismissed." He left the briefing room, his own departure followed in swift succession by the Ashkaarian and Ne'elatian delegations and all Starfleet personnel except Geordi and Lt. Worf.

Geordi stared wistfully at the door through which Ma'adrys had just departed. "Nothing for us to do now but wait," he said.

"You have no other duties?" Worf asked tersely.

Geordi touched the thready wound that Bilik's dagger had left on his neck. "Well, I suppose I do have business in sickbay." He, too, left.

Now the only persons remaining in the so recently crowded briefing room were Lt. Worf, Bilik, and Avren. The Klingon regarded the men suspiciously. "And you?" he asked. "Why have you not gone with your own people?"

"I don't think my people are in any hurry to see me just yet," Avren said with a note of self mockery in his voice.

"Nor are mine," Bilik mumbled, his head bent. Here was no irony turned inward, but only purest misery. "She hates me now. Why did it have to happen? Our lives were simple, they had direction, we could have lived happily if only we had been left alone. But no." His head came up suddenly and there was a dangerous light in his eyes. "This all began when she was first stolen away from Iskir. Stolen by *you!* You will pay for my sorrow!" He launched himself bare-handed at Avren and siezed the false shepherd by the neck, trying to choke the life out of him.

Lt. Worf was not about to stand aside and witness such goings-on. It was laughably easy for him to intervene, separating the two. "You," he informed Bilik, "will go with your own people. You have done nothing to inspire hostility in the Na'amOberyin, and the girl Ma'adrys is too intelligent to allow her personal feelings for you to interfere with more important matters. And you—" He turned to Avren.

"The—the Masra'et really won't behave as intelligently as Ma'adrys," the Ne'elatian agent said, rubbing his assaulted throat. "If you force me to attend their meeting, nothing will get done except maybe the passing of a resolution to skin me alive."

Worf sighed. "Very well. Then you will come with me."

"Yes, sir," said Avren meekly, and still fidgeting with the edge of his hat, he trailed after the Klingon.

Chapter Sixteen

"A WHAT?" AVREN ASKED, fascinated by the little animal in the tank.

"A hamster," Lt. Worf answered absently, distracted by the fact that he was having no luck whatsoever finding the item that he sought, a small figurine of Vulcan origin, one of the few art objects he had found worthy of owning. "It belongs to my son, Alexander."

"Really." Avren peered at the small ball of fur more closely. "I think it's dead."

"It is not dead, it is asleep. It sleeps much, conserving its strength for battle." Worf snapped out his reply. He was fast approaching the end of his patience. He didn't like being frustrated in this manner, and with warped logic he was beginning to blame his inability to find the elusive figurine on Avren.

Why did I have to bring him with me to my quarters? he thought ferociously. *He is no help, and he persists in diverting my attention. I should have placed him in the custody of Ensign Fougner when the call came from Alexander. She was just passing by us in the corridor when he contacted me. Better still, I should have told Alexander that he should know better than to interrupt my work merely because he had forgotten to bring that object to school with him today.* He yanked open a cabinet door with particular violence and there, on a shelf, the Vulcan figurine glimmered at him in austere elegance. At once he felt better, and his thoughts grew milder accordingly.

Ah, but the boy did *promise to show this to his classmates as part of their lesson, and he could not hope to leave the schoolroom to fetch it himself. He strove to keep his word in the only way possible. He did well.* Smiling with fatherly pride, Worf took down the figurine and turned to inform Avren that they could leave now.

"What are you doing with batlh-ghobbogh-yIH?" Worf bellowed.

"Ai!" Avren jumped at the Klingon's roar, sending the heroically named hamster flying. Fortunately for the beast, Avren had excellent reflexes. Tribble-who-battles-with-honor took only a short flight before the false shepherd clapped his hands around him once more. Fortunately for Avren, the hamster was still half asleep on re-entry and neglected to bite him. "Don't *do* that," he told Worf irritably.

Worf snatched the hamster from Avren's hands without deigning to respond. He replaced the creature in its tank, with only the slightest wince of pain crossing his face to indicate that his luck was not so good as Avren's. He considered his nipped finger and said, "It is a dangerous beast when aroused. I should have let you learn the hard way."

"That little fluffball, dangerous?" Avren laughed until Worf silenced him with a single look.

"I, too, made that mistake. It may not look dangerous, but looks deceive. I should not need to teach that to one of your profession."

"Point taken. Let me see that. I know a little about healing," Avren said, trying to make Worf permit him to examine the minor wound. Worf was less than cooperative, snatching his hand away from Avren indignantly. "Huh. Suit yourself. I know more than a few good herbal remedies, and I always carry my medicines with me." He grinned, snatching up his wide-brimmed shepherd's hat from a table and turning it so that Worf could see the little bunch of dried vegetation attached to the band. "See? Most of this is shepherd's herb, the stuff they use to brew up their ritual drink, but I carry a few other simples here. The difference is, *these* are useful. All shepherd's herb is good for is dulling the wits. Now a little pinch of this leaf moistened with water will stop bleeding quick as you—"

"I prefer to use our own shipboard medical facilities," Worf said gruffly.

"Ah. Well, I can't argue with that." Avren dropped the hat back onto the table just as the door hissed open.

"Father?" Alexander entered Worf's quarters and looked inquisitively at their Ne'elatian visitor.

"Alexander, what are you doing here? You ought to be in school."

"I told the teacher that you'd be bringing the figurine, but when you didn't come I was given permission to return to quarters and bring it myself."

"I could not find it immediately," Worf said gruffly. "There it is, on the table beside batlh-gobbogh-yIH's tank."

"So you are the master of that ferocious brute," Avren said, trying to keep a straight face. "I wanted to pet it, but your father seems to be afraid that the creature will tear my throat out as soon as look at me."

Alexander gave Avren one of those looks all children reserve for adults they think are just insane enough to be interesting. "He does bite," the boy acknowledged, "but not always." He reached into the tank and set the hamster down on the table. Immediately batlh-gobbogh-yIH scuttled onto the shepherd's hat and began to waddle around the brim.

"If you had a pair of them, we could make a fortune betting on the races," Avren said. He chuckled when the little animal found the bunch of dried flowers adorning the hatband and began avidly nibbling and stuffing them into its cheek pouches.

He stopped laughing when the hamster fell over on its side, black eyes staring at nothing.

"He's dead!" Alexander cried. "Father, Fido's dead!"

"batlh-gobbogh-yIH," Worf corrected his son automatically as he scooped up the still little form. Hands that had the strength to shatter bone handled the tiny creature with amazing delicacy and care. One finger lay lightly against the furry side until—

"He is not dead," Worf announced. "He is still breathing."

"What's wrong with him?" Alexander asked plaintively, for the moment forgetting that he was a young Klingon warrior-to-be.

"I—I don't know what to say," Avren stammered, frantic over what had happened. "I assure you, none of those plants are poisonous."

"Not to you," Worf said. "You had no business allowing my son's companion to ingest them."

"I swear, I didn't think any of them would harm him! I think the poor creature must've eaten some of the shepherd's herb. It's stupefied him the same as it does the Ashkaarians."

"Father, please can't we do something for him?" Alexander pleaded. "Maybe Dr. Crusher could help him."

Lt. Worf began to say, "It is not appropriate to trouble Dr. Crusher with a sick hamster," but before he had uttered the fourth word he saw the tragic look in his son's eyes. "It is not—Oh, very well," he said at last, and with the dazed batlh-gobbogh-yIH in one hand and the hangdog Avren lagging after, he led the way to sickbay.

Dr. Crusher examined her extraordinary patient with as much professional efficiency as she could muster without bursting into laughter. The hamster lay on its back, all four paws curled up, a vacant, amiable expression on its face. "Almost as if it's smiling at me," she observed aloud.

The hamster's whiskers twitched into a lopsided expression that was very like a drunken grin and a minuscule spasm shook its body.

"I do believe he's got the hiccups," Dr. Crusher opined. She looked up at a very worried Alexander. "What have you been feeding him?"

"I didn't do it," Alexander said.

"I'm afraid it was me." Avren stepped forward, fiddling with his hatbrim. "I didn't do it on purpose, though. The plant isn't poisonous to Ashkaarians. Even the sheep eat it with no ill effects, though it does slow them down pretty much if they find a big patch of it on the mountain. If I'd known it would hurt the animal—"

"You'll be happy to know that you haven't poisoned Alexander's hamster," Dr. Crusher reassured him. "But you *have* gotten him drunk as a lord."

"Drunk as a what?" Avren was puzzled by the alien figure of speech.

"What *I'd* like to know," Dr. Crusher continued, "is where you got the plant you say you fed him. You don't appear to be carrying anything with you."

"Oh. That. Well, you see, it's like this." Avren plucked the sprig of dried vegetation from his hatband and held it out for Dr. Crusher's inspection. He was explaining the properties of the various healing herbs with the enthusiasm of someone who enjoys hearing himself talk, but he was doing it for the benefit of an inattentive audience.

Dr. Crusher wasn't listening to Avren run on. Her attention was elsewhere as she studied the dried bouquet very closely, with a scientist's rapt concentration. One by one she separated the species comprising Avren's modest frippery on the examination station in front of her. Worf observed the process with both interest and perplexity. The individual samples of dried herb all looked pretty much the same to him.

Not so to Dr. Crusher. When she had gotten them all separated she selected one bunch in particular and held it up for more painstaking scrutiny. "That's the one the creature got a hold of," Avren said, eager to be heard. "Shepherd's herb, that's the stuff."

Dr. Crusher broke off one of the tiny branchlets of the plant, placed it in a clear slipcase, and dropped it into sickbay's specialized analytical unit. "Computer, DNA of sample submitted, evaluate," she directed, gazing intently at the display screen set into the wall above the input port.

"Working," came the disembodied voice of the ship's computer. There was a brief silence, followed by a detailed breakdown of the sample's genetic makeup, all of this accompanied by a video display showing the plant in its natural state. Dr. Crusher stared, then motioned for Avren to join her.

"Is that what your shepherd's herb looks like in the wild?" she demanded. There was so strong an undercurrent of urgency in her voice that the Ne'elatian agent found it hard to do more than nod assent. Dr. Crusher took a deep breath, let it out slowly, then touched her comm badge. "Crusher to Picard. We've found n'vashal."

As second in command, Riker was the logical choice to oversee the reconvened meeting of the Ashkaarian, Ne'elatian, and Orakisan factions in the briefing room. While he had never been one to shy away from a challenge, the manifest level of silent animosity still contained within those four walls made him wish that Captain Picard would join them soon, or at least Lt. Worf. For the moment there were no raised voices, no more threats, and yet the latent potential for further angry outbursts haunted the room.

They're all being so cursed polite *about this,* Riker thought uneasily. *It's not natural. If Rak Ti'ask's smile were any more forced, his teeth would shatter.*

"Your plan for the introduction of higher technology to Ashkaar is certainly worth consideration," Rak Ti'ask was saying to Hara'el smoothly. "And I swear to you that we have considered it. Udar Kishrit was most eloquent." He flashed his false smile at Udar Kishrit, who glowered back.

If looks could kill . . . Riker thought.

Rak Ti'ask ignored his leader's deadly scowl and continued. "We have put this to an official vote, and his arguments have persuaded three of our number to join their votes to his for initiating the mission to Ashkaar."

"Four out of six vote *for* the plan?" Riker asked hopefully. "Then that means you'll be going ahead with—"

"Alas, no." Rak Ti'ask's sigh was even less sincere than his smile, if that were possible. "It is written in ordinances of our people that a voice of *three* is needed to affirm any decision of the council."

"As with ourselves," Nish na'am said.

"With us as well." Hara'el blinked in mild amazement to discover this common thread still running strong through Skerrian daughterworlds so long kept apart.

"Do not feign compliance, Rak Ti'ask!" Udar Kishrit shouted. "You well know that it was *your* vote that destroyed the accord!"

"Was it?" Rak Ti'ask inquired mildly.

"You are opposed to making restitution to Ashkaar, yet when the tally was called, you voted aye. Do not deny it!"

"I would not deny it for the world," the younger Ne'elatian purred. "Three votes would have been enough to pass the resolution, even though three stood against it, for the affirming voice is always more pleasing to the Lady of the Balance than the dissenting one. And so I cast my vote in favor of bringing the Ashkaarian savages up to our level because that was the best, the *only* way to assure that it would never come to pass."

"Rak Ti'ask, I urge you to reconsider," Counsellor Troi said from her place beside Nish na'am. "The situation between Ashkaar and Ne'elat has changed irrevocably. Your worlds are no longer unknown and forgotten. The Federation will be watching what you do next, as will the union of Skerrian daughterworlds. What are you afraid of? That the Ashkaarians harbor a grudge and will act on it against you? There is no need to fear that. Ma'adrys shares her grandfather's gift for eloquence. She has convinced the Na'am-Oberyin to put aside their past grievances against Ne'elat for the sake of their people's future. They are your people, too, Rak Ti'ask!"

"I am willing to concede as much," he replied indifferently. "But they can afford to be magnanimous. The Orakisan's proposal is entirely to their advantage!"

"As the past was entirely to yours," Troi reminded him. "If you refuse to change your vote, you will only be adding to past wrongs."

"Ah!" Rak Ti'ask assumed a look of mock distress. "I never thought of it that way. But, oh dear. Lovely lady, you tell me that the situation between Ne'elat and Ashkaar has changed irrevocably. It is with more regret than you can *begin* to imagine that I tell you that an official vote of the Masra'et is *just* as irrevocable."

"Regret, my foot," Riker muttered to Data. "Either Rak Ti'ask learns to act more credibly, or he's going to get applauded where it'll do him some good."

"I believe that such unorthodox action would count as a violation of the Prime Directive," the android whispered back.

"Yes, but it'd be worth it."

"You speak too glibly, Rak Ti'ask," Udar Kishrit said. "As a member of the Masra'et you are entitled to use your vote as you think best, but to drag the Lady's holy name into your games, pretending you act exclusively in her service, this is vile. When we return, I will speak of this to the people. They will not dissent when you are removed from the council and I appoint another in your place."

Rak Ti'ask dropped his arrogant mask abruptly at Udar Kishrit's words. "You would not," he said, his voice shaking.

"I would. I will. That much lies within my power and you know it. Perhaps we have been wrong to limit the Masra'et to six souls if this is the harm one alone can do. The Ashkaarian council holds nine. The rule of three would still be possible and it would take far more than a single schemer to topple our hopes for a future truly blessed by the Lady."

"Udar Kishrit, *can* you do such a thing?" Geordi asked. "Just . . . appoint new members of the Masra'et?"

"I am the head of the Masra'et until my death or the people's petition. I am free to re-form it if that seems necessary. Our records teach that in ages past, there were times when the number of its members rose or fell, depending on the population of Ne'elat and following the judgment of its leader. Only the bovereem could intervene."

"So then, if the vote of a member of the Masra'et is irrevocable and you have the power to bring new members into the Masra'et . . ." Geordi grinned and said no more.

Udar Kishrit looked at the ship's chief engineer as if the man had spouted gibberish. Then by degrees he understood the idea that Geordi meant to give him, but could not elaborate out loud. "You," Udar Kishrit said, pointing to Nish na'am. "You shall join the Masra'et of Ne'elat and add your voice to the vote concerning Ashkaar."

"You would have this . . . of me?" Nish na'am asked. "But we are of different worlds!"

"And yet one people, as even your foes admit."

Udar Kishrit spared a cold look for Rak Ti'ask. "If you and the Orakisan ambassador will add your voices to those already favoring the plan—"

"Never!" Rak Ti'ask shouted, his face taut with rage. "If you open the doors of the Masra'et to off-worlders, you cut your own throat, Udar Kishrit, and I will rejoice to watch it happen."

"They dwell off-world, but they are still our kin. The bovereem will also say—"

But what the bovereem might say was drowned out in the uproar that ensued. Once again, everyone in the briefing room was trying to be heard at once. Riker leaned back in his chair wearily.

"I just *love* family reunions," he commented to Data.

"Do you?" The android glanced from one angry face to the next. "Why?"

Riker sighed. "Never mind." He was about to summon Security to the briefing room when the door slid open and Captain Picard came in, closely followed by Dr. Crusher, Lt. Worf, and Avren.

This time the sight alone of the Klingon was enough to tone down the general clamor, but when Dr. Crusher laid her sample of dried herbs on the conference table and made her report, backing up her conclusions with the aid of the table's holographic projector, the room fell completely silent. Ne'elatians, Orakisans, Ashkaarians, and *Enterprise* crewmembers could only stare wordlessly at the miraculous find.

"N'vashal," Commander Riker marvelled softly, contemplating the brittle, brown sprig rather than the projected image of the green, blossoming plant. "We must've seen this a hundred times on Ashkaar. How could we have missed it?"

"I am afraid that you exaggerate, Commander,"

Mr. Data said. "We saw the plant in question on approximately fifteen separate occasions, including our first introduction to Avren. However we were unaware that n'vashal has a radically different appearance in its dessicated form from when it is fresh and growing. We failed to make a proper identification because we had only the growing plant template as a basis for comparison."

"As you said, my friend," Avren remarked jovially to Worf. "Appearances deceive."

Worf, cradling Alexander's hamster in his hand, did not care for Ne'elatian agent's joviality. "I am not your friend."

"N'vashal!" Ambassador Lelys was wildly elated, and it showed plainly on her face. "Then we have succeeded. S'ka'rys will live again!" She turned to Nish na'am, who was seated between herself and Ma'adrys, and spontaneously clasped the Ashkaarian's hand with joy. "We will contact our superiors at once with the news, and as the duly designated representatives of the Orakisan government we can invoke emergency powers to effect an independent trade agreement with you. We can also grant you instant membership in the union of—"

"We can, but will we, Ambassador?" Legate Valdor said. He folded his arms across his chest. "You speak without consulting your associates, you are presumptuous. I will not allow my voice to feed your audacity."

"You would sacrifice the lives of our colonists just to teach me a lesson?" Lelys was incredulous. "We need this trade agreement with Ashkaar, and we need it now!"

"To obtain a plant that grows wild on that rude planet's surface? It belongs to no one. We could just take it."

"No, Father, we could not." Hara'el stood up and looked down on Legate Valdor. There was no anger in his eyes, but only sadness. "Do you hear your own words? We will simply *take* what we desire from Ashkaar, with or without their consent, merely because we *can?* No. That has been done to them already, and for too long."

"Boy, you speak of things you do not understand," Valdor growled.

"Do you not yet accept the fact that I am a boy no more? And I understand too well. Your heart is bitter, Father, because Lelys holds the title of ambassador which you feel should be yours by right, by merit. That will never be, not while you allow your own desires to distort your vision of our mission's purpose."

"What do you know of such matters?" Valdor muttered, looking away from his son.

"I know that if you do not join your voice with Ambassador Lelys's and mine to give something back to Ashkaar, you are unworthy of the greatest teaching I ever received: A good ambassador serves the power of peace, not the power of his own pride."

"And who filled your head with *that* precious thought?" Valdor spat.

Hara'el lowered his voice. "You did, Father."

Avren cleared his throat. "You know, it strikes me that I could be of a little service on the side of peace myself. I know where there are plenty of patches of shepherd's herb—I mean n'vashal—in my little part of Ashkaar. It's not all that easy to stumble across in the wild. Shy, I suppose." He grinned. "It likes gullies and out-of-the-way spots with more shade than sun and just the right combination of cold and wet. I'd like to volunteer to help lead harvesting expeditions, and I can lend a hand to the propagation of more n'vashal, too."

"You would do this, Avren?" Udar Kishrit regarded his erstwhile adversary with the beginnings of a grudging respect.

"It's the least I can do." Avren shrugged. "Can't exactly go back to my old line of work, now can I?"

"Well, Rak Ti'ask?" Counsellor Troi inquired gently. "Ashkaar will soon no longer be the barbarous world you think it is. Orakisa and the other Skerrian daughterworlds will see to that. They will come bearing gifts, new technology, medical aid, all in exchange for what only Ashkaar can provide. In time they will teach the Ashkaarians that their world has even more resources to offer in trade than only n'vashal. The power of Ashkaar will grow. They will remember their friends . . . and their adversaries. Which would you have Ne'elat be?"

Rak Ti'ask took a deep breath. "Udar Kishrit," he said, "although we cannot undo the defeat of the Orakisan's proposal, could we not take another vote on a—a somewhat different proposal along those same lines?"

Udar Kishrit smiled. "We can."

"I wonder how different this second proposal's going to be?" Riker remarked to Captain Picard.

"Different enough to satisfy protocol," Picard replied. "It appears that the contrary members of the Masra'et are more than willing to assume a benevolent role regarding their neighbors, as long as it is to their own advantage. *Plus ça change . . .*"

"The more it changes, the more it stays the same?" Riker raised one eyebrow, amused. "I don't think anything's going to stay the same for Ashkaar."

Epilogue

"Hey, Worf, who's your drinking buddy?" Guinan asked, leaning across the bar to set a glass of prune juice down in front of the Klingon.

"He is called batlh-ghobbogh-yIH," Worf replied, sliding a dish of peanuts closer to the hamster. "He has done much to earn a reward for his services to Starfleet." Tribble-who-battles-with-honor had recovered from his exposure to n'vashal, scented the peanuts, and plunged into them nose first, stuffing them into his pouches until his cheeks bulged out sideways wider than his plump hindquarters.

Guinan gave a low whistle of admiration. "Now *that's* ugly."

"It does not need to be attractive; it is practical, as is any truly great warrior," Worf explained, respectfully patting batlh-ghobbogh-yIH with a caution bred of many bites. "By enlarging its cheeks with supplies it not only carries more than enough provisions for any military campaign, it also makes itself fearful to behold, a terror to its enemies."

"Military campaign," Guinan repeated. "A terror to its enemies?" The terror in question sat up on its haunches and boldly twitched its whiskers at Guinan. She pursed her lips. "And they say you Klingons don't have a sense of humor."

"We do not need one," Worf averred, and set the sated hamster on his shoulder where the beast began to alternately groom himself and nibble on Worf's hair.

"Ooooookay." Guinan turned away, rolling her eyes, and surveyed the rest of her customers. There weren't all that many; things were fairly quiet in the bar at the moment. Besides Worf there were about three people from Security and a couple of Science personnel.

Then she noticed the couple at the most secluded table the bar could offer. It was Geordi La Forge and that Ashkaarian girl—what was her name?—oh yes, Ma'adrys. She looked like another person entirely now that she had put aside those flowing robes she used to wear. Instead she was clad in a serviceable jumpsuit rather like the Starfleet uniform, trim fitting and about as unremarkable. Her hair was pulled back and secured in a bun worn low at the back of her head, bringing out more of the beauty in her face.

"You do like it?" she asked Geordi, eyes shining. She seemed half afraid to hear his answer.

"Of course I do," he said, doing his best to cheer her. He clasped his hand over hers on the tabletop between them. "You're always the prettiest woman in the room, no matter how you wear your hair."

"Oh." Ma'adrys sounded a little disappointed. She pulled her hand out from under his and smoothed back a wayward wisp of hair that wasn't there at all. "Ambassador Lelys suggested this style. She said that as Iskir's first envoy to Orakisa and S'ka'rys, I should try to look more mature."

"Once you open your mouth and start speaking, no one will doubt your rightness for the job and no one will look twice at your hairstyle."

Despite this heartfelt reassurance, Ma'adrys bowed her head and folded her hands in her lap. Her mood troubled Geordi—her worries had always been his— and his chief desire was to discover the cause of her unhappiness and put an end to it. He leaned forward, reached out, and stroked her cheek lightly with his fingertips. "Ma'adrys. Dearest Ma'adrys, what's wrong? Tell me. Please."

The Ashkaarian girl jerked her chin up. There were tears misting her eyes. "Oh Geordi, I am so afraid!"

"There's nothing to fear. Ambassador Lelys will take the best care of you, and so will Hara'el. Look, I know you're all going to be put aboard a different starship in a couple of hours, but it'll be all right. It's necessary. The *Marcus* is one of the fastest ships in the fleet and the first shipment of n'vashal has to reach Skerris IV without delay. The *Enterprise* has been called elsewhere; we can't take you."

"No, no, that is not it at all." Ma'adrys shook her head, forlorn. "I do not go alone, Geordi. Bilik oberyin comes too."

"Bilik?" This was news to Geordi, news he didn't like. "Why? The Orakisans wanted only one Ashkaarian envoy, you."

"Where I go, he must go, though in truth and by right it ought to be that where he goes, I stay."

"No," Geordi said, and again, *"Why?* This doesn't make any sense. What there once was between you two is finished. You were never actually married to him, were you?" He needed to hear her answer, and he feared it.

"Not that," she replied, and he breathed again. "What binds us now does not come from the years before I was taken up to Ne'elat. This is new. Geordi . . . when Bilik held you captive, when he laid his knife to your throat, I was afraid. I thought he would kill you and so I—I spoke hari'imash, the oath of life for life, mine given to him in exchange for yours."

"What? But he can't hold you to that, can he?"

"To speak hari'imash is an ancient oath. If I do not honor it—" The tears spilled over, but her expression twisted from woe to anger before they fell. "Oh, *why* must I be bound by such a thing? It *is* ancient, a barbarous custom, and must I destroy my life for the sake something so—so antiquated? So outmoded? A relic of our long ignorance? It shames me to think that we still nurture such archaic ways. To speak hari'imash is like—the evening tale-tellings with the village children. Why must they gather to hear some elder recount the old lore when they could simply be taught to *read* it for themselves, like civilized people?"

"But Ma'adrys, you told me how much you used to enjoy the evening gathering, how much you learned from hearing the elders make the tales come alive for—" Geordi began.

She brushed his arguments aside. "Such things belong to the Iskir that was, not to the world that will be. No. Not Iskir. That name is as primitive as hari'imash itself. I will call my world by its proper name: *Ashkaar*."

"Proper? According to whom?" Geordi laid his hand palm upward on the tabletop, waiting for hers to come to him while he spoke on. "Listen to yourself, Ma'adrys. What are you saying? That the culture that produced you, and Bilik, and a spiritual life so rich it's nurtured *two* worlds is worthless?"

"I never—"

"Maybe what you've promised Bilik is too much. Maybe hari'imash will have no place in the Iskir of the future. But you can deal with it some other way than by turning your back on everything that's made you who you are."

"Who am I now, thanks to my oath?" Ma'adrys asked bitterly. "Bilik's toy."

"If that were true, would you still be your world's first envoy to Orakisa? Bilik would have said something, made some objection, backed it with your oath. Many things have changed since he tried to prevent you from becoming an oberyin in your own right. *He's* changed. Trust me, my love, he's too wise to think of you as his property."

Ma'adrys placed her hand in Geordi's and squeezed tight. "He had *better* not," she said fiercely.

"That's the Ma'adrys I know. Strong, proud, and— well, sometimes a little bit scary, but I still love you." Geordi smiled and cupped her face with his other hand, bringing her near enough for a lingering kiss.

"I will come back," Ma'adrys said staunchly when their lips parted. "No matter how long it takes, I will come back to you, my beloved, my starlord. This, too, I swear."

Geordi's comm badge chirruped before he could respond. "La Forge here."

"Mr. La Forge, the *Marcus* is within transporter range," Captain Picard's voice informed him. "All members of the Orakisan party should report to the transporter room immediately."

"Yes, sir. La Forge out." He touched the badge a

second time, then took Ma'adrys's hands in his. "It's time."

"You will not take me to the transporter room?" she asked.

"I'm afraid I can't. There's something I must attend to, a malfunction in—It would take too long to explain." He turned his head abruptly and noticed Lt. Worf at the bar. The Klingon was engaged in a losing tug-of-war with the hamster, which had decided it wanted to add a lock of Worf's hair to the booty already swelling its cheek pouches. "Worf! Over here!"

"Yes, Geordi?" Worf loomed over the couple.

"Would you escort Ma'adrys to the transporter room? If it's not too much trouble."

"I *know* what trouble is," Worf remarked cryptically, still tugging at the determined hamster. To Ma'adrys he said, "If you would come with me."

Ma'adrys stood. "Goodbye, Geordi. I will see you again." This time the tears fell freely.

"Goodbye, Ma'adrys," Geordi said. He did not rise, or make any move to hold her one last time. Instead he bent his head and remained where he was until the last echo of her footsteps vanished from the room. Only then did he get up and go to the bar.

Guinan put a drink in front of him. "I didn't order this."

"And you wouldn't if you knew what was in it," she retorted. "Drink it anyway."

Geordi shrugged, drained the glass at a gulp, and shuddered. "Well, you sure told me the truth about *that.*"

"Truth's the specialty of the house," Guinan said. "Not that there's much call for it, but still . . ." She picked up the dish of peanuts that batlh-gobbogh-yIH had pawed over and dumped it. "You know she's not coming back, don't you." It wasn't meant to be a question.

"That's not what she said," Geordi replied automatically. There wasn't a lot of faith behind his words, but he had to say them anyway.

"She's going to be traveling with him. That oberyin, Bilik, the one she used to have some kind of understanding with. First on board the *Marcus,* then on Orakisa, Skerris IV, wherever her new duties as an envoy take her, he'll be there too. A face she knows, a voice from home, someone who shares the same memories, someone familiar to turn to in a strange place. . . ."

"She said she'd come back," Geordi repeated.

"Yes," Guinan agreed. "That's what she said."

Geordi sighed. "She won't, will she?"

Guinan was silent for a moment, then she snapped her fingers against the side of Geordi's empty glass so that it rang with a single, pure, musical note. "Another? On the house."

"I could've made her stay," Geordi said, ignoring the invitation. "I had the chance. I could've told her she was right about that whole hari'imash thing, that she didn't need to honor an outworn tradition, that she shouldn't even give it lip service. Why stop there? I could've told her to let someone else be the first Ashkaarian representative to Orakisa, someone older, someone with more experience, an oberyin—*Bilik* oberyin. Why not? That would've gotten him out of the way permanently. I could've said something— anything—to keep her here with me. She would've listened. She loves me. Why didn't I say it?"

Guinan refilled Geordi's glass unasked and pushed it toward him. "Because you love her," she said quietly. "And because you knew that Ashkaar needs her."

Geordi's fingers linked around the glass, but he made no move to raise it. "I need her, too," he said, his voice hoarse. "I need her, and I let her go. Why, Guinan? Why?"

"Sometimes a man doesn't understand how much love is in him, Geordi, until he lets it go," Guinan said. "I can't say if that's any consolation for you, though. Maybe you should think of it like this: I've known a whole lot of people in my life who've given up the world for love, but you, Geordi La Forge—you're the first I've met who's ever found the greatness of heart to give up love for the sake of a world."

About the Author

ESTHER M. FRIESNER was educated at Vassar College, where she completed B.A.s in both Spanish and drama. She went on to Yale University, where within five years she was awarded an M.A. and a Ph.D. in Spanish. She taught Spanish at Yale for a number of years before going on to become a full-time author of fantasy and science fiction. She has published twenty-five novels so far. Most recent titles include *The Psalms of Herod* and *The Sword of Mary* from White Wolf and *Child of the Eagle* from Baen Books.

Her short fiction and poetry have appeared in *Asimov's, Fantasy and Science Fiction, Aboriginal SF, Pulphouse (The Hardback Magazine), Amazing,* and *Fantasy Book,* as well as in numerous anthologies. Her story "Love's Eldritch Ichor" was featured in the 1990 World Fantasy Convention book.

Her first stint as an anthology editor was *Alien Pregnant by Elvis,* a collection of truly gonzo original tabloid SF for DAW Books. Wisely, she undertook this project with the able collaboration of Martin H. Greenberg. Not having learned their lesson, they have also co-edited *Chicks in Chainmail,* an anthology of

Amazon comedy for Baen Books, and *Blood Muse,* an anthology of vampire stories for Donald I. Fine, Inc. They are currently working on *Did You Say "Chicks"?!,* the long-awaited sequel to *Chicks in Chainmail.*

Ask Auntie Esther was her regular column of etiquette advice to the SFlorn in *Pulphouse* magazine. Being paid for telling other people how to run their lives sounds like a pretty good deal to her.

Ms. Friesner won the Nebula Award for Best Short Story of 1995 for her work "Death and the Librarian" and in 1996 for "A Birthday," from the August 1995 issue of *Fantasy & Science Fiction.* In addition, she has won the *Romantic Times* award for Best New Fantasy Writer in 1986 and the Skylark Award in 1994. Her short story "All Vows" took second place in the *Asimov's* SF magazine readers' poll for 1993 and was a finalist for the Nebula in 1994. "A Birthday" was a finalist for the 1996 Hugo Award. Her *Star Trek: Deep Space Nine* novel, *Warchild,* made the *USA Today* bestseller list.

Ms. Friesner lives in Connecticut with her husband, two children, two rambunctious cats, and a fluctuating population of hamsters.

STAR TREK®
THE NEXT GENERATION™
THE
CONTINUING
MISSION

A TENTH ANNIVERSARY TRIBUTE

◆The definitive commemorative album for one of Star Trek's most beloved shows.

◆Featuring more than 750 photos and illustrations.

JUDITH AND GARFIELD REEVES-STEVENS
INTRODUCTION BY RICK BERMAN
AFTERWORD BY ROBERT JUSTMAN

Available in Hardcover
From Pocket Books

POCKET
BOOKS

1413-01

Coming Next Month from Pocket Books

STAR TREK®

ASSIGNMENT: ETERNITY
by
Greg Cox

Please turn the page for an excerpt from
Star Trek® Assignment: Eternity . . .

Kirk seized the armrest of his chair to keep from being thrown to the floor. On the opposite side of the chair, McCoy was not so fortunate. The ship's doctor staggered, then began to pitch forward. He fell toward the hard duranium floor, only to be rescued at the last second by Spock, who somehow managed to take hold of McCoy's arm while maintaining his own balance. *Good work,* Kirk thought as he struggled to keep standing. "Red alert!" he called out to his crew. Uhura, tightly holding on to the communications console, responded at once to his command. Red warning lights began flashing all around the bridge, accompanied by a high-pitched siren that drowned out the gasps of the other crewmen.

The vibration lasted several seconds, during which Kirk could feel the throbbing of the floor through the soles of his boots. Then the shaking began to subside, and the bridge gradually righted itself as the *Enterprise* stabilized its course. Kirk dropped back into his chair. "All stations report. What the devil was that?"

"Captain!" Ensign Chekov called out. "Sensors report a transporter beam of *astounding* power, a hundred times stronger than anything we've got!"

A transporter? Kirk thought. He had never felt a transporter beam like that, except for— His brain resisted the notion that occurred to him. *But that was three centuries ago!*

Spock's mind seemed to be racing down the same channels. "As I recall, Captain," he said, releasing his grip on McCoy, who had regained his balance, "we have experienced this phenomenon before—"

"Captain, look!" Chekov interrupted as two outlines suddenly materialized at the front of the bridge, only a couple of meters from Sulu's station at the helm. The figures were blurry at first, composed of a swirling blue energy, then quickly defined themselves. Alerted by his memory, Kirk recognized the intruders even before they fully solidified.

It was Gary Seven and his attractive young sidekick from the twentieth century. What was her name again? Kirk quickly retrieved the data from year-old memories. *Roberta Lincoln, that was it.*

But what were they doing aboard the *Enterprise* in this day and age? Kirk had never expected to encounter the pair again, let alone in his own time and on his own ship. Even their clothing, he noted, belonged on Earth a few centuries ago. Seven wore an antiquated suit and tie, while his female companion had dressed more casually in a loose-fitting, motley-colored shirt and a pair of faded denim pants. They both looked as if they had stepped out of some sort of historical costume drama.

Chekov leaped from his seat and drew his phaser. Sulu looked ready to do the same. Even McCoy instinctively placed his hand on the medical tricorder hanging from a strap over his shoulder. "Don't move," Chekov ordered the newcomers, "or I will fire."

Seven ignored both the young ensign's weapon and the blaring alarms. "Hello again, Captain Kirk, Mr. Spock," he said calmly. As usual, Kirk noticed, Seven had his cat with him. The sleek black animal nestled against Seven's chest, unruffled and undisturbed by its journey through time and space. By contrast, Roberta Lincoln looked around with wide-eyed astonishment; Kirk guessed she'd never seen the interior of a starship before. "Forgive the intrusion," Seven stated, "but I need your assistance."

"Captain?" Chekov asked, sounding confused. He kept his phaser aimed at the intruders. "Do you know these people?"

"You can stand down, Ensign," Kirk replied, rising from his own chair. Flicking a switch on the command functions panel on the starboard armrest, he deactivated the siren and blinking red lights. "Cancel red alert status." It occurred to him that few of the crew had actually met either Seven or Roberta; only he and Spock had actually beamed down to Earth during that mission. "I don't think you'll need that phaser. At least I hope not. Meet Gary Seven and Roberta Lincoln. They're time travelers from twentieth-century Earth, or so I assume."

Cradled in Seven's arms, the cat squawked, as if angry at being overlooked. Kirk didn't even try to remember the pet's name, although he found it slightly odd that Seven never seemed to go anywhere without the cat. *At least it's not a tribble,* he thought.

"Good Lord," McCoy said, staring in amazement at the strangers on the bridge. Kirk wondered if the doctor was remembering his own harrowing trip to Earth's Depression era, McCoy's only firsthand encounter with the twentieth century. "Kind of a long way from home, aren't they?" the doctor said. "In time *and* space."

That was certainly true, Kirk thought. Earth was hundreds of light-years away from their present location, not to mention a century or three removed from Seven's own time. *This must be serious,* he thought. Seven wouldn't have come all this way without a strong reason.

"Excuse me, Captain." Lieutenant Uhura spoke up from her post at the communications station. She pressed a compact silver receiver firmly against her ear. "Chief Engineer Scott is hailing you from Engineering. He wants to know what's happening."

"Tell Scotty the situation is under control," Kirk instructed.

"I'm glad you think so," McCoy grumbled. The doctor gave his captain a dubious look.

Kirk shrugged, then turned his attention to their unexpected guests. "All right, Seven, what's so important that you had to shake up my ship to get here?" His fists clenched at his sides. *That damn beam almost shook my ship apart,* he thought. Last time around, the *Enterprise* had intercepted Seven's transporter beam by accident. *Don't tell me that this was just another coincidence. I won't buy it.*

"I'm here on an urgent mission, Captain, the nature of which I can't fully disclose. Unfortunately, in this century, I don't have access to all the resources I had in your past, so I need the *Enterprise* to help me complete my mission."

"You'll have to tell me more than that," Kirk replied. He walked across the bridge, stepping up from the command module and circling around the navigation console until he was less than a meter away from Seven and his companions. "I suppose you are still working on behalf of some mysterious alien benefactors—"

Seven nodded.

"—whose nature and location you're still unwilling to divulge?"

"Exactly," Seven confirmed. "I trust you appreciate the delicacy of my position, Captain. As a visitor to your era, I don't wish to disturb future history any more than absolutely necessary. At present, your Federation remains unaware of my sponsors. Thus it is imperative that I do nothing to change that situation."

Kirk shook his head, scowling. "That may have been good enough back in the twentieth century, but not anymore. Your activities in the past are a matter of history; there's nothing I can do about them. But this is my era now—my present—and you're the one who doesn't belong here. And I don't like the idea of you, or the aliens you represent, meddling with our affairs. Humanity's grown a lot since the twentieth century. We don't need any cosmic baby-sitters these days."

"Actually, Captain," Seven replied, "that's exactly why I need your help. In this century, the human race has indeed graduated to a higher level of civilization, and no longer requires the intervention of my superiors."

"Well, bravo for us," McCoy said. He had remained within the circular command module, keeping one hand on the red guardrail just in case the ship lurched again. "Hear that, Spock? Modern-day *Homo sapiens* isn't nearly as primitive as you think."

"No matter what level of advancement, Doctor," Spock answered, not far from McCoy's side, "there is always room for improvement. Especially with regard to humanity's frequently unrestrained emotions."

"What's wrong with emotions?" Roberta blurted out. Her gaze, Kirk noted, kept drifting back to the points of Spock's ears. *Just wait till she sees an Andorian,* he thought. *Blue skin and antennae are even more eye-catching.*

"Please, gentlemen," Kirk said to Spock and McCoy. "Not now." He turned back to face Seven. "What are you saying? That the Federation is outside your jurisdiction now?"

"More or less," Seven said in a noncommittal manner. "That's why there is no organization or infrastructure in place to assist me in this era. My superiors, and my successors, are occupied elsewhere in the galaxy, safeguarding the development of sentient races that your civilization will not encounter for generations to come." Seven calmly stroked his cat's head as he spoke. "Given time, I could certainly acquire a starship of my own, and whatever equipment and personnel may be required to complete my mission, but time is exactly what is at stake."

"Meaning what?" Kirk demanded, growing annoyed by Seven's cryptic remarks. He was exhausted, the ship was facing a difficult rescue mission, and the last thing he needed now was a meddlesome time traveler with a secret agenda. True, Seven had proved trustworthy the last time they met him, but that didn't mean Kirk was ready to turn over the *Enterprise* just at Seven's insistence. *I need more than that,* he thought. *A lot more.*

Seven paused, weighing his words carefully. "I can tell you that I'm here to untangle a temporal paradox that threatens both our futures."

Kirk didn't like the sound of that. He knew, from painful experience, just how fragile the timeline could be. Memories of Edith Keeler came unbidden to his mind. "What sort of paradox?" he demanded. "Is something going to happen to change the past?"

"No," Seven said. "But your own future could be changed—has been changed—unless action is taken immediately. I have reason to believe that an event damaging the proper procession of history will originate several hours from now, at a specific location within this quadrant. Trust me, that's all you need to know, except for the coordinates of our destination."

"I need to know a good deal more than that," Kirk protested. "This ship is not going anywhere, except on its current course, unless I hear something better than a couple of ominous hints and warnings."

Seven refused to give in. "Think about it, Captain Kirk. Do you really want to know your own future?"

Look for STAR TREK Fiction from Pocket Books

Star Trek®: The Original Series

Star Trek: The Motion Picture • Gene Roddenberry
Star Trek II: The Wrath of Khan • Vonda N. McIntyre
Star Trek III: The Search for Spock • Vonda N. McIntyre
Star Trek IV: The Voyage Home • Vonda N. McIntyre
Star Trek V: The Final Frontier • J. M. Dillard
Star Trek VI: The Undiscovered Country • J. M. Dillard
Star Trek VII: Generations • J. M. Dillard
Enterprise: The First Adventure • Vonda N. McIntyre
Final Frontier • Diane Carey
Strangers from the Sky • Margaret Wander Bonanno
Spock's World • Diane Duane
The Lost Years • J. M. Dillard
Probe • Margaret Wander Bonanno
Prime Directive • Judith and Garfield Reeves-Stevens
Best Destiny • Diane Carey
Shadows on the Sun • Michael Jan Friedman
Sarek • A. C. Crispin
Federation • Judith and Garfield Reeves-Stevens
The Ashes of Eden • William Shatner & Judith and Garfield Reeves-Stevens
The Return • William Shatner & Judith and Garfield Reeves-Stevens
Star Trek: Starfleet Academy • Diane Carey

#1 *Star Trek: The Motion Picture* • Gene Roddenberry
#2 *The Entropy Effect* • Vonda N. McIntyre
#3 *The Klingon Gambit* • Robert E. Vardeman
#4 *The Covenant of the Crown* • Howard Weinstein
#5 *The Prometheus Design* • Sondra Marshak & Myrna Culbreath
#6 *The Abode of Life* • Lee Correy
#7 *Star Trek II: The Wrath of Khan* • Vonda N. McIntyre
#8 *Black Fire* • Sonni Cooper
#9 *Triangle* • Sondra Marshak & Myrna Culbreath
#10 *Web of the Romulans* • M. S. Murdock
#11 *Yesterday's Son* • A. C. Crispin
#12 *Mutiny on the Enterprise* • Robert E. Vardeman

#13 *The Wounded Sky* • Diane Duane
#14 *The Trellisane Confrontation* • David Dvorkin
#15 *Corona* • Greg Bear
#16 *The Final Reflection* • John M. Ford
#17 *Star Trek III: The Search for Spock* • Vonda N. McIntyre
#18 *My Enemy, My Ally* • Diane Duane
#19 *The Tears of the Singers* • Melinda Snodgrass
#20 *The Vulcan Academy Murders* • Jean Lorrah
#21 *Uhura's Song* • Janet Kagan
#22 *Shadow Lord* • Laurence Yep
#23 *Ishmael* • Barbara Hambly
#24 *Killing Time* • Della Van Hise
#25 *Dwellers in the Crucible* • Margaret Wander Bonanno
#26 *Pawns and Symbols* • Majiliss Larson
#27 *Mindshadow* • J. M. Dillard
#28 *Crisis on Centaurus* • Brad Ferguson
#29 *Dreadnought!* • Diane Carey
#30 *Demons* • J. M. Dillard
#31 *Battlestations!* • Diane Carey
#32 *Chain of Attack* • Gene DeWeese
#33 *Deep Domain* • Howard Weinstein
#34 *Dreams of the Raven* • Carmen Carter
#35 *The Romulan Way* • Diane Duane & Peter Morwood
#36 *How Much for Just the Planet?* • John M. Ford
#37 *Bloodthirst* • J. M. Dillard
#38 *The IDIC Epidemic* • Jean Lorrah
#39 *Time for Yesterday* • A. C. Crispin
#40 *Timetrap* • David Dvorkin
#41 *The Three-Minute Universe* • Barbara Paul
#42 *Memory Prime* • Judith and Garfield Reeves-Stevens
#43 *The Final Nexus* • Gene DeWeese
#44 *Vulcan's Glory* • D. C. Fontana
#45 *Double, Double* • Michael Jan Friedman
#46 *The Cry of the Onlies* • Judy Klass
#47 *The Kobayashi Maru* • Julia Ecklar
#48 *Rules of Engagement* • Peter Morwood
#49 *The Pandora Principle* • Carolyn Clowes
#50 *Doctor's Orders* • Diane Duane
#51 *Enemy Unseen* • V. E. Mitchell
#52 *Home Is the Hunter* • Dana Kramer Rolls
#53 *Ghost-Walker* • Barbara Hambly
#54 *A Flag Full of Stars* • Brad Ferguson
#55 *Renegade* • Gene DeWeese

#56 *Legacy* • Michael Jan Friedman
#57 *The Rift* • Peter David
#58 *Face of Fire* • Michael Jan Friedman
#59 *The Disinherited* • Peter David
#60 *Ice Trap* • L. A. Graf
#61 *Sanctuary* • John Vornholt
#62 *Death Count* • L. A. Graf
#63 *Shell Game* • Melissa Crandall
#64 *The Starship Trap* • Mel Gilden
#65 *Windows on a Lost World* • V. E. Mitchell
#66 *From the Depths* • Victor Milan
#67 *The Great Starship Race* • Diane Carey
#68 *Firestorm* • L. A. Graf
#69 *The Patrian Transgression* • Simon Hawke
#70 *Traitor Winds* • L. A. Graf
#71 *Crossroad* • Barbara Hambly
#72 *The Better Man* • Howard Weinstein
#73 *Recovery* • J. M. Dillard
#74 *The Fearful Summons* • Denny Martin Flynn
#75 *First Frontier* • Diane Carey & Dr. James I. Kirkland
#76 *The Captain's Daughter* • Peter David
#77 *Twilight's End* • Jerry Oltion
#78 *The Rings of Tautee* • Dean W. Smith & Kristine K. Rusch
#79 *Invasion #1: First Strike* • Diane Carey
#80 *The Joy Machine* • James Gunn
#81 *Mudd in Your Eye* • Jerry Oltion
#82 *Mind Meld* • John Vornholt
#83 *Heart of the Sun* • Pamela Sargent & George Zebrowski

Star Trek: The Next Generation®

Encounter at Farpoint • David Gerrold
Unification • Jeri Taylor
Relics • Michael Jan Friedman
Descent • Diane Carey
All Good Things • Michael Jan Friedman
Star Trek: Klingon • Dean W. Smith & Kristine K. Rusch
Star Trek VII: Generations • J. M. Dillard
Metamorphosis • Jean Lorrah
Vendetta • Peter David
Reunion • Michael Jan Friedman
Imzadi • Peter David
The Devil's Heart • Carmen Carter
Dark Mirror • Diane Duane
Q-Squared • Peter David
Crossover • Michael Jan Friedman
Kahless • Michael Jan Friedman
Star Trek: First Contact • J. M. Dillard

#1 *Ghost Ship* • Diane Carey
#2 *The Peacekeepers* • Gene DeWeese
#3 *The Children of Hamlin* • Carmen Carter
#4 *Survivors* • Jean Lorrah
#5 *Strike Zone* • Peter David
#6 *Power Hungry* • Howard Weinstein
#7 *Masks* • John Vornholt
#8 *The Captains' Honor* • David and Daniel Dvorkin
#9 *A Call to Darkness* • Michael Jan Friedman
#10 *A Rock and a Hard Place* • Peter David
#11 *Gulliver's Fugitives* • Keith Sharee
#12 *Doomsday World* • David, Carter, Friedman & Greenberg
#13 *The Eyes of the Beholders* • A. C. Crispin
#14 *Exiles* • Howard Weinstein
#15 *Fortune's Light* • Michael Jan Friedman
#16 *Contamination* • John Vornholt
#17 *Boogeymen* • Mel Gilden
#18 *Q-in-Law* • Peter David
#19 *Perchance to Dream* • Howard Weinstein
#20 *Spartacus* • T. L. Mancour
#21 *Chains of Command* • W. A. McCay & E. L. Flood
#22 *Imbalance* • V. E. Mitchell

#23 *War Drums* • John Vornholt
#24 *Nightshade* • Laurell K. Hamilton
#25 *Grounded* • David Bischoff
#26 *The Romulan Prize* • Simon Hawke
#27 *Guises of the Mind* • Rebecca Neason
#28 *Here There Be Dragons* • John Peel
#29 *Sins of Commission* • Susan Wright
#30 *Debtors' Planet* • W. R. Thompson
#31 *Foreign Foes* • David Galanter & Greg Brodeur
#32 *Requiem* • Michael Jan Friedman & Kevin Ryan
#33 *Balance of Power* • Dafydd ab Hugh
#34 *Blaze of Glory* • Simon Hawke
#35 *The Romulan Stratagem* • Robert Greenberger
#36 *Into the Nebula* • Gene DeWeese
#37 *The Last Stand* • Brad Ferguson
#38 *Dragon's Honor* • Kij Johnson & Greg Cox
#39 *Rogue Saucer* • John Vornholt
#40 *Possession* • J. M. Dillard & Kathleen O'Malley
#41 *Invasion #2: The Soldiers of Fear* • Dean W. Smith & Kristine K. Rusch
#42 *Infiltrator* • W. R. Thompson
#43 *A Fury Scorned* • Pam Sargent & George Zebrowski
#44 *The Death of Princes* • John Peel
#45 *Intellivore* • Diane Duane
#46 *To Storm Heaven* • Esther Friesner

Star Trek: Deep Space Nine®

The Search • Diane Carey
Warped • K. W. Jeter
The Way of the Warrior • Diane Carey
Star Trek: Klingon • Dean W. Smith & Kristine K. Rusch
Trials and Tribble-ations • Diane Carey

#1 *Emissary* • J. M. Dillard
#2 *The Siege* • Peter David
#3 *Bloodletter* • K. W. Jeter
#4 *The Big Game* • Sandy Schofield
#5 *Fallen Heroes* • Dafydd ab Hugh
#6 *Betrayal* • Lois Tilton
#7 *Warchild* • Esther Friesner
#8 *Antimatter* • John Vornholt
#9 *Proud Helios* • Melissa Scott
#10 *Valhalla* • Nathan Archer
#11 *Devil in the Sky* • Greg Cox & John Greggory Betancourt
#12 *The Laertian Gamble* • Robert Sheckley
#13 *Station Rage* • Diane Carey
#14 *The Long Night* • Dean W. Smith & Kristine K. Rusch
#15 *Objective: Bajor* • John Peel
#16 *Invasion #3: Time's Enemy* • L. A. Graf
#17 *The Heart of the Warrior* • John Greggory Betancourt
#18 *Saratoga* • Michael Jan Friedman
#19 *The Tempest* • Susan Wright
#20 *Wrath of the Prophets* • P. David, M. J. Friedman, R. Greenberger
#21 *Trial by Error* • Mark Garland

Star Trek®: Voyager™

Flashback • Diane Carey
Mosaic • Jeri Taylor

#1 *Caretaker* • L. A. Graf
#2 *The Escape* • Dean W. Smith & Kristine K. Rusch
#3 *Ragnarok* • Nathan Archer
#4 *Violations* • Susan Wright
#5 *Incident at Arbuk* • John Greggory Betancourt
#6 *The Murdered Sun* • Christie Golden
#7 *Ghost of a Chance* • Mark A. Garland & Charles G. McGraw
#8 *Cybersong* • S. N. Lewitt
#9 *Invasion #4: The Final Fury* • Dafydd ab Hugh
#10 *Bless the Beasts* • Karen Haber
#11 *The Garden* • Melissa Scott
#12 *Chrysalis* • David Niall Wilson
#13 *The Black Shore* • Greg Cox
#14 *Marooned* • Christie Golden

Star Trek®: New Frontier

#1 *House of Cards* • Peter David
#2 *Into the Void* • Peter David
#3 *The Two-Front War* • Peter David
#4 *End Game* • Peter David

Star Trek®: Day of Honor

Book One: *Ancient Blood* • Diane Carey
Book Two: *Armageddon Sky* • L. A. Graf
Book Three: *Her Klingon Soul* • Michael Jan Friedman
Book Four: *Treaty's Law* • Dean W. Smith & Kristine K. Rusch